THE BELL IN THE FOG

BOOKS BY LEV AC ROSEN

THE EVANDER MILLS SERIES
Lavender House
The Bell in the Fog

OTHER FICTION
Depth
All Men of Genius

FOR YOUNG ADULTS, AS L. C. ROSEN
Lion's Legacy
Camp
Jack of Hearts (and Other Parts)

FOR CHILDREN
The Memory Wall
Woundabout (with Ellis Rosen)

O/EN

THE BELL IN THE FOG

FORGE

TOR PUBLISHING GROUP
NEW YORK

This is a work of fiction. All of the characters, organizations, and events portrayed in this novel are either products of the author's imagination or are used fictitiously.

THE BELL IN THE FOG

Copyright © 2023 by Lev AC Rosen

A Forge Book
Published by Tom Doherty Associates / Tor Publishing Group
120 Broadway
New York, NY 10271

www.tor-forge.com

Forge® is a registered trademark of Macmillan Publishing Group, LLC.

The Library of Congress Cataloging-in-Publication Data is available upon request.

ISBN 978-1-250-83425-6 (hardcover)
ISBN 978-1-250-83426-3 (ebook)

Our books may be purchased in bulk for promotional, educational, or business use. Please contact your local bookseller or the Macmillan Corporate and Premium Sales Department at 1-800-221-7945, extension 5442, or by email at MacmillanSpecialMarkets@macmillan.com.

First Edition: 2023

Printed in the United States of America

0 9 8 7 6 5 4 3 2 1

For Sarah,

the most fatale femme I know

THE
BELL
IN THE
FOG

ONE

There's a crowd at the bar when I get inside, but I hang back, alone, and watch. There's a bucket swinging in my hand, rusted tin, filled with pinkish water, and my hands are dyed red. They match the walls of the Ruby, though it's so packed tonight, you can barely see the diamond wallpaper through the crowd. A constant hum of people talking over one another fills the room, pierced by a loud laugh here and there, like the church organ shrieking over the choir.

A few people stare at me—I don't know if it's the bucket or just knowing who I am, but they don't say anything. They look away, quick, back at a friend, or the stage, where the band plays "It's No Sin," the female impersonator's voice struggling to be heard.

People are dancing anyway, hands clasped, bodies close, men with men, women with women, some men with women, even. I haven't seen a mixed gay bar since the war, when women needed men to escort them in. All colors of people, too. Elsie has really gotten word out that the Ruby is the most welcoming queer bar in San Francisco.

Except maybe for me. News has trickled out about me, too—the gay PI with the office above the Ruby—but with it so has my past, and no one at a gay bar wants to get too close to a cop, even if he was kicked off the force for being caught in one. Especially not when he's holding a bucket of what looks like blood.

I push my way through the people who won't look at me, trying to be delicate, making sure the bucket doesn't spill, and walk over to the bar. Gene is pouring out drinks with steady hands that were trained for the scalpel before someone sent photos of him and a beau to his medical school. He looks gorgeous in the light. He glows. I know I should probably try talking to him more. But our kiss was months ago, and I was broken and bloody and glad to be alive. Since then, whenever I've gotten up the nerve to talk to him, he's smiled and laughed, same as he has with any other customer.

He looks down at the bucket I'm holding, and frowns.

"Need the sink?" he asks.

"If that's all right. I'm afraid I'll spill it if I try to bring it upstairs."

He moves to the left, making space for me, and I squeeze in next to him. Our shoulders touch and for a moment I think of asking him to dance, what that would be like, being out on the floor with him, shoulder to shoulder, arms around his waist. Like I belonged, I think. Like I was home.

I pour the red water out, and it sloshes loudly into the sink.

"That's not blood, is it?" a patron asks, watching. He's drunk enough to talk to me.

"Paint," I say. "Someone wrote some not-nice things on the building a few weeks back. No one else had time yet, so I washed it off."

"Aren't you supposed to be a detective?"

I shrug, not sure how to answer. The motion tilts the bucket a little harder and the last of the red water splashes back on me, hitting me in the face. The patron laughs as Gene hands me a towel.

"He is a detective," Gene says, as I wipe my face off, hiding my smile. I hand the towel back to him.

"Thanks," I say, and go to wash my hands off, too. I scrub, and the paint won't shift. My hands stay stained.

"Want a drink?" Gene asks.

"No," I say. "Thanks." I stand next to him a moment longer until he reaches past me to get a bottle and I realize I'm in the way.

I leave the bucket under the sink where it belongs and retreat to an empty table away from the bar. Gene shoots me a look when I get there, but I can't read it—maybe he's confused about my not wanting a drink. I try not to order drinks. Elsie said they'd be on the house, but considering I'm not bringing in much money, like she hoped I would, I'd rather not drain her cash and her liquor. I'm supposed to be paying her a percentage of my earnings from cases, but cases aren't exactly pouring in. As a cop, they used to find me; now . . . I'm not sure how to get them. I wait in my office most nights, and sometimes someone will walk in, but most nights it's empty, so I come down here, and stand to the side, hoping that'll drum up business somehow. Tonight I at least got to make myself useful when one of the cocktail waitresses mentioned the graffiti. At least I cleaned up something.

Elsie sits down next to me. "Oh, will you just ask him out already?" she says, lighting a cigarette. She's in a blue suit turned nearly purple from all the red light bouncing off the walls. Large ruby earrings sparkle from the shadows of her bob.

"What do you mean?"

"I mean it's been months of you two making baby eyes at each other and nothing happening. If you don't do something soon, he's going to assume you're not interested in him. It's nearly October already, Andy, get to it if you want to ring in '53 with him."

"I don't . . ." I shake my head and look back at him. He's laughing at something a guy at the bar said. Maybe I've been making eyes at him, but has he really been making eyes at me, or just staring at my stare? "How would I even do that?"

"What?" Elsie blows out a smoke ring. "What do you mean?"

"I mean . . ." I don't know what I mean. Two women, one in a suit, dance past us.

She sighs. "You just go up to him and ask him if he wants to get a drink."

"He works at a bar."

"Somewhere else." Elsie shrugs.

"But—"

"Elsie, Stan is trying to sneak another number into his set."

I look up at Lee, the showgirl who's interrupted us, and check for lipstick; deep red tonight. She's in a yellow halter-neck dress that sets off her cool onyx skin, and a black wig that's tied back in a bun with a large yellow flower. She sees me staring, and winks. I've met a lot of the showgirls and -boys in passing, but Lee has been the closest to welcoming. She told me flat out that when she's got the lipstick on, to call her miss, and when it comes off, to call him sir, and if I did that, we'd be pals. Easy enough to check. I don't want to mess it up and have the friendliest face in the hallway, maybe the whole city, stop talking to me.

"Oy vey," Elsie says, looking at the stage, where Stan, the female impersonator, is readying the mic for another number. "I'll take care of it."

"Sorry, Andy," Lee says, "didn't mean to steal her away."

"It's fine," I say, as Elsie stands.

"You have a fella waiting in your office, by the way. Nice shoulders."

"Sad or angry?" I ask. Those are the two types I get. Sad men, wondering if their boyfriends are cheating on them, and angry men, convinced their boyfriends are cheating on them. Cheap work, tailing men meeting other men, or going home to the wives they haven't told anyone about, but I can't be picky. I'm new at this, and I need to bring in whatever I can.

"Not sure." Lee shakes her head. "I think he came up through the garage, though." The ground floor under the club is a garage with an entrance in the alley. There's parking down there; my car, Elsie's, some others—but with it being out of the way and a bouncer in the stairwell keeping an eye out for the cops, it's an easy way up to my office without even setting foot in the club.

"Better get to work, then," Elsie says, walking away, "and ask him out." She glances meaningfully over at Gene.

"Ask who out?" Lee asks, grinning at me. "You finally find a boy you like, Andy? It better not be Stan."

"No," I say quickly. "It's . . . something else. Thanks, Lee. Sorry I won't get to hear you sing. I'll try to get down before your set is over."

"You'll hear me through the floorboards, honey," she says, walking after Elsie, her hips swaying. Gene's eyes flicker to mine for a moment as I pass the bar, or maybe I imagine it, and he's just staring at a drink as he pours it. I can talk to him later. Leaving a client waiting means they have time to reconsider and walk out. Elsie hasn't set an expiration date on this little experiment of having an in-house detective, but I must seem like a bad idea by now. I bring in enough to feed myself, sure, but her percentage is much lower than the value of renting me the space, and we both know it. How long before she decides my office and apartment were better before, as storerooms for booze?

I have to shove through the crowds, and by the time I get halfway upstairs to my office, I can hear Lee singing "How High the Moon." The floor above the club is just a hallway from one elevator to stairs, with dark purple walls, and lined with doors, most of them open. The two closest to the elevator are my office and apartment, respectively, but the other four are the dressing rooms, doors always thrown open, the hallway bustling with performers and musicians and sometimes waitresses here on break, or fans coming to leave flowers for their favorite performers. People laugh and talk as loudly as downstairs as they paint on makeup or fake mustaches, zip up dresses, button vests. At first, the chaos worried me, but it actually feels like home, the same sort of clamor as working at the police station, only now I'm not looking over my shoulder to see if they're realizing the truth about me.

Right now, the hall is filled with white feathers slowly floating down through the air and scattered on the floor like flower petals after a thunderstorm. I glance into one of the dressing rooms and see Walter trying to squeeze into a white dress that's covered in feathers. Sarah, already in a full tuxedo, is trying to pull up the zipper for him, but it's not going, and he hops up and down, hoping to make it fit, shedding feathers as he does.

"It fit last week," he says.

"You got fat this week."

In the next room, two female impersonators are peeling off their makeup, cackling at a joke I didn't hear. A male impersonator is leaning against the wall, smoking. When I nod, she nods back, which is something. They never nodded back the first few months I was here. Even if they're coming to terms with my old life, they don't love that I'm suddenly living and working next door. Clients don't love it, either. Even with a covert way up here, the way people gossip, you need to be careful.

But I'm the only queer detective in town, so some of them still risk it. Even when I'm not here, someone always tells me if a client shows up. It's still uncommon enough it's noteworthy. Not that the cases are. I'd thought I could do something here, maybe make up for who I was. But all I do is follow people, tell people who love them their secrets. I'm not helping out the way I wanted. No one even trusts me enough to ask me when they're in real trouble. Why would they?

Elsie had the door redone when I moved in, AMETHYST IN-VESTIGATIONS stenciled in dark purple. I don't love the name, but I get why she chose it—being affiliated with the Ruby, being another of Elsie's gems—it means I'm trustworthy, like the Ruby is. Most welcoming gay club in San Francisco, most welcoming gay PI, too. In theory anyway. Certainly not everyone is buying it, though, or I'd have more business. I wonder who's desperate or angry enough to come see me tonight.

There's a man sitting in the chair that faces my desk. His back is to me, but I can see he's blond, broad shouldered, tall. I close the door with a click and he turns around.

Oh.

The recognition hits like an anchor that's dropped too fast, crashing into the seabed, into both of us, sand flying up, fish fleeing, a heavy thud, and a scar on the ocean floor.

He looks just as shocked as I feel. Well, at least that's two of us.

"I didn't realize it would be you," he says, almost apologetically. He stands up. "I can go. I mean, I should go."

I think about letting him. He can drift out the door like smoke and I can go back to thinking of him as a sour memory. But I can't be turning down clients. And . . . I want to know. What happened.

I shake my head. "No, sit down. If you're here, there's not many other places you can go, right?"

"Sure, but—"

"James. Don't worry. I can help."

I make my face calm, professional, even smile a little, though it kills me, and I go around to my side of the desk. He looks almost the same, even though it's been seven years. He has gray creeping in at his sideburns, but is still shockingly handsome, with a square jaw and bright blue eyes that not even the dark circles can hide.

"So," he says after a moment, and I realize he's been looking at me the way I've been looking at him, finding all the changes, all the things that stayed the same. "Been a while, huh?"

I stare at him. I don't know what to say to that. He's the one who vanished. A faint whiff of him comes across the desk. Pine, the ocean. Just like he used to smell. For a moment, it's like the lines in his forehead and the grays vanish, and it's just us again, like when we were alone on base, or in the sonar cabin of the *Bell*, all our crewmates somewhere else. Just dim light, him, me, the sway of the ocean, our hands and bodies. He used to hold me tight when the ship really rocked. Kiss my earlobe.

I realize I haven't said anything, and so does he. "You look well," he says, smiling. He never could handle the silence. He always had to fill it with a grin or a joke or his mouth on mine.

"Thank you," I say. And as I get used to this—the two of us together again—I suddenly realize there's another presence.

"You ever hear from Helen?" he asks, as if sensing it, too.

I shake my head. "Not for years."

Helen had been the third of our motley crew—a member of WAVES, the navy women's auxiliary. Never went on a ship, but worked at Treasure Island, as a driver. After James vanished, though, we couldn't make the friendship work, just the two of us. The crater he left in our lives with his sudden disappearance, with us not knowing what had happened—it was so big, too terrifying to keep sidestepping. But I don't tell him all that. He doesn't get to know what he left behind.

Lee's voice comes through the floor, just like she promised, but it's muffled, the lyrics unclear. Just the sound of a voice, and music, too foggy to have any real meaning.

"Why don't we talk about why you're here," I say.

"Yeah. That's probably better than dwelling on the past."

"Sure," I say. "Better than that."

He swallows. He was barely prepared to do this, and then it was a swell of old memories that came in the door. I almost feel for him. But then I remember his bed on base, right next to mine, but empty one morning. Perfectly made. His luggage gone. His locker door hanging open, nothing inside. Not even a letter. Just emptiness waiting to be filled with fear and questions: Had they caught him? Was I next?

"I'm up for a promotion," he says finally. "Rear admiral, lower half."

"Oh," I say, trying not to look like I was just slapped across the face. "Congratulations. I didn't realize you'd stayed in the navy."

"Well, yeah," he says, tilting his head, confused. He used to do that a lot. "That's why I—" He stops himself. "After the thing with the spy, the brass noticed me."

I nod. He knew a little German from his grandmother. He'd never told anyone that—knowing German was suspicious during the war—but he overheard some supposed tourists speaking it on base, trying to get something to the mainland, and he'd reported it. He'd stumbled onto a spy, stopped a Nazi plot. But there was barely time to celebrate—the *Bell* left for Okinawa, our first real action since we'd enlisted, aside from escorting ships between San Francisco and Pearl Harbor.

We didn't get back until the end of '45. We spent our days looking for enemy subs and clearing out underwater mines around the coast—I ran the sonar, searching, and James was the captain's secretary. But we'd known each other before that. We'd come through training together. We were always together.

His eyes look the same now. He stares at me, waiting for a reaction.

"I remember," I say finally.

He nods, and takes out a cigarette case from his jacket pocket, offers me one, which I take. We tap our cigarettes on the desk almost in unison and then he takes out a lighter and brings it to his cigarette. Then, without even looking at me, without hesitating, he leans over the desk and lights mine, his fingers close to my mouth. I don't even realize how intimate it is until it's over. Old habits, memories our bodies haven't gotten rid of, the way alcoholics undo themselves drinking any glass put in front of them without realizing.

"Well . . ." he says, and blows smoke out between his lips in a long gust, "after that, I was on officer track. Worked hard. Kept my nose clean, y'know?"

"A change for you, then?"

He laughs, but it's sad. "Yes, well. That was the point. I mean . . . we all knew it wasn't going to last. The . . . openness. Right? The moment we took Okinawa I knew. The rules were going to change back as soon as we won the war." James always knew when the party was over. When to leave the bar before the raid, when to not go out at all. He said it felt like a thermometer, and the mercury was fun, release, going up up up . . . you had to leave before it hit the top. People like us, we only get our fun in doses, like junkies. Too much and you're dead.

"Just one of your feelings?" I ask.

He nods, cigarette smoke swirling around him at the gesture, like a frame around his portrait. "After we got back it was boiling. We'd gotten away with so much. Not every homosexual, I know. But you and me, we were lucky, Captain Teller didn't care much as long as we were good at our jobs. Some captains would have had us court-martialed just for the way we smiled at each other. With the war over, guys leaving, the navy bringing in those new shrinks to study us . . . it was time to go. No more fun for a while." He looks at me, a little sad, and then up at the ceiling. "Anyway, that's where I am today. Captain."

"That's fast," I say. "You must have really loved the job."

He doesn't wince at that, and I'm not sure he was supposed to. "Well, a lot of guys left after the war, and I'd already been to college. And I'm good at it, too. I always told you I would be if they'd given me a chance. And now there's this rear admiral spot. My name is being tossed around, now that Michaelson is retiring."

He pauses, takes a hit off his cigarette.

"Except?" I ask. "Someone make the captain spill about us?"

"Oh, no, I don't think . . . I mean, no one really remembers me then. I restarted. I was posted in the Atlantic until I made captain two years ago." He chuckles, low and familiar. "People call me Jim now. And with you gone . . ."

"Sure," I say, inhaling on my own cigarette. It's bitter.

"But there are some photos. More recent ones."

"I thought you said you kept your nose clean."

"I did. I do. But you know how it is, Andy. You go weeks, months, and you start to feel . . ."

"Yeah," I say, remembering how it felt at the station, the nights I was off duty and felt like I barely existed. "It doesn't feel like that if you're more open about things, for what it's worth." I decide I don't like the cigarette and twist it out in the ashtray on my desk. I haven't kissed anyone since Gene but I don't feel that ache, that loneliness like I used to. I haven't needed to shove myself against another man just to feel my own skin.

"Well . . . that must be nice," James says. He looks around my office and I follow his eyes: coatrack, desk, ashtray, pens, paper. On a shelf are some books my friend Pat lent me. I keep it discreet in here. Nothing personal. Still feels odd to have him looking around, like he might find something.

"I never got married, you know," he says, turning back to me. "I didn't want to do that to a woman, unless she was in on it. I suppose I could have asked Helen, but . . ."

"But that would have been even more trouble," I say.

"Yeah, she was always trouble." He smiles, inhales on his cigarette.

She'd recognized us from base, and come up to us one night

at a gay bar, fearless, to offer us a ride next time we were headed out—provided we escorted her in. The gay bars were more mixed then, men and women, and it suited us all to pair off, for appearances. But we got close. She was funny, flinty, wild both in a car and out of it, always going for the girls with boyfriends, husbands, diving out a back window when he came home. She'd pick us up from our hotel at the time we'd agreed, her blouse still half-unbuttoned from having to run.

"So the photos?" I ask, suddenly missing her more than I missed him. She didn't vanish. I let her slip away.

"Yeah, right." He nods, then puts the cigarette out. "Me and a professional. Not someone I picked up in a park or anything, not some punk looking to roll me. He's a fairy I see sometimes. Discreet. But then these photos came the other day. Not from him, I don't think. They're not signed. Tells me to leave ten grand in a locker Wednesday or else they get sent to the admirals. I'll get dishonorably discharged, maybe court-martialed." His voice is getting higher, reedier. "Andy, I don't have that kind of money. What am I supposed to do?"

"Why are you so sure it's not from the hooker?" I ask.

"Danny's a good guy. And I pay him well enough—why turn on me now?"

"He could need a payday—could be he's being blackmailed himself. Or he's moving, or just got tired of it and decided to cash out. Could be he only just got a camera."

"I don't think he—"

"What, another feeling?"

"I've never been wrong." He crosses his legs and starts rubbing his hand on his knee, like he's polishing something. His nervous tic. "Though I haven't been able to get in touch with him, either."

"Okay. You have the photos?"

"Do you really want to see them?" We lock eyes and I think about it. I don't.

"Do you know where they were taken?"

"Yeah. A hotel I use. Fake name, and he comes up later, we don't go in together. And the hotel never asks questions."

"What's the hotel?"

"It's on California, just east of Pacific Heights."

"Okay, but what's it called? I'm going to have to go there."

He looks away, won't meet my eyes. "The Belltower."

A laugh rips out of me like a knife.

"It just seemed like a good sign."

"Sure," I say. "You know what room they were taken in?"

"I always ask for the same one. High up enough there aren't other buildings out the window. Room 608."

I start jotting down notes. "And how did you meet, exactly? Did he have a madam or handler?"

"No, no, he was on his own. I met him at a bar—not a queer one. But he spotted me anyway, y'know, like we used to do with—" He stops. The past keeps pouring out of him, and he knows he's going to choke on it.

"You have a phone number, and address?"

"Just his phone number." He rattles it off, and I write that down, too.

"All right," I say.

"So you'll take the case?"

"I'll do what I can. I'm fifty bucks a day, plus expenses." It's higher than I usually charge. I'm entitled to some pettiness.

"Fine," he says. "But I need the photos—the negatives, too—by Wednesday or else . . ."

"I can't make any promises. But five days should be enough time. And if it's not, I can watch the locker, find out who's blackmailing you, get the money back."

"I don't have money like that, I can't even get it together."

He looks so sad for a moment, so scared, I feel a need to protect him. To hold him. He must be so desperate if he came here—a club where setting foot inside could get him fired if anyone saw. Then I remember that I felt the same way when he vanished, terrified that I would be next. The pity fades.

"We'll figure something out if it comes to that. But let me poke around first. Could just be Danny, desperate, and I can scare him off. All right?"

"Yeah . . . yeah." He takes a deep breath, goes to take out his cigarette case again, then stops. "You always looked out for me, Andy. I guess this is . . . just like old times."

"It's not, James."

"Maybe it could be?" he asks, standing. He takes the pen out of my hand and writes a phone number on the pad. He bends his body over the corner of the desk to write, and without the furniture between us, I can smell him clearly, feel him. Touch him if I wanted. There's a spot on his spine where if I ran my fingers, he would melt. I could take him to my room across the hall, better than the cheap motels we used. It would be easy, I think. He wants me to. The memories are like magnets, trying to snap our bodies back together.

He drops the pen. I look up at him. I think for a moment he's going to kiss me, and I don't know if I want him to or not.

"I'll be in touch," I say.

"I don't know if I'm glad or terrified that it ended up being you," he says softly.

"Only queer detective in town."

"I know. People talk about it. But I never thought . . . What did you do? After?"

"I left. I became a cop. That didn't work. Here I am."

"Do you hate me?"

He stares at me, narrowing his eyes a little, willing an answer out of me, but I don't know if he wants a yes or no. Below us, Lee is singing another song: "That Old Black Magic." The music rises up like perfume.

"Not anymore, James. It's been seven years. We don't even know each other."

It's a lie. He knows it's a lie as well as he knows me. Or some version of me. Some version of me that's already reaching up, hungry mouth first.

But that version of me isn't here, not now. We stare at each other a moment longer. Then he turns and goes.

I sit alone in my office long enough I hear the music downstairs end, and a little while after that the door creaks open and Lee peeks in.

"I thought you'd be back down at the bar to hear me sing."

"Oh." I look up. "I'm sorry, Lee. I heard you through the floor. You sounded great."

"You okay? I saw the light on, but the door is open. You don't usually just wait in here alone."

"I . . . The client," I say, looking up at her. "I knew him. Ages ago. In the war."

"Never knew he was gay?"

I laugh. "I knew."

"Ex-boyfriend, then?"

We never called each other that. Hearing the word now feels cheap to describe what we were. I shake my head. "I don't know."

"Well . . . you take the case?"

"I gotta earn my keep."

She steps in and sits down opposite me. When Lee was first so nice to me, I thought maybe she had a crush, but over the months, I've realized that's not it. She likes my job. Always asks me questions about the cases, even throws out theories. The attraction isn't me, it's the office.

"So what kind of job?"

"Blackmail."

"Oh." She raises her eyebrows. "You have one of those before?"

"No. But I didn't tell him that." I crack a smile. "Charged him twice my usual rate."

She laughs. "Leads?"

"The man he was with, the hotel he was at."

"Exciting." She slowly takes off her wig.

"We'll see."

"All right," she says. "You sure you're okay?"

"Sure, sure," I say, waving her off. "It was just . . . seeing a ghost, you know?"

"Oh, I know all about that," she says, standing up. "Plenty of my ghosts waltz into this place every night. But"—she smiles—"there was a very nice-looking man at the bar tonight. So I'm going to go take off my lipstick and put on a suit and see if he wants to dance with me. Even if it is to Stan's singing. You should come down."

"I will," I say. "Just give me a few."

She shrugs and walks out of the office. I stay there for a while longer, breathing in the smell of pine and the ocean.

TWO

When I finally get downstairs, Lee is on the dance floor, in a suit and out of makeup, his arms around a tall and handsome man who smiles at him. They're one of just a few couples left on the floor, the earlier crowds having faded as the night did. At the bar, Elsie and Gene are chatting. Some people are nursing drinks alone, and there's a couple kissing in one of the shadowy corners.

Stan is back with the band, singing "All My Love." He's not as good as Lee. I wish I'd been down here for her set. I walk over to the bar, Elsie looking me up and down.

"You don't look good," Elsie says. "You okay?"

Gene immediately reaches over the bar and puts his hand on my forehead.

"Doesn't feel like a fever," he says, taking his hand back. I realize my own hand has reached up a little, as if to take his, so I rest it on the bar.

"Just the new client," I say.

"Who does he want you to follow?" Gene asks, voice a little hoarse. If there's one person who hates my cheap little tail-jobs more than me, it's Gene. That's another reason I haven't asked him out. He says he understands why I take the cases, that he knows I hate them, too. But he knows better than most what happens when secrets get out. How dirty these cases are. Well, at least this one isn't.

"Actually, he might be in real trouble," I say, and Gene looks up, eyes curious. "I might finally get to help someone."

"Yeah?" Elsie swirls her drink. It's mostly empty, her usual, a highball, and it smells like oranges, washing away the pine. "And get paid?"

"Yeah. Double. I know him. Knew him."

"Really?" Elsie's eyes widen in shock with a hint of amusement. "What, was he an ex?"

I don't say anything, but my eyes go to Gene, who has suddenly started cleaning the glasses that are lined up under the bar, dipping them in under the faucet and then rubbing them clean with a towel.

An ex-friend maybe. My closest friend. My lover. We were together from my first week of training, when he came out of the showers in the bunk, towel wrapped around his waist, dancing like he was a striptease at a boys' club, the other guys playing along, whistling, hooting. He and I met eyes, and in that moment we both knew. We were stuck together. Until we weren't. "Ex" doesn't feel like the right word for it. I just shake my head, noncommittal.

"Oh," Elsie says. "Sorry, I didn't think you had any . . ." She shakes her head, then turns on me, glaring. "And no more cleaning up the nasty words someone painted on the building. People saw you dragging that back through the bar and thought you'd killed someone."

"I wanted to help," I say. "It had been there for weeks."

"You are helping. But that's not your job. It had been there for weeks because it was small and red and it made other would-be defacers feel like they didn't have anything to add. If I wanted it gone, I would have asked one of the busboys." She pats me on the cheek. "Stick to what you're good at."

"Defacers?"

She smirks, then glances at her watch. "It's a word, right there in the dictionary," she says, then downs the rest of her drink. "I should get going. I promised my girl I'd be home tonight. You good to close up, Gene?"

"Sure," Gene says.

She stands, and as Gene turns back down to the glasses, looks from him to me and raises an eyebrow. I sigh, and she shrugs, our entire conversation silent.

"Bye, boys," she says, before turning and walking out.

"You want anything?" Gene asks when she's gone. His shirt is unbuttoned now, and his undershirt has a low collar, showing off the edges of his clavicle, shining with sweat. "I know seeing an ex can be . . ." He takes out a glass and pours me some whisky without even waiting for an answer. I take it and down it.

"Thanks," I say, wiping my mouth.

"It was a bad breakup?"

"There was no breakup," I say.

He raises an eyebrow.

"He just vanished one day. I thought maybe he'd been caught and . . . I put in for early discharge. Before they could give me the blue ticket. I was terrified. I joined the police to hide, thought I could throw people off the scent." I stop and look up at Gene. He's staring at me, listening. I let my finger trail the cold edge of the empty glass. "I turned my life to ash because I thought he'd been taken. But this whole time it turns out he'd been . . ."

"Caught?"

"Promoted."

Gene winces in sympathy and pours me another shot. I stare down at it.

"He's up for another promotion," I say. "Rear admiral."

Gene snorts. "Really?"

"I know, but it's a big job. But . . ."

"You don't want him to get it?" Gene asks, and his eyes are

staring me down, brown so dark they look black, like they're pulling something out of me just to fill the space. "You don't want to help him?"

I look away. "I don't know."

It's the wrong thing to say and I know it as soon as it escapes me, but it hovers there, the way the truth always does when it's spoken too loudly.

"Thanks for the drink," I tell him.

"Andy—" he says, like he's going to apologize to me. But that's just embarrassing for both of us, so I get up. He beckons to me, but then the lights start to flicker—the code for a police raid. The music stops. Everyone immediately separates, standing apart from one another, nervous. Walter takes a badge from his feathered cleavage that says "I am a man" and sticks it to his dress—a trick Elsie stole from José at the Black Cat. Legally, bars are allowed to be queer now, they can't shut us down just for having gay people inside. But cross-dressing can be deception, which is an arrest. Dancing and hand-holding can be improper acts, which is an arrest. And then there's worse than just arrest.

"Go," Gene says to me, but I'm already heading to the stairs. The thing about being a former cop who was fired after being caught in a raid on a gay bar is that all your old buddies on the force would love to win bragging rights for breaking your face. They don't know about my new job or home, but if they did, they'd be here every night trying to shut the Ruby—and me— down permanently. I pull out my key to Elsie's apartment—the one place the cops can't go. Technically my apartment's a residence, but it's also renovated storage, so they can search it, and if they find me in there, some old pal on the force who knows me, they might take me in for fun. No way I'd survive that. There's no safe place for me, not really. But hiding in the shadows, relying on Elsie—it's the best I've got.

This is the ninth raid since I've been here. I hope it isn't because they've heard about me, some rumor. But I don't think that's it. Elsie used to be able to hold the cops off with bribes, but the money for those bribes came from blackmailing some people we both liked and she'd stopped it when I'd caught her. She said she could handle it. I wonder exactly how wrong she was.

Elsie's place is clean, quiet. I don't snoop, I don't turn on the lights, I just wait by the window. When the police leave, I watch them stream out of the building like a river of navy. They don't have anyone with them, which means everyone got apart in time, everyone was separate, alone, and there was no reason to make an arrest and close the place down. It's safe, for tonight.

When I get back down to the Ruby, I only peek in, the door covering half of me. Everyone looks rattled, but no one is hurt. The cops like to smack people around sometimes, hope someone will fight back and they'll have their reason to shutter the club. But it's late, and the club was mostly empty, so maybe it didn't seem like much fun. And now the music is playing again, and Lee and his man are on the dance floor, arms around each other, smiling as brightly as they can to scare away the shadows the police left behind.

I glance at Gene, but he's mixing someone a drink, and what do I have to say to him, really? What could I have done if they weren't okay? So I let the stairwell door close. It's time to call it a night.

Upstairs, the feathers have all sunk to the floor. Just a few performers are left, washing their faces, changing back into street clothes, vanishing into the night. They always look saddest leaving.

I unlock the door to my apartment, across from the office. It's just a small studio with a bathroom off it. I've decorated more in here; there are some of Pat's books, a photo of my parents, and a record player. It's the first thing I bought with my money once I was out of the navy. Plenty of records—that's where my money goes after food and Elsie's cut, if I have any left.

I strip and lie on my bed, above the sheets. The window is open and a faint rattle of traffic rolls by outside. The Ruby's sign glows red right out my window, staining the room pink where it's not black. It smells like liquor and makeup from the hall, seawater and gasoline from the street. I close my eyes, and memories swell back up, his hand in mine. His lips on mine. Moments in the dark alone in the sonar cabin I operated on the *Bell*. Moments not alone, in hotel rooms on leave, other men we brought back sometimes, or just his hand on my thigh in a club, Helen smoking on my other side, chatting up a woman.

We were happy, somehow, then. It doesn't make any sense.

I will the memories away, push them aside, and instead wonder about the case, then about Gene, and then I wonder what his hand would feel like, if I'd taken it when he touched my forehead. How soft his hands would be. If his wrist would taste of salt.

The next morning, after uneasy dreams about James and photos that left me feeling seasick, I need to get out into the air. I shower and head down the street to the diner I've been having breakfast at every day since I moved in. It's the kind of greasy spoon where the vinyl of the seats creaks under you like an old floorboard, but the food is cheap and the waitresses aren't chatty. No one knows me, so I just eat alone, and read the paper if someone leaves one in the booth, and the headline isn't about moral deviants, which it is at least half the time these days.

But today, when I walk in, I see I'm going to have a companion. She sticks out like a tiger in a room full of housecats. The white scarf wrapped around her blond hair and the sunglasses might be disguising her face enough no one recognizes her from the papers, but it's also drawing more attention to her. Margo was never good at being subtle.

I sit down across from her and try to keep my expression level. "You in trouble again?"

She keeps her sunglasses on, but I can tell she's rolling her eyes behind them. "Sort of. Not me, though."

I nod, wondering who at Lavender House could have gotten mixed up in something. I'd met Margo, Elsie's girlfriend, working my first private case, for her mother-in-law. She hadn't liked me at first, been like rough ice. I'm proud I got her warmed up to the place where the ice cube starts to get slippery. "Cliff?" I ask.

"No, no one from the house, Andy . . ." She looks down at her nails. "I got Elsie to drive me into town today. I told her I wanted to do some dress shopping. Henry is coming to join me in a few hours. We're going to pick out wallpaper."

"Redoing something at the house?" Wondering if that's what they need me for—day labor. At this point, I'd take it.

"Just a room," she says, looking away. "Pearl asked if you were getting fed enough, and Elsie said you went to the same little diner down the street every morning, if you're wondering how I found you."

I nod. "You could join the team, if you wanted. Be a junior investigator."

She looks at me like I just told her she has a roach on her face. "No."

The waitress appears and asks if we want anything, so I order scrambled eggs, toast, and coffee. When the waitress turns to Margo, she shakes her head, as if horrified by the idea.

"So this visit—what is the trouble?" I feel myself tense up; Margo doesn't usually beat around the bush like this.

She smiles a little and lowers her sunglasses enough to look me in the eye. "It's you."

"What?"

"Elsie would never tell you, but you're hurting the business."

I shake my head. "The place was packed last night."

"Maybe." She shrugs. "But not as packed as it used to be. Apparently word is that she's housing a cop, and people don't love that, for obvious reasons."

"Ex-cop."

"I know," she says, a little angry. "Look, I'm not telling you to leave. I'm just telling you that you need to be doing better. I've been floating Elsie a little money, but I can't do that much longer. There are . . ." She stares down at her hands—white gloves. "Expenses."

"Doing better how?"

"Getting enough clients to help Elsie cover the loss of business. Her bribes to the cops to hold off raids have gone up, too. And if they find out about you—"

"Yeah," I say.

"So you need to make this worthwhile for her. I mean the idea . . . you helping people . . . like us. It's a good one. But it only works if they trust you. And it's not going to happen just because Elsie does."

I sigh, and the waitress puts down my food and walks away. Suddenly I'm not hungry.

"Thanks for telling me," I say.

"I knew you'd want to know," she says, starting to get up.

"Hey, wait, no, stay awhile. Get a coffee. Tell me how everyone is."

She smiles at that, almost a big one, but she shakes her head. "I need to meet Henry. And everyone is fine, Andy. Pearl wants you to come for dinner one night. Just call us up, say when."

"I will," I say. She tilts her head like she doesn't believe me. I will, one day, though. I just want them to have a little more time without me, the reminder of the murder that brought us together. And maybe I want a little more time in the real world before going back to their home, which wasn't just a secluded mansion, but was protected and caged. If I go back too soon, I don't think I'll be able to leave. But I don't belong there.

She takes her coat off the rack, white, with fur trim, and slips it on. She looks at me again, evaluating.

"I don't usually say this kind of thing," she tells me, "but I agree with Elsie, for what it's worth. I think you're in the right place. Just make sure everyone else knows that."

"Yeah." I nod. "Thanks. Hey, I'm on a case now. Maybe that'll help."

"I hope so," she says. And then she's gone.

I turn back to my eggs and shove them down so I don't get hungry later. Elsie believes in me, and I've been letting her down more than I knew. Sure, she could probably just go live with Margo, hide away, but that's not Elsie, and the Ruby is her home. The home she welcomed me into, and where I'm not providing my keep. I'm not sure how to fix it, but I know I have to. The best way I can think of to start is with the case. Five days—no, four now—to find those photos, or James won't pay me a thing because he'll be in a brig somewhere. I can see him, in one of the cells they have at Treasure Island, cold, wet, dark, the kind of feeling that creeps into your soul. Even with all the things I feel about him, I don't want that for him. I don't want it for anybody. I remember what it's like to be dragged out and beaten when your colleagues find out the truth.

I take the streetcar to the civic center. The library is just off the town hall, and the air smells sweet, earthy with falling leaves. San Francisco in the fall never really reaches autumn the way it does in those East Coast postcard photos, but if you've been here long enough, you spot the differences—the few leaves that tumble, the way the wind blows harder. Summer is hot and bright, a party on the beach, but the fall is smoking in an alley. I like the fall better.

I walk into the library, down the stairs between those lonely murals. I like the murals, the sea one especially. The women, in different frames between the columns, looking at that flat blue-gray space that somehow has no color and all the colors at once.

Downstairs I dig out the reverse telephone directory and spend a while searching through it until I have the address that matches the phone number James gave me. The professional he's been screwing. Danny.

James always liked variety. During the war, he was my everything—my buddy, my best friend, my lover—but it was never exclusive. Didn't mean it wasn't close, though. War does things to relationships, being locked away, surrounded by death. I spent every day looking at the sonar equipment, waiting for the solemn ping. Waiting to miss one and for us to snap apart in the ocean. James waited with me. That bonds you in ways beyond sex. Knowing you might die together. That you probably will.

Danny can't be all that to him. I bet he's pretty, though. James always liked them pretty.

The address is in Potrero, so I get back on the streetcar and take it to Townsend, then cross the bridge. It's getting on toward noon and the sun is hot here, even though it's fall. The buildings are squat in the light and the smell of the bay, salt and smoke, wafts over everything. I find Danny's apartment building—red bricks, built along the side of a slope, so it looks crooked. The door is propped open with a rock, and a woman in curlers leans out the front window, smoking. She narrows her eyes at me as I approach the building.

"Who are you here for?" she asks.

"Danny," I tell her.

"He hasn't been home in a while," she says.

"Just need to leave him something," I say.

"I hope it's money for rent," she says. "Apartment 6. That girl has been living there, though."

I almost ask what girl, but I suspect that would draw more attention than I want, so I head upstairs to meet her myself.

He's on the top floor, and the stairs creak as I climb them. I knock on the door. Beyond it I can hear the faint static of a radio, maybe a newscaster. The door opens a crack; one large dark eye stares up at me. She has a full face and dark hair, and her skin is pale enough that her eye and hair look even darker by comparison. I can't see much more of her, but she's in black. She doesn't say anything.

"I'm looking for Danny."

"He's not here." Her voice is quiet, like she doesn't want anyone else to know, even though the woman in curlers seemed to think it was common knowledge. She blinks, but doesn't close the door. She seems worried, so I do my nicest smile.

"I'm a private investigator," I say. "Maybe I can help?"

She opens the door wider, enough I can see her. She's got one of those faces where she could be eighteen or thirty, but she's clearly been crying. Her hair is pulled up on top of her head in two waves, the rest falling down her back, and her black dress is dated, a little prudish, and makes her figure—all curves—seem like something she's ashamed of. Probably not in the same line of business as Danny, then.

"My name is Andy," I tell her.

"I'm Donna," she says after a moment. She swallows. "I'm Danny's sister."

"Can I come in?" I ask.

She nods and opens the door wider, stepping aside. I walk in. The place is shabby, but tidy. I wonder if that's him or her. There's an open window with pale-green drapes hanging limply over it. Then there's a bed, a sofa, a radio softly playing a jingle. The bed is made, could have been slept in, but the sofa has a dent for a head in one of the pillows. She's sleeping there, waiting for him to come back. Otherwise the place is more plain than I expected. No scarves over the lamp in the corner, no air of cheap cologne. But then, that could be Donna's tidying up.

I turn around as she closes the door.

"You've been staying here?" I ask.

She nods and goes to sit on the sofa. "I come in now and then. I still live with my parents, in Burlingame, but I take the train in once a month to see Danny. He leaves a key under the mat for me . . . but this time he wasn't home."

"Did you call first?"

"Oh, sure. Four days ago. And he said he'd be here when I came in—day before yesterday. But he wasn't. I mean sometimes I get here and he's not back for a few hours. I think he likes it that way, because he knows I'll clean up . . ." She smiles a little, then immediately frowns. "But he hasn't come back yet. Is he in trouble? Is that why you're here?"

"I don't know yet," I tell her honestly. "He's part of a case I'm working, but I have no reason to think he's in trouble. But I do need to find him, so if I do, I'll send him back to you."

She nods. "I can't pay—"

I shake my head. "Don't worry. This is part of another case, someone's already paying me. But you can help me out by answering some questions, letting me look around."

"All right," she says. "Do you want some water, or a Sanka?"

"Sure, a Sanka would be swell," I say. She looks relieved at that and goes into the tiny kitchen off the main room. I follow her and watch as she sets the kettle on. She takes out two mugs.

"Do you know what your brother does for a living?" I ask.

"He's a waiter," Donna says, nodding at the mugs. "But he wants to be a singer. He says there are bars and cafés and stuff that he's going to try to sing at, he just needs to know the right people."

"Sure." I nod. "So waitering is a good way to earn money and meet them."

"Exactly." She smiles up at me. "My parents . . . they think he's a bit of a layabout. But he's got a great voice, really."

"I believe you," I say. "What sort of things does he like to sing?"

She turns back to the mugs. "Oh, you know, old stuff. The kind of things everyone is singing nowadays."

The kettle starts to whistle and I decide not to push more on the singing. She seems almost embarrassed all of a sudden, when a moment ago, she was proud. I wonder if the songs he sings are women's songs—if his performance is in drag. She doesn't know I'm gay; she wouldn't want me to know that. But I can't be sure enough to tell her why she doesn't have to worry.

She pours the water into the mugs and then takes out a can of Sanka and stirs it in, then hands me a mug.

"Do you know where he was a waiter?" I ask.

She shakes her head. "He never took me. Said it wouldn't look good to eat where he worked."

"Sure," I say, "but he never mentioned the name?"

She sips, then shakes her head. "He must have, but I can't remember. Something with an *R*, or a *K* at the start? It might have been a name. Or a street name." She shakes her head and frowns. "I'm sorry. I want to be helpful, I do."

"That's all right," I say, walking back out to the living room. "Maybe I can find a pay stub or something. Do you mind if I poke around?"

She sits down on the sofa again, putting her mug on the little wooden table in front of her.

"I suppose," she says. "If you think it will help."

"It will." I nod, already headed to the dresser by the bed.

"Just . . . don't stare if you see something strange, please. He'll be so mad if I let a man he doesn't even know poke around his stuff."

"I won't tell him," I say, smiling. There's a framed photo on the dresser: Donna and, I assume, Danny. They have the same dark eyes and hair, same cream skin. He's pretty, not muscular, but soft looking, with a coy look and full lips. I can see why he caught James's eye.

"So you two are close?" I ask, trying to focus on why I'm here.

"Oh, very. Danny is my best friend. We're twins, and you know what they say about twins being inseparable? It's all true." She smiles faintly, proud of that. "Do you have siblings?"

"No."

"Oh. Well . . . sometimes it can feel like it's you and them against the world. Nothing bonds you closer."

I nod and open the dresser. I can feel Donna's eyes on me, so I keep talking.

"Did you know many of Danny's friends?"

She turns her head, her eyes drifting off, like she's trying to remember, or come up with a lie.

"I've met a few now and then, but not closely. He never threw parties or anything while I was here—I mean, there's not much room for it."

I nod, sliding open drawers. Undershirts and briefs, some sweaters. In one drawer I find three matchbooks from bars: Shelly's, the Silver Jay, and one that has no name, just an image of a pair of women's cat-eyed glasses. I pocket that one when Donna isn't looking, and write down the names of the other two bars in my notepad.

"You find something?" she asks.

"Just some matchbooks from bars and restaurants. One might be where he worked. Did he smoke?"

She looks down at her coffee, embarrassed again. "Sometimes. I didn't like it. It smells so bad."

"It doesn't after you get used to it," I say, moving to the closet. "So what exactly did he say last time you spoke, do you remember? He mention going to work, or meeting anyone?"

"No," she says, "nothing like that. Just 'can't wait to see you,' and then he had to go because he had to get to work."

Just clothes in the closet—nothing especially outrageous, either. I go through the pockets of the hanging pants, but nothing.

"That was during the day?"

"Yes. He usually worked during the day. Lunch crowds. Only worked at night on Thursdays and Fridays. Then Saturdays were his night off."

I pick up my mug and sip it, sitting down next to her. There's not much else to go through. "When you got here, did you tidy up?" I ask.

She frowns. "Was that bad?"

"No. But did you throw anything away?"

"Oh, I . . . yes." She stands up and goes back into the kitchen and comes out with a wastebasket. "You need to go through his trash? Really?"

"I admit, it's not always a great job," I say, taking the basket. It's small, and there's not much in it. Candy bar wrappers. Another matchbook, this one empty. The Ruby.

"Is it exciting?" she asks. "The job?"

"Oh, now and then," I say, picking up the matchbook and turning it around in my hand. Someone has drawn an X inside it. I pocket it, and keep rifling through the trash.

"You ever solve something like a murder?"

I nod. "Sure. Once on my own, and a lot more times when I was a cop."

Her face goes pale faster than she can look down at her mug this time. "You were a cop first?" she asks, lifting it to her lips and taking a long drink.

"For a bit, yeah. That make you nervous?"

"Oh, I . . . I don't know. A little. I don't like violence."

I pull a scrap of white fabric out of the trash and look at it, not sure what it could be from.

"That's mine," she says, seeing what I'm looking at. "I like to sew. Make all my own clothes and some of Danny's—" She cuts off suddenly. "Just a few of his shirts. When I come to visit, we usually go shopping for fabric together. He takes me to Gump's, or sometimes City of Paris." She takes the fabric and pulls it between her hands. I don't know much about fabric, but it looks flimsy, cheap. "This was for a shirt for him. It was on sale, but it's good quality. We got it last weekend."

"I thought you said you only come up once a month."

She turns back to her mug and lifts it to her lips. "Did I?" She sips. "I mean, usually. I try to get up whenever I can."

"What stops you?" I ask.

"Oh, Mom and Dad need help with the store. We sell farm supplies." Her voice goes flat as she says it. "I wanted to move out, come to the city like Danny, but . . ." She shakes her head. "My parents would have hated that."

"Did you finish the shirt?" I ask. "I didn't see anything like this fabric in the closet, so could he be wearing it?"

"Oh," she sips again, "I didn't think of that. He could be. He'd better not be ruining it."

She frowns, then giggles a little, like it's a joke. She puts the mug down and then turns back to me, her eyes wide. "Danny will be okay, right? Nothing bad happened to him?"

She reaches out and puts her hand on mine. It's my turn to look down at the mug. "I don't know," I say, because it's honest, even though it'll break her heart a little. "He could be mixed up in something bad, and something bad could have happened to him. I wish I could promise . . ."

She pulls her hand back and stands up, turning away. I can hear her sniff, hold back tears. "I understand."

"I'll do everything I can, though," I tell her. I thought it would sound heroic to say that, but it just sounds sad. "Maybe I should get your information—phone number back home, in case you have to go back to your parents. Then I can let you know if I find him."

She nods, her back still turned to me, and then turns around. I hand her my notebook and pen, and she writes down "Donna Geller" and a phone number. Geller. I don't think James knew Danny's surname. If he did, he never mentioned it.

I take the pad back and put it in my pocket. "Thanks."

"Can you tell me . . . what the case you're on is?" she asks.

I shake my head. "No. But I promise to tell you if I find Danny."

She nods, solemn. "Thank you for that."

"Here's my card," I say, taking one out. Elsie had had fancy ones made up with the Ruby's name, but I made up some simpler ones, just my name and number, to give out to people who don't know the kind of clientele I work for. I suspect Donna knows more about her brother than she's been letting on, but I hand her one of those anyway, just in case. "Call me if he comes back, or if you think of anything."

"I will," she says.

"I'd better get going. Thanks for the Sanka."

"Sure," she says, but she doesn't look up at me as I leave.

Outside, the woman in curlers must be on her fourth or fifth cigarette, judging by the pile of stubs under her windowsill.

"She still up there?" the woman asks.

"She's his sister. She's waiting for him to come home."

"Sure," she says, not looking me in the eye. "We're all waiting for someone to come home, right?"

I don't have an answer to that, and I don't think she really wants one, so I walk away. Danny is vanished, and all I have as leads are some matchbooks for clubs. But I'd be willing to bet his singing career was female impersonation, and Donna knows that, even made his dresses for him. A nice girl from the country who comes up and helps out her fairy brother with his dreams of singing while dressed like a woman. That's love. The indent on the sofa pillow was so empty.

I walk till I'm on China Basin Bridge, looking out at the harbor, and I can see a big freighter heading out, piping smoke and streaking the sky gray as it moves. The water is flat otherwise, unbothered. I want to find Danny for the girl waiting alone in the apartment, hoping her brother will come home, as much as I want to find him to help James. James who has four and a half days till his life explodes.

THREE

I stop at a diner for lunch before heading back to the Ruby. Elsie is auditioning a new act, a singer, a woman, maybe Chinese, who's singing "Mona Lisa" as the house band backs her up. I sit next to Elsie and listen for a few minutes. She's got talent, a beautiful voice, real longing as she sings.

"Like her?" Elsie whispers, leaning into me.

"Yeah," I say.

She nods, and when the woman finishes, we both applaud. "You sound great, and I'll give you a forty-five-minute set tonight for four bucks, but make sure you have some dance numbers in there, too," Elsie says. "We'll see how you do in front of a crowd."

"I'll do fine," the woman says with a grin.

"Then I'll put you in the rotation," Elsie says. "Get you a few sets a week. But you gotta make people dance. This place is about bringing joy, not just reminding us about our unrequited longing."

"Also, dancing makes them thirsty," I add.

Elsie elbows me. "It's about joy. This is the one place we can have it."

"I've always found unrequited longing to be a kind of joy," the singer says, smiling and stepping down from the stage. "But I love a girl I can't have." She winks and Elsie laughs. "See you tonight, then."

Elsie grins. "You'll go on at eleven, so get here at ten if you need to change or do your face."

"Thanks. You really won't regret it."

They shake hands and the singer leaves. Elsie turns around to me. "You didn't ask out Gene."

"I'm working," I say with a sigh. "Can we talk about that later?" I fish out the matchbook from Danny's trash and show it to her. "You know a Danny Geller?"

She takes it and flips it over, thinking. "I remember the name. I always remember the Jewish names." She narrows her eyes. "Yeah. It was an unusual act. Too vaudeville. Him and his sister. Dressed the same, did harmonies. Andrews Sisters minus one."

"His sister?" I ask. "Donna?"

"Sure, sounds right. Pretty young thing, dark eyes and curves. I wanted to like it, but his makeup wasn't good, her voice was better . . . it just didn't mesh. I told them to practice, invited them back to see some of the boys here, maybe refine their act a little. Find out where to get a real wig, nicer fabrics for their dresses—the whole thing was kind of threadbare. But they never came back."

"When was that?"

"A while now. Maybe a month?"

"And you told them if they had more money their act would be better?"

She crosses her legs. "I didn't say it like that. And if that were the only issue, I would have given them an advance, brought them on. But it was more than that. They just didn't have it."

I nod. "So he never applied for another kind of job here? Bartender, waiter?"

"No." Elsie shakes her head. "Why? What's he got to do with your case?"

"He's missing," I say. "I found some other matchbooks, though. Only one I didn't recognize." I take out the matchbook with the pair of glasses on it. "Which one is this?"

Elsie frowns. "Yeah, that's not for you. Cheaters. Women's place, mostly. Some tourists. Old bar, been here years, in some way or another. They don't like me much—I hired away a lot of their talent. You should ask Lee. He used to work there."

"I thought you said it was mostly women."

"The entertainment was more varied. But the clientele is mostly queer women, yeah. If you go check it out, they're probably going to be chilly to you."

"I've dealt with cold welcomes before. Your girlfriend, for one." I think of Margo, in the diner, but I don't mention it. She came to me in private as a favor, and Elsie wouldn't have liked it.

Elsie grins. "Ahhh, she wasn't so bad to you. You know her and Henry are doing it—going forward with the adoption. I'm going to be like . . . an auntie or something." I grin, something warm inside me. So that's what the new expense was—and the new wallpaper.

"Not a mother?" I ask.

Elsie brings her hand to her mouth in mock shock. "Evander. She hasn't made an honest woman out of me yet."

"I don't think anyone could do that," I say, standing. "But I'm happy for them—for you, really. Your family is growing."

"It is," she says, looking satisfied. "Always growing." She looks me up and down, satisfaction turning to smugness.

I roll my eyes. "Lee in yet?"

She glances at her watch. "He'll be here in half an hour to rehearse. Speaking of, I should go check the dressing rooms are clean."

We walk together to the elevator.

"So when are you going to ask out Gene?" she asks, after the doors have closed.

"I don't . . ."

"Is this about the client, your ex?"

I look down at the elevator floor. The chime dings and we get out.

"Look," she says, turning to face me and blocking the way to my office. "You're good by me, Andy. You did a lot for my family, and I think you can do a lot for everyone in our family, the bigger one, I mean. But you gotta be part of it. Just because you know the kind of life you want to live now doesn't mean it's going to happen. It's not a bus stop. It's a bus. You have to actually get on the thing. Gene, this client, someone else . . . I don't care. But stop standing on the sidelines downstairs just watching everyone else, okay? It's bad for business. Both of ours."

"I know," I say, thinking of Margo again. "Look, if you want me to take off—"

"That's not what I said," she says, turning away, heading for the dressing rooms, stopping in the first one. "Did someone murder a bird in here?" she says, not to me especially.

I go into my office. I know she's right. And I'm happier than I was when I met her, happier being honest about myself. But I also know who I was, and what I did—or didn't do—as a cop. I didn't warn people of raids when I could have. I didn't help, because I was only looking out for myself. Who am I to help anyone now? It makes me feel weak when I think of it, like I've taken a beating and I'm about to pass out. You don't get to eat at the table if you saw someone poisoning the food and didn't say anything.

I sit down at my chair and look at the phone numbers James gave me. There are two. I try the top one first, but it just rings, so I try the second, and a man's voice picks up.

"Naval Station Treasure Island," says a polite young man. "This is the office of Captain Jim Morris, who's calling?"

My throat goes dry hearing the name of the place, and for a moment I can't speak.

"Hello?" the voice asks again.

"Tell him it's Andy," I say.

"Just a moment."

He has his own office, his own secretary who's devoted enough to come in on a Saturday. He has so much success that I'm never going to see again—a job in public, money, the ability to go to the police and not get beaten by them for asking for help. He might have to hide part of himself in the shadows, but the rest of him is shining bright in the sun. That's what he traded me in for. That's why he left without a goodbye. A good life. The kind I'll never have.

A moment later, he picks up.

"Hi, Andy," he says. His voice is warm and wet, but I can hear an edge in it, too, the performance he used to do. "I really can't talk long."

"I understand," I say, hearing an edge in my own voice. I take a breath. I shouldn't be so angry. Until half a year ago, I was striving for what he has—living it, even. But I never gave up on someone I loved to get there. If he ever loved me.

"Never know when someone else might pick up, or walk in," he says in a near whisper.

"Even on Saturday?" I ask. "Why are you even at work?"

"I don't have much of a social life," he says. "And when I come in, people come in to try to impress me. Impress the people I'm trying to impress, too." He says it softly, sad, like he wishes he weren't one of those people.

"You all right?" I ask. It comes out of me before I have time to think of it. Just hearing that tone in his voice made me worry.

"Well . . . I don't know. It's nice hearing your voice, though." He takes a deep breath when I don't respond to that. It's nice hearing his, too. "Do you have good news?"

"No news yet," I say. "Just that I stopped by Dan's place. He wasn't in. Hasn't been for a while, so I'd better find him."

"Sure, sure," he says.

I don't say aloud he's the best lead, and him having vanished like this isn't looking good. That maybe what I thought would just be breaking into some guy's house and stealing the negatives has turned into something more worrisome. People only really go missing for two reasons: to hide from someone, or because someone has taken them. Either way, the case is a lot more dangerous if he's really missing and not just sleeping it off at some john's house. And with his sister in town, that seems unlikely. So Danny is gone, and I only have one other lead.

"I need to go by the . . ." I pause, working out a code. "The place where that picture you told me about was painted. I know I haven't seen it yet," I say. "But I'm going to do some painting tomorrow in the spot you recommended. I'd like to know what angle you were at."

"Angle?" He pauses. He must be holding the receiver right up against his mouth because it's like he's breathing in my ear. "Oh, sure. Well, if you're looking out at the city, it was . . . painted to your right."

"Sure," I say, thinking I understand. "I'm going to do that tomorrow probably."

"That'll be four days—can you go tonight?"

"It'll be easier to see the room during the day," I tell him. "Trying to get in to see a room at night, when they're busiest, most on guard for . . . visitors—"

"Sure, I get it," he says quickly.

Neither of us hang up and I wonder if he can hear me breathing the way I can him. If he can hear my pulse, which is far too loud.

"I wish . . ." he says. "I wish I had looked you up first when I'd come back here. I think I missed out on something."

And with that, it's like a rotten smell fills the room. He left without a word, but he wished now he'd come back? Why doesn't he wish he'd never vanished? Wish he'd never left me terrified in the dark?

The fear slams back into me, his empty bed and locker when I woke up, knowing he'd been caught, that he'd break, that I was next, sure to be locked up, blue ticketed, with no money, and no way to get a job because of what was on my record. I hadn't been able to feel my fingertips the whole day he vanished. I'd kept dropping things. And all that time, he'd just decided I didn't deserve a goodbye. That he wanted to have a nice normal life and he was fine to burn our relationship down as he took it. I can feel the anger in my chest turning my breath ragged.

"I'll call again when I know more," I say. "Bye, Jim."

I say his new nickname with as much venom as I think is allowed, professionally, and hang up. Then I lean back in my chair and light a cigarette and inhale. It hits like a bullet, and I sigh in relief. I should just ask him why he left like that. I was suddenly alone, aside from Helen, who dealt with his disappearing act by trying to pretend he'd never existed. I used to go to bed on the ship, on the base, and if he was nearby, I'd look over at him and know that even if I died tomorrow, he was a good thing in my life. He was something I'd had, in all the senses of the word, a home I'd found. And that made the risks worth it.

Joining the police made sense. Helen hated the idea, said I'd be going from one prison to another. I knew she was half-right, of course. But what she didn't understand is that no one would suspect if I were a cop. And besides, as a cop, I'd have the inside information—I'd know which clubs were going to be raided, who was being tailed. I'd know how to stay safe. And I'd still get to help people. That's what I told myself.

Helen made me go out to clubs while my discharge request was processed, to try to talk me out of it. Thought if we had enough fun, I'd want to just give in, and become a bouncer or something.

We were on leave. She had a car. We drove into town and went around to clubs, always careful to look like a couple when needed, her picking up women, me picking up men. It was the same as we had done with James, but without him it just wasn't right. It was like dancing without a partner. You know all the steps, but without his hand on your back, there's just a cold spot on your spine. It made me shiver, even more afraid.

All of it comes back to me, even the parts I'd forgotten, but that cold spot was always there until I came to the Ruby. And that was because of the way James vanished. And all this time, he's just been . . . living a good life. It makes me want to throttle him. To quit the case and let him get blackmailed. To let him know what that fear is like until it beats him down like it did me.

But I want to hand Elsie some real money, and even if I hate him, he only has four days, like he said, so I'm going to do it, no matter how many bad memories it stirs up. The *Bell* was a beautiful ship, painted in blocks of black and white. Dazzle camouflage, they call it. It's supposed to make the ship blurry on the horizon, like it could be a trick of the light, but up close, you can see the broad black-and-white bands, curved to pass over the ship like shadows from a blind. I need to see the past from a distance, like a blur on the horizon.

So I take out the matchbooks and make a list of the clubs. Cheaters was the one with the glasses. Shelly's. The Silver Jay. They all have drag acts sometimes, they all have waiters. It's possible none of them were where Danny worked. It's possible he didn't work as a waiter at all, and Donna was just lying to me because she thought I'd find the whole thing perverted.

What I need to do is go around to all the clubs, find out who hears the auditions, see if they were shopping this double act around, or if Danny really was waiting tables somewhere. I need to find out who saw him last, try to find out where he went. Maybe he's just spending a week with a rich john somewhere. Maybe he has no idea about the blackmail.

Downstairs I hear the band kick up, and Lee's voice vibrates through the floor. I grab the matchbooks and head downstairs.

He's on stage, not in makeup yet, just wearing a collared shirt and pants. He's conducting with his hands—he never does that when he performs, then it's always for the crowd, but rehearsals are for the band, who are keeping time with him. He's doing a rendition of "The Glow-Worm," like the Mills Brothers and McIntyre, but jazzier. I haven't heard him sing it before, and by the way the band is reading the music as they play, I'm not sure they have either. Lee probably wrote out the arrangement himself. His other job is in the back room of a music store, loading clarinets and sheet music, or something like that. He says he reads it all in his free time. Marks it up, sees how he would sing it. And if he likes it enough, he does.

I wait until he's finished. They stop and start a few times, but after a little while he comes over and pours himself a glass of water behind the bar. He looks me up and down.

"You want something," he says after a long swallow of water.

I lay the matchbooks out in front of him. "You ever performed these places?"

He looks them over. "All of them. Why?" He glances up at me, his eyes narrowing. "This for a case?" He's already smiling.

"There's a guy I'm trying to find. Danny Geller. Know him?"

Lee shakes his head. "Have a photo?"

"Tall, fit, dark curly hair, dark eyes, pale skin, has a sort of superior smile in every photo I've seen of him."

"Honey, that's a lot of people," he says, looking a little annoyed. No, disappointed. I should have a photo to flash like in those detective stories. I'm definitely not living up to the role.

"Well, I need to find out who saw him last. He might have auditioned at these places, or he could be a waiter at one of them."

Lee's smile grows bigger. "You want me to take you around, introduce you to the folks who do the hiring, don't you?"

I nod.

"And I'd be helping on a case?"

"You would."

"Do I get paid?" he asks, raising an eyebrow.

"I'll buy you a drink at each one," I say, tapping on each of the matchbooks.

He pauses, pretending to consider, his lips pursed, but I know he's in. Getting to work on a case is too exciting for him even if he's not sold on me yet. It's what he's been hoping for since I set up shop.

"My set is over at nine tonight. After that I'll show you around."

"Thanks," I say, grinning. "And . . ." I flinch at what I'm about to ask. "Since you know everyone here, if you maybe could help me . . . convince them I'm trustworthy?"

He scratches his chin, like he's trying to decide what I'm asking. I wait. I know it's a lot to ask and I have nothing to give, really.

"Drum up some more business, you mean, so Elsie doesn't throw you out on your ass?"

"So people trust me enough to hire me, even with who I was."

He smiles, a little solemn, and nods. "But you're going to tell me all about your cases, then. Since *Black Mask* stopped publishing last year, I miss my mysteries."

"As long as you don't break client confidentiality, then as far as I'm concerned, you're part of the team."

"Oh, the team. I'm your girl Friday, then?"

"Depends if you're wearing lipstick, I guess," I say.

He laughs. "Then you better prepare, we're going to have a fun night tonight." He turns away and walks back toward the stage, already conducting with his hands again.

I watch them practice for a few minutes longer then go upstairs to take a quick nap. It's going to be a long evening.

After Lee has performed his set and taken his makeup off, we head out into the night.

It's dark, but the city is still alive, people sitting on fire escapes smoking as we walk down the hills away from the Ruby, and up some others. It's not a far walk to Shelly's, the first place on the list. As we talk I hear the murmur of laughter from open windows, blending with the buzz of traffic. Leaving the financial district and heading into North Beach, the buildings aren't as tall, so the neon lights are more often street level and cast the sidewalk in a rainbow of colors, their buzzing adding to the hum of the city.

I know Shelly's pretty well, but it's amazing how different it seems with Lee. It used to be people barely met my eye until they wanted something else. We never talked. It was all silhouettes and smoke in the dark, waiting for the right moment for a whisper, a meeting in the bathroom or the alley or a car. But now, Lee is greeted by the doorman with a grin and a hug.

"Lee! How are you doing?" he asks.

"Oh, I'm getting by," Lee says. "Who's on tonight?"

"Some new guy. Lester something. He sings real nice, but he doesn't know how to wear a dress."

"Well," Lee says, smiling, "he'll grow into it."

"You looked good in a dress from day one," the bouncer says.

"I was born for it," Lee says, waving him off. "Is Shelly around?"

"Yep, he's in his usual booth."

The bouncer waves us in. It's a golden sort of place, with

wood-paneled walls and the windows blocked with yellow curtains. Candles are at every table, and the electric lights are dim, except on stage. It smells like cigarettes and gin, the way most bars do, but there's something spiky in the smell, like lemon, that makes it all feel warmer. Or maybe that's just the love Lee gets walking around the place—everyone waves, some people stop to kiss his cheek.

"You know everyone," I say.

"Everyone wants to be friends with the showgirl," Lee says. He points at a booth where an older man sits alone, watching everyone, and smiling. "I'll be over there. Get me a Singapore sling."

I laugh and go to order Lee's drink from the bar, getting myself a soda water, to keep my head clear. On stage, a man with a nice voice and an ill-fitting dress is crooning "That Lucky Old Sun." I look around the bar at a few couples dancing, some straight couples gaping at them—tourists coming to watch us like animals at the zoo. The place isn't as fancy as the Ruby, it's more homey, but it's been here twenty years, while the Ruby is just three years old, so I guess that's to be expected. Everything here is well-worn, and the couples here are older. Next to me at the bar are two guys in their fifties, maybe sixties, gray hair, laughing at a joke one whispered to the other. Their hands are laid over each other on the leg of the one farther from me. Looking at them I think about James again, about the gray in his hair, about us sitting in this exact bar nine years ago, one of our first nights on leave after we'd been stationed at Treasure Island.

We'd come here and held hands and flirted with each other, and other men, and then gone to a hotel together. He has a callus on the side of his finger that would always rub the back of my hand, rough. I've been back alone so many times since James vanished that his ghost had faded, but now that he's returned, so have these memories. But they feel different now. They still make me angry, a little sad, but . . . there's hope in them, too. Stupid hope that drips, like a wave of it just hit me.

The bartender puts the Singapore sling down in front of me, and I think he's glaring, like he knows who I am—who I used to be. I pay and walk over to Lee, presenting him with his drink. The man across from us, Shelly I assume, looks me over, his grin fading. He's older, a narrow kind of guy who still has enough hair for a decent comb-over and looks good in it. An old-fashioned pencil mustache gives him an air of foppishness that my old cop buddies would probably have zeroed in on and hassled him for, but he wears it with pride. He looks me up and down and his eyes narrow.

"Lee says you're the gay detective we keep hearing about."

"That's me," I say.

"You've been here before. I know your face. I never knew you were a cop."

"He's not anymore," Lee says. "And they beat him pretty bad when they found out."

"I never ratted anyone out," I say. "I just kept to myself. I was afraid to make friends." I swallow.

"He doesn't even remember the time I tried talking to him," Lee says with a grin.

"What?" I ask, turning suddenly. Lee ignores me, still talking to Shelly.

"He was another guy then. I like him more now." He sips his drink.

"You knew me?" I ask Lee again. I flip through my memory like a book, but it's all silhouettes and blurry photos. So many men I didn't know, didn't want to know. It feels like a kick in the ribs thinking one of them could have been Lee. He deserves so much more than to be a silhouette.

He looks at me from the side, grinning. "Honey, plenty of people knew you on sight. Not your name, or anything else. There were rumors you were a cop, but also rumors about what you liked to get up to, so no one knew what to make of you. But you were cute, and you were easy. That made you notable to a certain demographic."

"We never . . ." I start.

Lee throws his head back, cackling. "No. I was never that desperate. I bought you a drink, you drank it, looking at me. I asked your name, you said you didn't do names, so I walked away."

"Sounds like you were a charmer," Shelly says.

"I don't know how much better I've gotten," I say, "but I'm trying."

"He was something," Lee says. "But like I said, I like him now. And he has some questions about a case he's working . . ." He nods at me.

"Do you know a Danny Geller?" I ask Shelly. "Young, dark hair. He and his sister Donna might have auditioned as a double act. Or maybe he was a waiter?"

"Oh." Shelly nods. "Yep, I remember the act. I liked the idea. Neither of them ever worked here, though, not as waiters, either. I told them to make some changes, get some new wigs, and come back with it again, but they got huffy with the critique. He stormed out and she got real quiet and left after him. I think she was scarier."

"Why's that?"

"Just the venom in her eyes. Neither of them liked being told no. And a few nights later I found the back door busted—not open, but like someone had tried to open it. They'd spray-painted some impolite words on the door and around it, too."

"When was this?" I ask.

Shelly looks off, remembering. "Three weeks, I think? Not too far back."

"And that was it?" I ask. "No more trouble since?"

Shelly shakes his head. "I'd be happy if they never came back, honestly. He made a real scene exiting. Said I'd 'rue the day.' Who talks like that?"

"Sounds like he was made to perform," Lee says.

"Well, not here," Shelly says.

"Did you ever see him after the audition? Maybe he stopped in to try to cause a scene? Sometimes vandalism is just the first part. He's angry, he comes in, you're angry—"

Shelly cuts me off with a laugh. "No, no. I've seen plenty of drama from folks who don't get a shot. All bark, no bite. Just . . . never saw him again. Maybe he wasn't even the vandal. Or her. Could have been some kids, some angry straight people. Sorry if that's not helpful." He nods toward the stage. "But what do you two think of this guy, though?"

"I like him," Lee says, turning carefully to me and looking me in the eye. This is a test.

"He's got a good voice," I say, looking at the singer. He pulls at the side of his dress. "I think he's doing the drag because it's what he thinks he's supposed to do, though. Doesn't seem comfortable. Try putting him in a suit."

"Not sure that's our kind of act," Shelly says.

"His makeup is good, though," Lee says. "Think he can do the suit and the face?"

Shelly grins. "Yeah, that might be something. Like the male impersonators. Like that old movie with Anna Lee but backward. I'll talk to him. Thanks, fellas. Sorry I couldn't be more help in your case, though."

"That's all right," I say.

"Give him your card," Lee says. "Good to spread some business around."

I laugh and take out a card and hand it to Shelly. "Like the man says."

"I'll keep you in mind," Shelly says. His voice is too neutral for me to know if I've made a good impression, but I think that if I had, I'd know it.

We shake hands and then Lee finishes the rest of his drink in one swallow. We're about to get up when a bell rings and Lee pulls me back down into my chair. I look up and watch all the dancers switch partners with a practiced ease. Not men with men and women with women anymore, now all the couples are male-female, still dancing in time.

"Careful," Lee whispers. The door opens and some cops come in. I recognize one of them, my old partner, Lou. He doesn't spot me and I turn away quick, feeling my heartbeat speed up, my breath turn scratchy in my chest. My rib starts to ache with the last time I saw someone I knew on the force.

"Check the dressing rooms, the bathrooms," one of the cops says. Shelly stands and goes over to the cop in charge. I watch out of the corner of my eye, keeping my head down, my shoulders slouched. I don't know any of the other cops aside from Lou, who went to check the bathroom. I hope no one is in there—I hope no one is about to be caught the way I was.

Shelly has a soft conversation with the cop, some murmurs, a few bills exchanged.

"All right, nothing here," the cop calls out to the rest of them. They file out as quickly as they came in. Lou never looks back and I take a deep breath when he leaves.

"You okay?" Lee asks. "Your hands are shaking."

"I knew one. If he'd spotted me . . ."

Shelly sits down. "If you hadn't looked so frightened, I would have said you were part of that," he says.

"He knew one of them," Lee says.

"If I'd been spotted . . . last time they broke bones. And that was just on the street."

Shelly nods. "They busted my jaw once. I had to eat through a straw for a few months. Here . . ." He snaps his fingers and a waiter brings over some glasses of whisky. The couples have all switched back to their rightful partners. I down my drink greedily, the warmth of it hitting my chest, slowing my heart enough I start to feel normal again.

"You're too scared to still be a cop," Shelly says.

I flinch. "Sorry. Probably not what someone asking for detective work should do."

"Maybe, but our kind of folks wouldn't want the cops involved anyway."

"He's good at his job," Lee says. "You okay?" he asks me again. I try not to picture this through his eyes—he wanted a mystery story with a stoic PI and he got me cowering in the corner the moment the cops came in.

So I nod like it's all fine. I survived again. I feel the hit of relief, the one that made me kiss Gene once. I smile. "I got through another one. Sorry if I looked like a wreck."

Lee raises an eyebrow like he doesn't quite believe me, then shrugs.

"I've seen worse," Shelly says.

"I've been worse," Lee says. "Want to go question the next bar?"

"Yeah," I say. "Nice meeting you, Shelly."

"You too, Detective. It was nice meeting you, really."

I shake his hand once, and then we head out. Outside the air feels fresh and the cops are gone.

"You sure you're okay?" Lee asks. "We can do the others tomorrow or something . . ."

"No, no." I shake my head, then chuckle. "I'm really fine. Like after a scary movie. The adrenaline, you know. I want to do this."

I smile into the night air. I can taste the wind like metal on my tongue.

"You never told me that," I say to him, putting my hands in my pockets. "About how we met before."

"I wanted to wait until I could really embarrass you with it," he says, strolling ahead. Our next stop, the Silver Jay, is down in the Tenderloin, so we walk down Market, through more neon lights and crowds of people out trying to take in the sights, same as us. It gets quieter as we move farther from downtown and the air gets colder, reminding me how close winter is.

Lee doesn't seem to mind, though—he's wearing a blue suit with a matching hat and as we walk and talk, I spot a few white women staring at us.

"You going to be okay in the Silver Jay?" I ask. "It's still whites-only, isn't it?"

"Not for the entertainment," Lee says with a sigh. "It's no problem. We'll go in the back. They know me."

I don't say anything, and Lee turns to me. "You want to ask about that?"

"What?" I say.

"Performing someplace I can't have a drink?"

"Well, you don't have much choice, right? Unless you didn't want to sing there."

Lee nods. "That's why I stopped. The manager, Bert, he's . . . fine. Pay is fair. It was a good place to get started, try some stuff."

"You always wanted to do this?" I lower my voice to a whisper. "Sing in women's clothes?"

"Sing in *my* clothes," Lee corrects, his voice normal, unashamed. "And yes. I've been singing and wearing heels since I was old enough to talk and walk. My mother thought it was the cutest thing. We hid it from my father, though, until he caught me when I was nine. He said he loved my voice, but I was too old for dress-up. Made me join the church choir. And a robe was enough like a dress I liked it for a while. But after school, I made my way up here. They said it was a wide-open town, you know, and I knew by then what I liked and what I wanted. Got a job bussing tables at Shelly's, met some of the other female imper-sonators, learned where to buy dresses, wigs, how to put them on. I auditioned at the Silver Jay first, though, because it's a different crowd. Didn't want anyone I knew to see if I embarrassed myself. Did that about a year. Then had the nerve to audition for Shelly. Two years there, then started taking shows other places. But Elsie came to me, promised me a weekly schedule, steady, good pay. Been there almost two years now."

"I wish I'd had that nerve," I say. "I mean, I knew what I was, but . . . in the navy it was different."

"That's what I've heard. They tried drafting me, you know. Didn't pass the psychological evaluation. Told that man exactly what I liked."

"On purpose?" I ask.

"Sure. I know other guys who did the same. Why not? The army wasn't going to tell anyone if you never joined up or tried to get a government job. And I'm an entertainer, not a killer. Even those boys in the theater division the army's got, they need to use guns, too. And I was happy up here, working at Shelly's. Besides, no need to envy me. You got to where you are, just took a longer route. But it's your route. Always was going to be."

"You think that?" I ask. "Really? I can think of a hundred things I could have done differently." I think of the two men next to me at the bar, their hands overlapping.

Lee shakes his head. "Well, you can't do them differently now, can you?"

I shrug, thinking of James in my office, the smell of pine and the ocean. "You never know."

"Yes, I do," he says, a laugh in his voice. "There's never any going back."

Suddenly I realize something. "If I was so rude to you when we met, why were you so nice to me when I moved in? Just the detective thing?"

"I do love those novels," Lee says. "I was serious about missing *Black Mask*. I used to put money aside so I could buy every new issue. So that's part of it. But I also figured if Elsie brought you in, you must be all right."

"You trust her judgment that much?"

"She hired me, didn't she?" He grins. "But yes. Elsie has been hiring smart—Gene, an almost doctor, to man the bar. Cocktail waitress who was a nurse in the war for good measure. She leaves the garage door unlocked before we're officially open and makes sure people know it's a place to come if they're running. She built that place like a fortress then threw a party in it. Jury's still out on what you bring to either of those, but I'm hoping you'll impress me."

We're nearly at the Silver Jay now, a small club in an alley with a door only marked by a gray bird painted on it. I follow Lee around to a side door farther down the alley behind a dumpster where the saltwater smell mingles with rot. I step on a wet, empty pack of Luckies.

Lee knocks on the side door, waits, then knocks again. I've only been here a handful of times. It's a younger, rougher crowd. Some bikers, some businessmen. No women, no tourists. The female impersonators almost always model themselves after movie stars.

"It's hard to see you performing here," I tell Lee.

THE BELL IN THE FOG   55

"They're not as rough and tough as they look in there. They just like to play pretend."

The door opens a crack and a face peeks out.

"Tell Bert that Lee is here," Lee says sweetly. The door closes and opens again a minute later. A thin guy with a bad toupee and a cigar steps out and leans against the alley wall.

"Well, well, well, look at this chicken come home to roost."

"I'm too old to be a chicken now, Bert," Lee says, folding his arms. "And you're no chicken-hawk."

Bert breaks into a grin and reaches forward to hug Lee, who hugs him back.

"You trying to pick up some side shows or something?" Bert asks. "You're always welcome here, but I can't pay what the Ruby does."

"That's sweet, but no. I'm showing a friend around. This is Andy. He's the PI. You heard?"

Bert looks at me, unimpressed. "Oh, sure. One of our usuals hired you, found out his boyfriend had a wife. Was crying about it for days."

"Sorry," I say, rubbing the back of my neck.

"Don't be, he drank more than ever." He shifts his weight a little, leans back on the wall. "So you used to be a cop?"

"Not anymore, though," I say. "Got caught in a raid."

Bert nods and then turns his head and spits on the sidewalk. "We all get caught in raids sooner or later, right? Some guys here, they'd really go for the cop thing. You should come in for a drink."

"Thanks, but I'm working," I say, not wanting to leave Lee.

"Oh yeah?" Bert frowns. "So whaddya need? I'm not a snitch, though, so don't think I'm going to help you—"

"I'm just looking for a guy named Danny Geller. He was a waiter somewhere, but also he and his sister had this double act they were shopping around."

"Oh yeah, I know Danny." Bert nods. "He was a waiter here until about a month ago. He and his sister auditioned and I told them, I *told* him, I like him, but the act wasn't for us. Too old-fashioned. Who knows who the Andrews Sisters are anymore? We need something fresh. You see that new movie, *Monkey Business*? I want a guy who does that Marilyn Monroe. These guys would get a kick out of that."

"But is he still working here?" I ask, hoping I finally have a lead.

"No, sorry." Bert tosses his cigar stub on the ground and crushes it under his toe. "After I said no to the show, little asshole stormed out, said he wasn't coming back. That was a month ago. Haven't seen him since."

I sigh. "Anything you can tell me about him? What was he like?"

"I can tell you the safe was cleared out that night—he had a key, so I lost all that cash and had to change the locks. The owner didn't like that. If you find him, I'd like to know where he is. I can pay."

I tilt my head, not agreeing, but not saying no. "So you were angry?"

"Don't try that shit." Bert rolls his eyes. "I haven't seen him, so there's no way I could have made him disappear."

"I wasn't trying anything," I say, putting my hands up. "Just want to get a sense of who he was. You're saying he was a thief."

Bert nods. "He always talked about being a star one day, living the high life. Kinda assumed his break would come any day and it would be big. Haughty. That's why he didn't take the rejection well, I think. Didn't see it coming. But the guys liked him, he was a good flirt. He probably turned some tricks on the side."

"Did he have a pimp or anything?"

"Nah. It wasn't his real business. Just another side hustle. He was going to be a star, after all."

"Did your boss, the owner, ever meet with him?"

Bert and Lee laugh together.

"The owner is straight, Andy," Lee says.

"He just likes making money off us, doesn't want to screw us," Bert says.

"Yeah. Well"—I take another card out and hand it to him—"if you think of anything else, or you hear from him, please let me know."

"And you can hire Andy here if you need any mysteries solved," Lee adds.

"Sure," Bert says, though he sounds skeptical. "Well, good seeing you, Lee."

"You too," Lee says. Bert goes back inside and Lee turns to me.

"We should hit the last club, just to get a time line," I say.

"And because you promised me a drink at each one—two at Cheaters since you couldn't buy me one here."

"Sure," I say, and we start walking, leaving the stench of the alley behind. "I don't get it, you seem like pals. Why doesn't he let you drink in there?"

Lee's eyebrows raise and he looks at me as we walk. "Don't do that."

"Do what?"

"Act stupid to make me like you. You're not stupid, and I already like you."

"I wasn't—"

"Sure you were. You know why I'm allowed to perform in there but not drink. You're playing innocent so I'll think you're just the least prejudiced gentleman in the city. Don't do that."

"I guess I just feel like, at the Ruby, we're all . . . together. Us against the world, united by . . . what we are. I don't understand why it isn't like that everywhere."

"It's a nice thought, Andy, but being gay doesn't make us all the same. Treating people the same makes us the same. Up until now, you've treated me with all the respect a lady requires of a gentleman. So don't quit now."

We walk north again, toward the water. The smell of the ocean gets stronger as we walk, and the neon signs fade away, like we're getting farther from the surface.

"You're right. Sorry."

"The world is what it is, Andy. You can hate it with me—that's fine, I like that—but don't pretend like you're only just seeing it for the first time because a colored man is next to you."

I don't say anything. He's right.

"You'd never turn away a colored man who tried to hire you, right? Or woman?"

"No," I say immediately. "Of course not."

"Then come on, Cheaters is just a few blocks from here," he says.

"Elsie said Cheaters is women only."

"Not only," Lee says. "But mostly. Male impersonators are their stars, but they'll hire anyone as a warm-up. Their headliner for the past few years is the owner now. Bought it from Cheryl about a year or two back, I think? I don't know this new woman so well, but after her show she might be willing to talk if we go by her dressing room."

"So this one will be harder."

"Or more fun," Lee says. The chill has gotten more pronounced and the fog is starting to come in now, making the light on the streets hazy, almost like you can touch it, or breathe it in. The dark around it feels the same, though. I think of Bert and Shelly. Bert definitely had a reason for getting rid of Danny, and Shelly didn't seem to love him either. If Danny is dead, he doesn't have any shortage of suspects lining up who could have killed him. He seems the type to attract them.

But Donna was the one who scared Shelly. Bert didn't mention Donna at all. And she lied to me not just about her brother's show but how she was part of it. The neon fog seems to dim as we walk.

"Here we go," Lee says, coming to a stop in front of a small dark door with a neon sign in the shape of the cat-eyed glasses from the matchbook. He knocks on the door, and a panel slides open, someone looking at us through it.

"This isn't a place for you," comes a low female voice.

Lee turns and peers at the eyes. "Is that Bonnie?"

"Lee?" The door opens, and standing inside is a tall woman in a man's suit. "Well, look at you. Barely recognized you out of a dress."

"I'd barely recognize you in one," Lee says. They smile and shake hands. "This is my friend Andy. He's that detective, you know?"

"Oh, I heard," Bonnie says, looking me up and down. "He's a cop."

"Former," I say, getting tired of repeating it.

The woman spits on the ground at my feet. "You bring this guy here, Lee?"

"He's okay, Bonnie, I promise."

"How many of my friends have you arrested?" Bonnie asks, leaning toward me, her face inches from mine. "How many did you pound into the sidewalk?"

"None," I say, staring at her, unblinking. "I never participated in those raids. Never hassled anyone."

"But you let it happen," she says, not moving.

I look down. "Yeah, I did. I wish I hadn't. I was different then. And scared."

Lee reaches out and squeezes my arm. "Bonnie. You know what it's like. You were engaged to a man once, one you hated, because of your mother, if I recall correctly. We gotta give second chances."

Bonnie leans back and I look up. She's studying me. "I don't like it, but for Lee, okay. You can come in. If I find out you're blackmailing or anything like that, though, I'll hunt you down and kill you. I protect these girls, you got it?"

"I do," I say with a nod.

She sighs, and steps to the side. "And no pestering the clients looking for business. People come here to relax."

"Actually," I say, "I'm here on a case, not to drum up business."

"We were hoping to talk to the new boss," Lee says.

"Well, she's just about to go on, so you'll have to wait."

"Thanks, Bonnie," Lee says.

"Enjoy the show," Bonnie says, stepping aside. We walk past her into a dark, narrow hallway that I follow Lee down. It ends in a gauzy curtain that he pulls aside. Past it is a small and packed bar. There's a stage and small black tables set up in front of it, no room for dancing. The walls are paneled in dark wood, and the lighting is dim, so the room feels close, cave-like. But it's strangely elegant, too—women in suits and bow ties go from table to table, serving drinks. The lights overhead look like a chandelier. Lee pulls me over to the bar, where we stand for a moment, and he orders a drink I pay for. Then he spots a few empty chairs at a table and takes me over to them. We sit down just as the lights dim.

The whole room goes quiet. A band gets on stage and starts playing in the dark. I recognize the song by the first few notes and chuckle. "My Buddy." It's a wartime song. First in World War I, but then again during II. Everyone sang it. The army and navy played it for us, almost made it like the theme of the war. We even were supposed to have buddies, to pair up with our best friend. We had buddy books to introduce us to the guys in our unit. Everything was My Buddy.

And it's one of the gayest songs ever written. James, Helen, and I used to sing it to one another, with faux longing, and laugh.

Every time it came on we danced. I liked the one Harry James and His Orchestra did best, with Frank Sinatra singing, and it sounds like this will be similar.

The lights come up, and I can't help it, I laugh. On stage is a sailor. Full uniform, back turned to us. She—I assume she—starts to sing.

"Nights are long since you went away, how I think about you all through the day . . ." and then she turns to face the audience. "My buddy," she sings, but for a moment I can't hear her.

Because it's James.

"My buddy, no buddy quite so true."

I take a deep breath as I realize it's not James. It can't be James, obviously. I just saw James, and his hair has gray now, and he's older. This looks like James years ago. My James.

She starts walking down off the stage and seems to spot me as she sings, walking closer. I still can't get over how she looks. It's uncanny.

"I miss your voice, and the touch of your hand," she says, reaching our table, she leans forward, putting her hand on mine. "I long to know that you understand."

She looks deep into my eyes, and I look deep into hers, and realize I do recognize them. Not James. Helen.

"My buddy," she sings, taking her hand back. "My buddy, your buddy misses you."

FOUR

She finishes the song to a room full of applause. I don't clap. I narrow my eyes at her. I take a deep breath, but keep it shallow so she can't see the surprise. I haven't seen her in five or six years, and here she is, on stage, dressed as a sailor and looking like the man who left us both behind.

"Ladies, and ladies dressed like gentlemen, welcome. I'm James Bell," she says. I take another deep breath to keep my face still at that detail. The makeup is intentional. People clap louder. She looks over at me and cocks an eyebrow. The same expression she always gave me when she pulled up in the jeep, still a mess, thrilled by the trouble she'd narrowly avoided. But this time, she just sings.

She's good, and funny, making small talk between sets, flirting with women. Her eyes keep coming back to me, but she never engages. I wonder if she's nervous, too. Her act certainly says . . . something. Is she still talking to James? Has he seen it? Or is this all just some joke no one else is in on?

When she finishes up, she doesn't linger, just vanishes through a side door.

"She's good," Lee says. "Pity she's the owner now, she'd kill at the Ruby."

"She was never really the kind who stayed put long," I say. "So maybe there's a chance."

"You know her?"

A waitress comes by, a rose in her lapel, and she smiles at me. "James would love it if you would visit her in her dressing room."

"Both of us?" I ask.

"Just you."

"I guess you do," Lee says. "Well, I'm going to enjoy my drink and mosey back to the Ruby when I'm done. You good without me?"

I nod. "Thanks, Lee."

"You can thank me by swinging by my dressing room later and telling me everything that's going on. Let me in on the story a little."

"I will," I promise, and get up to follow the waitress. She leads me through the side door Helen went through and down a dimly lit hall to a room with a big star painted on it in gold. She knocks twice, then walks away.

"That you?" Helen calls from inside.

I open the door and go in. It's a nice setup, cozier than the rooms at the Ruby, with blue-and-white wallpaper, thick navy carpeting, and one big vanity lit up with bulbs around it. The mirror is pointed at the door, so when I walk in what I see is her eyes meeting mine as she takes off her makeup. Half her face is James, and half is Helen. She grins and turns around then runs up to me, wrapping her arms around me.

"I knew it was you," she whispers in my ear. She sounds almost like she's going to cry, and I wrap my arms around her, too, squeezing tightly.

I missed her, I realize. She was my best friend besides James, once. But then, I don't know her anymore either, any more than I know James. And that act . . . like a ghost coming to life on stage, a haunting I'm trying to avoid.

She lets go but keeps her hands on my arms as she steps back, looking me up and down. "You got old," she says.

"And you got . . ." I tilt my head, not sure what to say. "James-like."

She barks a laugh and turns back to the vanity. "My little tribute," she says, sitting down and using tissues and creams to wipe the rest of her face clean, and I can't read her expression enough to know if her little tribute is one that really makes her laugh, or makes her angry, or even sad. I'd guess all three. "Sit, sit." She motions at an armchair in the corner. I can still see her face from it. "So why'd you finally look me up? It's been a long time."

"Well, you didn't exactly want to see me," I say.

"No." She stops cleaning her face and gives me a hard look. "That's not what I didn't want. I didn't want you to become a cop. I still wanted to see you."

"Well, I'm not a cop anymore, so I guess we can both be happy." I smirk.

"No? They find out about you?"

I let that hang there, and she turns around.

"I'm sorry, Andy. Really. I can't imagine what they did to you."

"I'm all right, thanks," I say, wincing slightly at the memory.

She studies me, as if trying to figure out if it's true, then turns back to the mirror. Her hair is pinned up to look shorter, and she takes a pin out, letting it fall to her shoulders. It used to be red. It looks strange blond. Like a bad photo.

"So why are you here now?" she asks. "Need a job? I need a man up front to pour the drinks—a woman can own a bar, but not tend one, legally, if you believe it. They think we'll slip stuff in people's drinks." She grins, as if she likes the idea. "If you know how to do that, I'll gladly hire you, or if not, we always need folks to help load and unload stuff in back, clean up."

I shake my head. "No, no, I was fired a few months ago. I have a job already."

"Oh, too bad. I could use someone smart helping me run things."

I raise an eyebrow. "Unloading and cleaning up is helping you run things?"

"Well, I wasn't just going to offer you a manager job upfront. Needed to know you could be helpful around a bar. But I guess since you have a job, it doesn't matter. What are you doing, anyway?"

"I'm a PI," I say.

She freezes, her eyes going wide. "The gay detective? At the Ruby? That's you?"

I nod.

"Oh . . . Andy, I could kiss you, it's the perfect gig for you, but I could slap you for setting up with Elsie instead of me."

"She's the one who offered." I shrug. "And she's got the space for the office. And I like her. She reminds me of you."

"A compliment and an insult in one breath," she says with a little frown, taking the last of the makeup off. "That's the Andy I know."

"How'd you get here, anyway?" I ask. "Last I saw you, you were a bookkeeper at Gump's."

"Ugh." She rolls her eyes. "That was so boring. Gave it up after three months. I came in here one night—it had a different name then. Might have been a different place. But I met the owner, the one before me. Cheryl. We hit it off. Not like that, just like friends. She told me I had a spark, I should put together an act. So I did. Tried a few others before I landed on James, but he was a hit. The wartime thing made 'em laugh. Moved up to headliner, and Cheryl took me under her wing—said she'd created me. Taught me how to run things. So when she and her girl decided to move down to LA, she let me buy her out."

"Just like that, huh?"

"I always liked making a scene, you remember. Looking for trouble. I get to do that on stage, but it's . . . safer. Not safe, none of this is safe, but it's safer. I've grown up, Andy." She stands, and puts her hand on her hip, smiling down at me. "Proud of me?"

"Yeah," I say. "This is quite the place. And quite the act."

"Thanks." She goes behind a pair of folding screens in the corner. "So what are you here for then, if it wasn't to check up on me? Working a case?"

"Yeah," I say, watching the sailor suit she had on get flung to the floor. "For James, actually."

She's silent. It's like the whole room seems to hold its breath. I think of her show again, of how she got after James disappeared, sullen and angry. She'd loved him, too, if differently than I had. When he disappeared, I was terrified so I closed myself off, turned off my life. It was an armor. What has she forged from his abandonment? If that show is anything to go by, it's some kind of weapon—with a sharp edge.

Eventually, I can hear her move again, and she steps out from behind the screen in just a dressing gown, her face a mask of coy amusement. "So he's back in town, huh? And he just came running back to you?"

"No, not like that," I say.

She picks a cigarette case and lighter up off the vanity and offers me one. I take it and she lights us both. "So like what?"

"Just a client."

She laughs, longer this time. "Sure, Andy." She takes a long drag and blows the smoke out as a ring. "He bother explaining why he vanished in the first place?"

"Yeah," I say, taking a drag off the cigarette. "He had a feeling, and got offered a promotion."

"That's all he said?"

I nod.

"Well fuck me," she says, and opens a cabinet under the vanity. Inside are some glasses and a bottle of rye. She takes two glasses out and pours, then hands me one. "Good stuff," she says. "Not for the patrons."

We clink glasses. "To reunions," I say.

"Old friends," she says, downing her drink in one gulp. I sip mine. It's smooth, but strong.

"I gotta ask, though," I say as she pours herself another. "The act? James Bell?"

She chuckles, low and rough. "Yeah. You should tell him to stop by and watch."

"What is it, though? Some . . . joke?"

She shrugs. "I guess. And I was feeling angry after he left. After you became a cop. I tried an Andy Bell act, too, but it wasn't as fun. James was always more . . ."

"Outgoing," I say. "Let's say 'outgoing' or you're gonna hurt my feelings."

"Sure." She laughs. "Anyway, he was a better act. Started as a little fuck-you to both of you for leaving me for the normal world, but it's turned into a real thing. Plus, 'My Buddy'—"

"Gayest song in the world," we say in unison. She raises her glass again and toasts mine.

"I guess you're back now, though," she says. "Gay detective. And James must be, too, if he's hiring you."

I tilt my head. "I don't know about him. But I'm trying. It's hard after so many years. I haven't had a queer friend since you and James," I say, and let that hang a moment. The meaning of it—that I haven't had a friend in years, not a single one who knew me. "Well, until recently, I mean. Now I have a few."

"Who was the guy you were sitting with?"

"Lee. A friend. He sings at the Ruby, offered to show me the clubs."

"That's Lee? We never met, but he's a legend, y'know."

"That's what I learned tonight, yeah." I sip my drink then take another hit on my cigarette. "Been going around to all these clubs where everyone knows him and giving out my card. He's trying to get me more business."

"That's nice of him. And he can definitely do that. But I can help, too. Let me see the card." She curls her hand at me, palm up, and I take out a card and put it in her grip.

She reads it and sneers. "Over the Ruby," she says. "Trust nose-in-the-air Elsie to come up with some fancy phrasing like that."

"You'd like her," I say.

Helen rolls her eyes. "Maybe. Doesn't matter. She's the competition."

"There was the other reason I was out tonight. The case."

"James's?" She frowns.

"You know Danny and Donna Geller? They auditioned for you, maybe? Did a sister act, but one's a brother."

She nods. "Oh, sure. Donna is in here a few times a month. When she auditioned I was kind of shocked. Good voice, too, nice dresses, wigs . . . but her brother . . . and that's what made the act queer, y'know? I took her aside, said if she butched it up a little I'd hire her alone, but she didn't like that. She wanted to do it with him. And he just doesn't have it. Drama, sure, but no charm. Some guys think being good-looking is enough. I felt bad telling them no. They in trouble?"

"Danny is missing," I say. "But Donna comes in here alone?"

"Oh yeah, and she's popular," she says with a wiggle of her eyebrows.

"When did they audition?"

"Last weekend. But Donna has been in almost every night since. I'll bet she's down there right now."

"Really?" I ask. So she didn't just get into town. "She seem upset or anything?"

"She's drinking more than usual, but I don't ask why, I just take her money."

I nod. Drinking away fear for her brother? Nerves? If he is blackmailing James for money to shine up their act, she'd probably know about it, too. Or at least know he's up to something funny.

"But you haven't seen him?"

"Not since the audition."

"Has anyone left graffiti, vandalized the place, any trouble like that?"

She cocks an eyebrow. "No." She almost sounds insulted. "I mean, nothing out of the ordinary."

I sigh. I still have the hotel tomorrow. "Well, thanks," I say, standing up. There's an ashtray on her vanity and I put my cigarette down in it. She takes my wrist, gently.

"Do me a favor," she says, staring at my hand, "don't tell James? About the act, I mean. Or even that you saw me. You know how he can get."

"What do you mean?"

She looks up and narrows her eyes, studying me.

"That time at the Farallones. You remember."

"The guy who tried to roll him?" I ask. "I was really drunk. I mean, I know it wasn't his best moment." The memories are just snippets in the fog of how drunk I was that night, but it was one of the last nights we went out before James vanished, so what I remember I've gone over so many times it's stuck to the inside of my brain: the Farallones, a hotel over in Sunset, been around since the thirties, one of those places built near the beach, but not so near it was fancy. It was in disrepair during the war, and no one asked questions about who was going to what room for what. A good place for us. We went there a lot. Helen had brought a girl back with her, and James and I were sharing a guy we'd picked up. But I hadn't even gotten my undershirt off when I heard the scream.

"He knocked out some guy who tried to roll him," I say to Helen, shrugging. I remember the water in the sink running pink as he washed the blood off. "It was understandable."

She opens her mouth, then closes it again, as if she's changed her mind.

"What?" I ask. "I know my memory is hazy, but—"

She sighs, lets go of my wrist. "You were drunk. It's better you don't remember it, honestly. Just . . . it was vicious, Andy. He could be vicious is all I mean."

"I remember that woman, trying to get out the window on a dare."

"Suzanne." She smirks. "I heard her husband died. She's still in WAVES. Maybe I should look her up . . ." She shakes her head, and looks back up at me. "But just be careful, okay?"

I nod, but her eyes won't meet mine, like there's something else she's hiding. I never saw James get violent except that night. He wasn't cold-blooded. I knew that for sure. He was hot-blooded, through and through.

Except when he left.

"I promise, I'll be careful," I say.

"No, you won't." She snubs out her cigarette. She fluffs her hair then looks up at me, a sad smile on her face. "I can tell already, he's got his hooks in you again. There was always something about you two. You were my closest friends and I could never get as close to either of you."

"Well," I smirk, "we did have a special relationship."

She laughs. "Not the sex. Just . . ." She waves her hand in a circle, linking James and me in an eternal spin with it. "Something there."

"Maybe," I say. "Maybe it's gone now, though."

She shrugs and lifts her glass. "Maybe." She doesn't sound like she means it. "It was good seeing you, Andy. Don't be a stranger. And if you ever get sick of working for Elsie, I'd be happy to set you up in one of our storerooms."

"You should come to the Ruby some night. See my office. From what I hear, you're important in the community. I could use your help getting word around that I'm trustworthy. I need the work."

"Maybe," she says. "I'll think about it." She grins, and winks at me in the mirror. "But no way I'm visiting the Ruby. Now get going, I need to change and show myself downstairs so no one forgets who runs the place."

I smile and we lock eyes in the mirror for a moment. I feel a familiar warmth run through me. Friendship, maybe.

It's colder in the hall. I walk back the way I came, wondering about James, Helen, some night he beat a man at the Farallones, and why she's so scared remembering it. You never could tell with Helen, though. She'd go for the most dangerous girl at the bar, the one with a husband, a navy boyfriend, and seduce her like it was a game, but the one time she got a flat tire driving us around she burst into tears about how she was going to get in trouble until we changed it for her.

She didn't have a good explanation for her James Bell act, either. Under the warm old feeling of a friendship coming back, there was something rotten. After James vanished she was so angry at him. Just mentioning his name made her press her nails into her palms hard enough to leave marks. She could be wrapped up in all this . . . I shake my head. That's a leap right now. I can't let the past get mixed up in this case; I'm looking for a blackmailer, and I'm looking for Danny, to figure out if he is the blackmailer. That's it. The Farallones, Helen, James—it's all the past. I reach the door to the bar and turn the handle. I'll leave the past in the past.

Back out in the bar, Lee is gone already, but since Helen said Donna liked to stop in, I scan the room for her. I spot her, but only after my eyes had run over her twice. She looks different. Gone is the mousy old-fashioned dress. Now she's in a form-fitting number with a tight skirt to just below the knees and a wide collar extending from a low neckline. Her makeup is different, her hair is different. And when she spots me, her expression is different, too.

She's standing at the bar and turns away with a sigh as I walk toward her. Her drink is half-empty and smells like smoke and wood. All around us are women, talking and laughing, more than a few eyeing Donna. But she ignores them, focusing on her drink, trying to ignore me, too. The lights go dim and on stage, another male impersonator appears, and starts singing "It's the Bluest Kind of Blues" in a low, smoky voice. She's got a full top hat and tails, and a curled mustache painted on. I watch for a moment, then turn back to Donna.

"So," I say. "You were shopping an act around."

She opens her mouth like she wants to say something, then closes it again, rethinking it. Finally, she turns to me. She looks annoyed.

"Look," she says, "you said you were police. I was being careful. You going to turn me in? Turn this whole club in?"

I laugh. "Nah," I say. "I'm gay, too."

That shifts her body, shoulders more toward me. "A gay cop? Like the kind who blackmail people or get clubs raided?"

"No, and a former cop. I was caught in one of those raids."

She snorts a laugh and sips her drink. "Poor baby," she says, sarcastic. "What'd they do when they caught you?"

"Well, I had to find a new job."

She laughs again, still nasty. "Your sob story needs work."

"You want to feel my cracked rib?" I ask her. "It healed a little funny. Aches in the rain."

She rolls her eyes. The singer on stage is still crooning, sad.

She's not looking at me, but her expression gets more solemn. "Look, I told you mostly the truth. I just didn't tell you about me. Or Danny. That we're gay."

"Another part of being twins?"

"I don't know." She shrugs. "Honestly, I don't mind the idea of having sex with a man, it's the idea of talking to one I hate."

"You're talking to me," I say, trying to be charming.

"You're talking to me," Donna corrects. "I'm responding because I don't want to make a scene. Yet."

"Look, I really am trying to find your brother. Seems like you'd want that, right?"

She slams her hand down on the bar and glares at me. "Of course I want it. We finally were getting everything we—" She stops, frowns. "Yes. I want him back. I don't know where he is, though."

"Do you know why he vanished?"

"Is this usually how you do your job? Bothering people into telling you things?"

"It's part of it."

"So what have you bothered out of people so far? What do I need to tell you to make you go away?" She turns back to her drink, sips it.

I nod. She's not going to be charmed. "I know your brother was blackmailing his johns. I'm guessing that was to get money for new wigs, better fabrics for your costumes for the show?"

"I didn't know how he was getting the money," she says very evenly.

"Photos of him with other guys."

"Why would he do that? It would ruin him as much as the men."

"Well, your brother wants to sing as a female impersonator. These guys had careers, families. Stuff they could lose."

"We were going to be famous. Female impersonation acts are going big, you know. Not just at the gay clubs. They tour the country, doing cabaret acts. You see the table up front tonight? On the straight and narrow. People love to watch us. And they'll love to watch me and Danny."

"Yeah," I say. "I've spent all night running around to clubs you've auditioned at. Sounds like you have potential. But think of the time I could have saved looking for him."

"Potential?" She doesn't try to hide the bitterness in her voice.

"We're a good act. Funny. So Danny's wigs are a little messy. I make the costumes, I can't be a hairstylist, too. They just couldn't see it. We just needed a little more money." She pauses, swirls her drink. "Danny said he had a way. I didn't ask questions. All we needed was one chance. Once the crowd saw us, and loved us . . . we'd go right to the top." It's a mantra, the way she says it. Practiced, rehearsed. Maybe a promise between the two of them.

"I don't doubt it," I say.

"Don't patronize me," she sneers. "You were a cop. What did you ever do for anyone?"

"I solved some cases . . ." I say.

She laughs again. "Some cases. How nice. For pretty young girls in trouble?" She relaxes her face, flutters her eyelids, and suddenly she's the same girl she was at the apartment, all innocence. "Oh no, I need a big strong detective to help me out," she says. She frowns, the act falls, she drinks some more. "Please. Those girls can get anything they want."

"That why you put that act on?"

"It's the only way to survive," she says. "That, or be famous for being a character. Mae West. Marlene Dietrich. The only way to have any chance at being able to be yourself is to be famous. Regular girls have to be . . ." She puts the innocent eyes on again. "Sweet little damsels like me." She drops it. It moves back and forth so fluidly. "Otherwise, we're never going to get anything out of life."

"So the show was your ticket out?" I ask.

"And Danny's. It's the same for men, isn't it? That's why you're a butch strapping man. Act a queen, and Danny always does, and you're going to get beaten to death . . ." She chokes on the last word, her eyes going watery. She looks away.

"Is that what happened to him? Is he okay?"

"What the fuck do you care?" she says, staring at her drink.

"I can help," I say.

She stands up. "You can't help anybody. A fucking cop."

I'm usually all right about taking a beating, fists or words. But those words hit right where it aches, and I don't have anything to say back.

She bends one of her collar lapels back, revealing a buttoned pocket, which she takes some cash out of and puts it on the bar. She slips off her chair and is gone faster than I expected. I turn to follow her and knock a woman holding a drink, who scowls at me. I apologize before I turn back to follow Donna.

The audience is thick, though. I push past people, looking for her, but I don't spot her by the door until she's there, and I'm still in the crowd. By the time I get out onto the street, she's gone. I look up and down, but don't even see her silhouette on the sidewalk. Still, I run to either end, I look down the streets, I listen for heels on pavement, but all I can hear is traffic. She's gone. I clench my fists in my pockets, frustrated.

They needed money, he was a drama queen, who stole sometimes, and made enemies. She lies like it's doing her hair. She said they were close—to something. Their show? They finally had enough money? Who did they blackmail for that?

I have nothing, I realize. Just an empty stomach queasy from the drinks I had, and a real bad feeling about what I'm mixed up in. She was right, even if she was just flailing, trying to hurt me. I can't help anybody. So I turn into the night and walk back to the Ruby.

When I get there, it's still going strong. Gene is at the bar, but I can barely see him for the crowd, and he doesn't even notice me. On stage is the girl Elsie was auditioning this afternoon, but now she's done up, wearing a tux, her hair slicked back. Her singing is great but all I can hear is an empty street and Donna's footsteps echoing in the dark.

FIVE

At the diner the next morning, I eat quickly while going over what James had told me—the Belltower Hotel. Room 608. Photos taken from the right if you're looking out the window.

The Belltower turns out to be a nice-enough-looking building at the edge of Nob Hill, all white and six stories tall, higher than all its neighbors. It's also at the top of a hill, built along the slant, so it looks a little crooked from the outside. But inside, the first thought that hits me is how much James has come up in the world. This isn't the Farallones, with its moldy wall-to-wall carpeting, peeling wallpaper, and one weaselly little guy behind a desk. It had been beige art deco buildings built around a parking lot, like the whole point of the place was to leave it.

Here at the Belltower, the whole point is to stay. High ceilings, tiled floor, and a fancy rug with a sofa and tables with magazines for people who are waiting. Behind the desk is a pretty young woman who beams at me the moment I come in. It's not the Ritz, but if James is making enough money to stay here regularly, no wonder somebody thought he could afford that blackmail payment.

I approach the young woman at the counter and give her my best smile.

"I'd like a room," I tell her.

"Of course, sir. For how many nights?"

I cock my head. I could expense a stay to James, but there's no way I can front the money for even one night. Should have thought of that.

"Is there any way to see the rooms before I pick one?" I ask, making my voice delicate. "I have very specific requirements for my comfort, you understand. My analyst says I need to be high up, for one."

"Well," she looks behind her at a door marked OFFICE, then back at me, "that's unorthodox. We have a few rooms available on the sixth floor, if you'd like. That's as high up as we go."

"How about room 608?" I ask. "It's a lucky number. If I could see it first." I give her all my charm, but she just blinks nervously.

"Let me get the manager," she says, and slips away into the office. I peek over the counter at the guest book while she's gone, but I don't spot Danny Geller's name. He'd be using a fake one, but there aren't any Daniels or Dans. I turn my head like I'm looking at a painting of a boat on the wall when I hear the door click open. A man comes out, sixties, with round glasses, a full head of hair only gray at the temples, and a warm smile. He's handsome, in that older way. He makes you feel taken care of just by smiling.

"Hello, Mr.—" He pauses, waits for me to fill in the blank.

"Mills," I say. He reaches across the desk and offers his hand. When I shake it, he puts his other hand over ours and squeezes.

"Sidney Cardwell," he says. "Shall we?" He gestures to the lounge and then steps out from behind the desk. I follow him over to a corner, but he doesn't sit, so neither do I.

"So you'd like to see room 608," he says. "May I ask why?"

"Lucky number," I say.

His smile doesn't falter, but I get the impression he doesn't believe me. "Have you stayed with us before?" he asks. "I don't remember you, and I'm good with faces."

"No, I haven't," I say.

He looks me up and down, focusing on my shoes, then my suit and tie. I suddenly wonder if a navy suit with a cornflower blue tie was too much. "No . . . but you're not police, either."

"I—"

"Your shoes are, but your wardrobe isn't staid. The clothes seem like hand-me-down, too, so I don't think you're our usual clientele, but you are a friend of Dorothy."

"Well—"

"Please"—he raises his hands, palms forward—"don't worry. So am I."

"Ah," I say, taking him in again. One of us. "Well, then maybe I can be frank with you."

"I think it'll work a lot better than telling me 608 is your lucky number."

I smirk. "I'm a PI. A client is being blackmailed with photos taken in your hotel."

He blanches at first, then shakes his head and looks down. He puts his hand to his forehead like he suddenly has a headache, and sits down in one of the chairs. "I knew it," he says softly, clasping his hands in front of him.

"You did?"

"When you asked for 608 . . . We recently discovered some holes in the wall between 608 and 606. Small ones, but large enough someone could take photos through them. So we, ah . . . have those rooms closed for the time being."

"Well, I wasn't going to sleep there anyway," I say with my best smile.

He laughs. "No, I suppose not. You'd like to see them?"

"If I can," I say.

"Certainly. As long as . . . we value discretion here, Mr. Mills. You're not about to report anything you might find to the author-ities?"

I shake my head. "They don't like me very much."

"I heard about you at Shelly's," he says, standing. "The de-tective. I didn't think . . . perhaps I should have called you the moment I found the holes." He walks over to the elevator and we get in together. "Our clientele isn't exclusively gay," he says in a whisper, even though the doors are closed, "but we get some. Often with that boy."

"Boy?" I ask.

"He never checks in. But I remember faces. I always see him in the lobby after someone I think might be one of us books room 608. They're discreet, and the money is for a night, not an hour. We're not that kind of hotel. But these things happen even at the best places. I suppose I could have stopped it, but . . . I feel for those men." He chuckles. "And the boy is good-looking, too, so I don't want to stop them from getting their money's worth."

The elevator clanks open and we walk down a long hallway of anonymous doors and dark carpeting. When we stop in front of 608, Sidney takes out a key from his pocket and opens it. I walk in and turn on the light, and he follows me. The room is nice and vague in the way hotel rooms are. There's one window looking out at the city, a bed, a chair and a desk, an ashtray with matches that have the Belltower logo on them.

"You ever spend time with him?" I ask. "The boy?"

Sidney gasps. "Mr. Mills. I'm not that sort. I have a long-time . . . paramour. We live together."

"I'm sorry," I say. "Didn't mean to offend."

He laughs. "Honestly, it's flattering, thinking someone my age would have the wherewithal for him."

"Have you seen him in here recently? The boy?"

"No, not for a few weeks. But he doesn't have a set schedule." He laughs again.

"He's got dark hair, pretty face?" I ask, as I look around the room. The photos were taken from the right, James had said. I walk over to the wall, and there, small, and blending in with the pattern on the wallpaper, and just at the corner of a framed picture on the wall. Another boat.

"Yes, that's him. And I see you've found . . . ah."

I stare at the hole. It's big enough to stick a small lens through, with the right camera and attachment. I've seen something similar before, back on the force, though in that case it was the hotel manager himself who'd drilled the holes.

"If you straighten the picture out," Sidney says, "it covers the hole. Same on the other side. I guess our decorating style didn't help."

"Folks like this know how to hide the holes," I say, poking the hole with my finger. "They would have found a way even if the walls were bare. The question is how they knew what was happening in this room in the first place."

"Wouldn't the boy have been in on it?" Sidney asks.

I turn to him, and nod. "Or someone else who was here all the time, noticed things, figured out what was going on, how to make an easy payday."

He frowns. "Mr. Mills, I know you're a private detective, but there's no need to talk like a dime-store novel. I assure you, I had no idea."

"None?" I ask, turning on him. "Someone must have been coming in around the same time as the boy to take the photos. Someone who knew. You already told me you noticed him, so it could be you, or maybe someone on your staff who noticed him, too. That's the most likely explanation."

He turns red, then white. "I . . ." He sits down on the bed, shaking, and for a moment, I think I'm about to get a confession, that he's going to say it's all him. But he swallows and looks up at me, eyes wet. "I would never, Mr. Mills, I assure you. And the staff . . . I can't imagine any of them. None of them are . . . like us, for one. They're all young, a little naive if I'm being honest, but good people. Even the bellboys." He sounds pleading, but sincere.

I sit down on the bed next to him. "Then tell me, who checked out 606 whenever someone had 608? You must have noticed someone, the way you clocked the kid. Otherwise, it's probably someone here."

"No, no . . ." He swallows, looking down again. "No one here. I would notice if they were gone for long, too." His back turns straight, and he looks up at me. "There was a young woman who would come in, yes, and take room 606. But she's . . . a woman, Mr. Mills. She's not going to . . . She seems so sweet. She's not a modern girl. Her hair, her clothes . . ."

"Dark hair, full figure?" I ask.

He nods. "She was so charming whenever she checked in. Said she liked 606 because she and her husband had stayed there once, and now that he was gone, she could get lost in the memories of that trip . . . but I never put together that she was always there when he was. It's only been a few months of her showing up, you know. The boy has been coming and going for over a year."

"I think they only decided to cash in recently," I say, standing up and going back over to the hole. I feel the inside of it with my finger. It's still a little rough. Probably been there a few months, but not so long it's turned smooth with age.

"I just can't believe it. A woman. Involved in . . . not just criminal activity but . . . our criminal activity."

"If it helps, she's one of us, too."

He looks up at me, confused. "Really? I can usually spot that."

"Just saw her drinking last night at Cheaters," I say. "I'm told she's popular."

He sighs. "I feel like such a fool." He shakes his head. "No, I was being indulgent, because I knew if I exposed the boy or those men that they'd just go somewhere else. Here, at least, if the police came in, I could send someone up to knock on their door. I was ready. I mean, I don't approve of prostitution, but I understand . . . it's so risky. Terrible things can happen. I wanted to look out for them."

I nod. "You wanted to do right by our kind of people, I get it, Sidney. Don't beat yourself up." He's doing more than I ever did, after all.

"I wish it were that easy, Mr. Mills."

I go over to him and put my hand on his shoulder. "It's not, but I'm telling you, as a professional, this isn't your fault. Got it?"

He looks up at me and we stare for a moment, unblinking, and he smiles a little. "I do appreciate that. Is there any other way I can help?"

"I want to check out next door, too, if that's all right?"

"Of course," he says, standing. We leave 608 and he unlocks 606 next door. It's practically identical.

"These rooms were cleaned, I assume?" I ask, looking at the perfectly made bed.

"Of course."

"Anything get left behind?" I bend down to look under the bed. Nothing.

"No, I'm sorry."

"That's all right," I say, standing back up and going over to another picture of a boat on the wall. This one is in a storm. I move it aside, and there's the hole. This one is bigger, so the camera can fit in, the lens right against the inside of the wall next door. All it would take would be a rod to push the painting on the other side out of the way, then the right kind of lens. The photos wouldn't be great, but they'd be good enough. And the hole is bigger, but under the painting, no one would have spotted it.

THE BELL IN THE FOG 83

"I should get back down—is there anything else you need?" Sidney asks, from the doorway.

I shake my head. "I'm just going to look around, see if your cleaning staff missed anything," I say. "If that's all right? You said the rooms weren't in use."

"Oh no, not until we have the repairman in. He has to fill the holes and then patch the wallpaper, which he needed to find. It's such a hassle. If I see either of those two again, I'm going to give them a bill for all this."

"If you see them again, call me," I say, taking out a card and handing it to him. "Don't do anything else, okay?"

"Oh," he says, suddenly nervous. "Yes. Do you think they could be dangerous?"

"I don't know," I say. "But just to be on the safe side."

He studies the card, then pockets it. "Let me know if you find anything, please," he says. "Just in case."

"Of course," I say.

He turns and leaves and I spend the next hour or so going through the rooms, even unmaking and remaking the beds, but I don't find anything. I make sure to put everything back before I leave—Sidney seemed like an okay guy, so I don't want to make his life harder. In the lobby, I give him a brief shake of my head and he nods. We don't need to talk more than that.

Donna is her brother's accomplice. But then why wouldn't she know where he was?

There's a clock over the door out, and it's already after noon. Three and a half days until they ruin James's life, and I already let her get away once.

I take the streetcar back down to Potrero and let myself into Danny's building again. When nobody answers his door, I take out some lockpicks and let myself in there, too. Empty, but looks the same as before, a dent in the pillow on the sofa, a perfectly made bed. The only thing odd is a half-full mug of Sanka on the table, still a little warm, like she just ran out. I wait around to see if she'll come back, but she doesn't.

Now that I know they're blackmailers, I don't feel so bad giving the place a rougher search. I look under the mattress and sofa cushions, push aside clothing in the closet, tap the walls and floors for hidden nooks, but I don't find anything. Which makes sense. If the photos were here, Donna probably never would have let me search the place the first time.

I clean up, and try waiting awhile, but she still doesn't turn up, so I let myself out. She'll probably be back at Cheaters tonight, or someone there will have a clue. And if not, I'll come back. Unless she's gone missing, too, she'll turn up eventually. She was never hiding.

I stop for lunch at my usual place before heading back to the office. Lee is sitting at my desk when I go in, waiting for me. He's in a dressing gown but no makeup yet.

"You're here early," I say to him. "Don't you usually go on at eight or nine?"

"Elsie said someone canceled, needed a fill-in at five. And I believe as your new girl Friday I get to know what you've been up to," he says, folding his hands in front of him and putting his chin on them. I smile and sit down opposite him.

"What do you want to know?"

"How you know Helen, for one."

"Oh, it's a long story. Wrapped up in this case, too."

"Well, I promise confidentiality, but that means it's time for you to spill."

I grin and tilt my head. Lee was helpful last night, and I trust him. "As long as you don't think I have the money to pay you."

He throws back his head and laughs. "I've heard what you make. I do much better singing," he says.

"Fair enough," I say, and I lay out the case for him, including my own past with James and Helen. Lee stays raptly at attention the whole time. "So now I just need to find Donna again," I say. "And I know her address and where she's been most nights. So that's the plan. Sound good?"

"Sounds like you are far too close to all this," Lee says, arching an eyebrow. "I don't think you should have taken the case at all."

"I need the work."

"Sure," Lee says. "I get that. But look at you, you haven't even noticed that Helen is the only one they auditioned for who they didn't seek revenge on, assuming that bit of cleaning you did the other night was their gift to Elsie. No theft, no break-ins, no graffiti for Helen. Either she's going to get hit tonight or she knows a lot more than she's telling you."

I open my mouth to respond, but he's right. I should have noticed that, but talking with Helen again felt so comfortable, and James . . . I've been distracted by the past.

"You're right," I say. "I should talk to her tonight."

Lee nods. "I better go put my face on, but I expect updates." He stands and goes to the door, but as he's almost out it, the phone rings, and he pauses, lingering.

I pick it up. "This is Andy," I say.

"Hey Andy, it's Helen." Her voice sounds nervous. "Did you talk to Donna last night?"

"Yeah," I say, looking up at Lee, who's still watching. "But she got away from me before I could get any useful information out of her."

"Well, I found her," Helen says softly. "She's out by the alley, the side door where we load the booze in. She's . . . remember what I said about Suzanne's husband? She's in the same condition."

I swallow and I can feel my eyes go wide.

"I was hoping you might be able to help me out," Helen says.

"I'll be right there," I say, hanging up.

Lee looks at me, curious.

"Donna is dead, in the alley outside Cheaters," I tell him, putting on my coat. His face goes gray with shock.

"Be careful, Andy," he says, "Helen could have killed her."

But I barely hear him, I'm already gone.

The sun is going down when I get there, and the sky is an angry red. When I knock on the back door, tucked in a thin alley, it cracks open, and one of Helen's eyes—bloodshot—stares out. She opens the door enough for me to come in.

We're in a storeroom. Shelves of booze line the walls. And in the center, lying faceup in the same old-fashioned black dress she wore when I met her, is Donna.

"I moved her in here," Helen says. "I didn't want anyone to see."

"How was she positioned?" I ask, kneeling down to touch Donna's wrist. She's cold. Been dead at least since this afternoon.

"She was curled up. I thought maybe someone had fallen asleep drunk when I saw her."

I carefully move the body, looking for what killed her. There's a soft part of her skull that shouldn't be soft, a little blood there. I swallow.

"Poor Donna," Helen whispers.

I look her over again. No pockets in her dress. "Was there a purse?" I ask.

"I didn't see one," Helen says. "Should I go check?"

I look up at her. She's in a men's undershirt and dungarees, her hair pinned back. Her pants are clean, so she hasn't been kneeling in the alley.

"Sure," I say.

"Andy, you're looking at me like I did it," she says, her voice nervous.

"Did you?" I ask, standing up.

"Andy." Her face grows hard. "I've done things I regret, and I admit I'll do what I need to to survive. But . . . Donna was a nice girl. I had nothing against her."

"She didn't come back, break in? She's been doing that with the clubs who turned the act down. If you thought she was a burglar—"

"I swear, I just found her in the alley. She wasn't there last night."

I think about last night. How I should have gone back to Danny's place then, pushed her for more information. I sigh.

"If someone dumped her there," I say, "they might have called the cops. They could be trying to frame you."

She goes pale. She was never great in a crisis. Her instinct is always to get clear, even if it leaves the mess for somebody else.

"Okay, so . . ."

And I guess it works. I'm about to clean up another one. "Go check for a purse. You have a car?"

She nods.

"Bring it around. As close to the door as you can get it. We're going to have to move her. I don't know where to, but if this is a setup, getting her gone is most important."

She nods, and leaves. I kneel down again, studying Donna. Her eyes are closed. Someone did that. I check the rest of her for marks, but there's nothing. I remember her collar last night— Donna doesn't keep things in a purse. I carefully feel around her collar, and find a small button on the back of it, just like in the other dress. I unbutton it; there's some cash inside. So I try the other side of the collar. Another pouch—this one with a key inside. Before

I have time to look at it, though, I hear the door open behind me, so I pocket it.

"No purse," Helen says. "My car is right up against the door."

"Help me lift her then."

"Okay," she says. We carry the body to the door. She opens it, and parked right in front of us is a small red car, the trunk open. The trunk is lined in black fabric and looks endless. It hits me what we're doing. Hiding a body. Hiding a murder. Donna wasn't good, but she was one of us. And I'm about to help erase her. I taste bile on my tongue.

"Andy?" Helen asks, and I realize I've been staring too long. I put the body in the trunk and slam it closed. I look up at Helen. Her hair is falling out of her bun in pale strands. She looks on the verge of tears. "I should leave a note," she says. "Tell the girls I'm just checking . . . something. I'll make something up. Warn them we might have a raid."

"Good idea," I say. "I'll wait."

"Andy." She looks at me and there are so many emotions flying over her face. "Thanks." She goes inside before I can respond.

I'm sweating and take my coat off, getting out a handkerchief. My nose is running, too.

Helen comes back a minute later and gets behind the wheel, and I sit next to her.

"I thought of a place," she says, and starts the motor. I watch her, but she keeps her eyes ahead. How would she know a place to dump a body?

We're quiet, and neither of us turns on the radio at first. She heads down along Mission, driving out of San Francisco and to South City, where the smokestacks rise up like bars of a cage.

"This is a good place," she says.

"How do you know?"

"It just is," she sighs. "No one is here at night. Water and ware-houses."

If we could go to the police, I would, but they'd just use it as an excuse to shut down Cheaters and then once they found out Donna was a regular, would have just never bothered. I saw it enough during my time on the police. They called it a "homo-cide." Said it was justified. When I tried actually investigating one, try-ing to solve that case, my chief told me to let it ride or people would get the wrong idea.

So I did.

I was supposed to be better now, I was supposed to help gay people now. And all I can do is stuff the body of one in a trunk and drive away. Outside the houses fade, and I can smell the wa-ter turn dirtier. I used to have faith in something as an inspector. After I'd done the long work of finding the murderer, gathering the evidence, I'd turn it over to the DA, and I'd trust that jus-tice would be done. Not every case led to a conviction, but I still always believed there was something to the system there. Some reason for what I did. But that's not how it is for us, and now I'm actively taking away the chance for the system to even try to do its job.

I'm taking justice into my own hands, I realize. I'm making myself a promise that I'll find out who killed Donna. I'm not sure it's one I can keep. It's definitely not one I'm getting paid for.

Out the window it's mostly factories and warehouses. She drives close to the water. So that's where we're putting her.

"How'd you think of this place?" I ask.

"I just did," she says, her eyes on the road, cheeks flushed. "And I know what you're thinking, and yes, there's something I'm not telling you but it doesn't matter now. It can only hurt. So just help me. For old times' sake?" Her voice gets higher at the end. Scared.

"Sure," I say, but we both know that's not the end of it.

We don't pass anyone on the street for a while, and then we're up against the water. It's dark now, too. She pulls to a stop and kills the motor, then turns to look at me. Her eyes are dry now.

"Before we do this, I want to make sure you know it wasn't me," she says. "I swear it, Andy, this one wasn't me, and I need you to believe that." She holds out her hands for me. "So check my hands, her body, whatever you need to. You always saw things no one else did. That little sonar, the ways other men and women would stare, or not. So look me over, Andy. Tell me you believe I didn't do this."

I look her over. Her hands aren't clean—she picked through the trash for the purse. Her pants and shirt are clean, though. No blood, but she could have washed, changed before I got there. And that's if there was any splatter to begin with. Head injuries, if the object is blunt, can crush the skull without very much blood at all.

"I have no reason to have wanted her dead," she says. "She wasn't breaking into the club in that dress, either, so it wasn't me thinking she was a burglar. Someone just left her there."

"Who?" I ask. "Who's out to get you and Donna?"

She shrugs and drops her hands. "I don't know. Maybe there was a fight back there, or maybe someone just figured it was the best place to drop her because she's been in so much. Maybe someone wants to frame me and just picked her at random. I don't know, Andy. I don't know I don't know I don't know."

Her voice gets higher again and I take her hand. She goes quiet, and looks at me.

"I don't think it was you," I say. And I'm mostly sure I'm right. "But you are hiding something."

She takes a deep breath and a single tear leaks out of her left eye. She brushes it away with her wrist as she turns away from me. "I'm hiding so much, Andy. It would take years to tell you all of it."

"Helen . . ."

"If you believe me about this, then that's what we need to focus on now, all right?"

I pause. It's my last chance to stop, to take the body to the police, to make sure she finds her way home. But then Helen will probably end up in prison. So will I.

"All right," I say.

"Thank you," she says softly. "Now we should . . . do it."

I nod, and we both get out of the car and open the trunk. It's quiet and we don't speak as we do the awful thing. Watching Donna go under, her eyes still closed, I think of the bodies I've seen brought out of the water, about how once I thought of killing myself by throwing myself into the bay. She sinks slowly, but she'll bounce back up again soon. Helen wades in and pushes Donna farther out, and I watch her vanish and hope that despite everything she's done, whatever is next for her is better.

Helen wades back out of the water and stands next to me.

"They'll find her soon," she says, "and think she floated down from the city."

"How do you know that?"

She doesn't say anything, just gets back in the car, passenger side this time, slamming the door.

I get behind the wheel and start the car up, heading back to the city.

"If the world were just, I could have gone to the cops," she says, her voice matching the engine's growl.

"I was thinking the same thing," I say.

"I don't know how you ever could have joined up with them," she hisses.

"Do you want to fight right now?" I ask. "I'm out. I'm trying to help people. I just helped you."

She sighs, then slams the side of her fist against her window. "I know," she says finally. "Sorry. I just . . . hate this. Our lives are criminal because they make us criminals. It's why we can't go to the police, why Donna won't . . ." She hits the window again, but it's weaker this time, and the sound rings out empty in the fog.

I don't say anything, and she reaches forward and turns on the radio. "Can we play the old game?" she asks. "To take my mind off it?"

"Sure," I say.

She turns on the radio. It was something we used to do together, something she and James used to make fun of me for. The radio plays a few bars and she turns it off again.

"'Mockin' Bird Hill,' Patti Page," I say. She turns it back on and the song continues playing. It takes her a moment before she realizes I'm right, but then she laughs.

"I'm glad you can still do that," she says. "You wouldn't be you, otherwise."

"I might lose my hearing one day," I say.

"Maybe." She leans her head on my shoulder, the radio keeps playing. Outside, the smokestacks are a forest, but we're soon out of it, and driving back into the neon of San Francisco. The fog is strong tonight, almost like cotton candy, the way the light hits it. I pull up next to the alley behind Cheaters, and Helen sighs.

"I need to change. I'll probably get sick from this."

"I don't see any police. I don't think you've been raided yet."

"We'll see," she says. "But you should go. You shouldn't get wrapped up in this if there is a raid." She squeezes my arm. "I don't want to know what your former colleagues would do to you."

"They broke some ribs on my left side last time," I say. "I guess they could do the right, make it a matched set."

She laughs. "Don't joke. After what you did tonight for me, Andy . . . thank you."

"Just let me know if you learn anything else—if you get raided, or don't, or you find something, okay? This is linked to my case, somehow."

"I will. You should come by for a drink after the decommissioning ceremony. If we're still open and I'm not in prison."

"The what?" I ask.

She raises an eyebrow. "James didn't tell you? They're decommissioning the *Bell*." She pops open the glove compartment and shows me a formal navy invitation.

"I've changed addresses, if they even sent me one . . ." I reach out and touch the seal on the invitation, feel something heavy in my chest. The *Bell*, decommissioned—embossed right there.

"Some of the girls mentioned it the other day—the ones who risk coming in, I mean. I had them get me one. I can get one for you, too, I'm sure."

"I didn't know," I say. I feel like all the breath has gone out of me.

"Well, I thought I'd stop by. I know I wasn't on the ship, but . . . you were. James was. It was part of the family, too."

"Yeah," I say. "A family funeral."

We're quiet at that. Wrong joke to make.

"I'll try to be there," I say. "Thanks for telling me."

"Come on, go home," she says, opening her door. "You've had a long night. We both have, but I have to put on my face and sing in a few hours, unless that place is already swarming with cops."

"Well, without the body, they have nothing to use to shut you down permanently."

"I'm sure they'll come up with something."

We get out of the car and she heads inside and I wait for a few minutes, then walk around to the front. A few people are going in and out. Looks like a normal Sunday night. If the body was dumped there, whoever did it either didn't call the cops or the cops didn't believe them. But then why leave Donna there at all? And if she was murdered in that alley, why was she there? In that old-fashioned dress? Too many questions.

I fish in my pocket and take out the key and look at it in the dim light. It's a locker key. Number 34. But what does it open?

SIX

There are a lot of lockers in the city, so I pocket the key for now. I deserve a drink after the night I've had. The Ruby seems even more full than usual when I get there. Lee is on stage singing her heart out to her version of "The Glow-Worm," and I nod at her. She winks at me when she spots me, but then I head over to the bar. Gene smiles at me, and I melt a little. He's in a white shirt tonight, unbuttoned a few places, maybe more than he realizes, and I stare at the V of his chest for a moment, think about running my hand over it, before looking back up into his eyes. He looks at me like he's happy to see me. I don't know if anyone else does that. Maybe Elsie, Lee, but . . . not the way Gene does.

"You look tired," Gene says. "You just want a nightcap?"

"It's been a long few hours," I say, feeling the weight of it all come down again. Gene had banished it all with a smile, just for a second. I wish I could do that for him, too. "Something to make me forget them would be nice."

He smiles and mixes something up, crushing leaves into ice, and making him smell like mint. I watch his arms as he turns the muddler, muscles swelling as they fill out his sleeves. He sets the drink down in front of me. "Mint julep. It won't make you forget, but I think it'll help you sleep through this when you head upstairs."

I nod. Does he mean he wants me to leave?

He stares at me, waiting for me to drink it, and I do. It rolls down my throat like liquid sugar. "It's good," I tell him.

He smiles and opens his mouth, but then someone else calls for another drink, and he laughs, turning away from me. I watch him mix a drink for another guy, smiling at him the same way, and so I turn to watch Lee. She's like a siren on stage, and the crowd is mesmerized. Some aren't even dancing anymore, just watching her go. I sip and watch and try not to wonder about my choice tonight, about what kind of man I am. On the police, it seemed easier—catch bad guys, put them away. But of course, it wasn't actually easier, it just felt that way because of the rules they lived by. Rules I violated every time I went to a club or bar and met a man in a bathroom stall. Rules that turned on me when they found me.

And rules I followed, and never protected other gay people from.

But now there are no rules, and a young woman is dead and I helped hide her body. I feel lost, like I'm listening for a ping on the sonar and nothing is happening. I know there'll be one soon, soon, some guidance, soon . . . but nothing.

"Hey." I turn around, it's Gene again. "You okay? You look . . ." He shakes his head. "Something."

"I don't know who I am right now," I say.

He doesn't seem at all shocked or confused by that. He just nods. "Yeah, it happened to me, too, after I got kicked out of med school, started working here. It was like I had to rebuild everything. I've been . . . sort of waiting for you to get there."

"Waiting?" I ask. "For me to realize I'm lost?"

"You can't find yourself until you know you're lost," he says. He reaches out and puts his hand on my forearm. I feel his heat through my sleeve, and look down at it. "And these cases you've been taking . . ."

"I didn't like them either," I say, "but I owe Elsie—"

"I get it," he interrupts, squeezing my arm.

I want to kiss him suddenly. I want to put my arm around his waist and pull him and kiss him, like I did months ago. I want him to make me forget tonight. I don't move.

"I'm glad you're working something real now, too. But . . ." He takes his hand away and I watch it go, loneliness filling me up like a sinking ship. He starts to wash another glass.

"How did you find yourself?" I ask.

"I didn't. I built myself. I decided who I wanted to be in my new life." He shrugs. "I still have to do that, but . . . I think I'm doing all right."

"More than," I say, smiling.

Gene laughs. "Finish your drink, and go to bed. You've clearly had a long day."

Suddenly the lights flicker on and off and Gene sighs. I'm about to make for the stairwell, but the elevator opens immediately and a couple of cops pull out. They're young, eager, the kind who would volunteer for a raid on a Sunday, hoping it would earn them a promotion. I've seen rookies like them lot—they're usually the cruelest. But I breathe a sigh of relief when I don't recognize any of them.

Everyone on the dance floor has managed to pull away from one another in time. Everyone lined up and separate, so all the cops can do is hassle us. Nothing lewd here.

"Check the bathrooms," the cop in charge says to one of the others. "These perverts like to do their business there."

The crowd stares at the cops, who spread out and weave through us, knocking into folks. No one speaks. The Ruby is silent aside from the cops' heavy footsteps.

"You a man or a woman?" one of the cops asks someone.

"Woman," she replies. "I'm a male impersonator, this is for work."

I glance over at her. She's in a suit, short hair, but she's not one of the male impersonators. No one is going to tell the cops that, though.

"Freak," the cop says, and shoves her down. She falls to her knees.

"Hey," Gene says, coming out from behind the bar. "Don't hurt anyone."

The cop turns to look at Gene, happy to have a target now. "You're not the club owner, are you? I know it's a woman, but who can tell in this place."

"No," Gene says, "I'm just the bartender."

I want to get up and go stand next to him, but I know if I get hauled in, I'm done for.

"And you don't want me to hurt anyone?" the cop asks.

"We're not doing anything wrong," Gene says, and I know he's trying to sound firm, but his voice wobbles.

The cop turns to one of the men he's standing next to and without warning, punches him in the face. The man doubles over, collapsing to his knees. Gene runs over to him and helps him lie carefully on the floor.

"Oops," the cop says. "Didn't see him there."

The officer who was in the bathroom comes out and shakes his head.

"Well, we were checking for immoral behavior, but I guess we didn't find any, legally speaking," the lead cop says. "But we'll be back." He looks down at Gene. "Tell your boss to stop skimping on her payments. There's a pervert tax in this city."

Gene just stares back.

The cops pour back into the elevator, like poison being drawn out of a wound. Everyone is quiet until Lee, still on stage, motions to the band, and they start playing again. Then it's like we all start up again, plugged back in. I rush over to Gene and help him move the punched guy over to the bar, where Gene takes out some bandages for the cut on the guy's forehead, and some ice for the bruise.

"I thought I was going to die," the man says.

"Well, you didn't," Gene says, glancing at me. "You're alive, okay?"

I remember him patching me up a few months ago, me feeling the same way, asking to kiss him. Maybe that's what he's remembering, too, but his eyes go back to the man who needs his attention, and I can't read his expression to know if the memory is pleasant or annoying.

"You need anything?" I ask Gene. He doesn't look at me as he applies a bandage, just shakes his head. I know I'm just in the way, but I linger anyway, knowing that this wouldn't have happened if it weren't for me, that I'm draining Elsie's finances enough she can't bribe the cops anymore.

Around us, people start to dance again, but it's half-hearted. A lot of them leave. No one wants to try to find fun in the evening anymore. It smells too much like despair, like powerlessness. On stage, Lee does her best, singing her heart out, but the room feels emptier and emptier, and even when there are some dancers left, it's like the whole club is a pit we've all fallen into.

I watch Lee sing a few minutes more, trying to make everyone feel better, watch Gene fuss over the guy who got knocked down and the girl who was shoved, making sure everyone is okay. They're helping. What am I doing? What can I do? A man is being blackmailed for who he is. A woman was killed. I have no idea who did it. And then this happened, and all I could do was watch.

I'm useless. So I go upstairs.

I check my office before locking it for the night, but it's empty when I flick on the lights.

"Andy?" comes a whispered voice. I look around, and he

uncurls himself from under my desk: James, his hat crumpled and low on his head, scarf dragging down one shoulder. "I heard the key . . ." He stands up. He's corpse-white. "I heard the raid and thought . . . I hid. But no one came in, and then the music restarted and I thought maybe it was safe but I couldn't . . ." His legs shake and he catches himself on the desk. I reach out to grab him and lower him into my chair. He stares up at me. Even his lips are white.

"They're gone now," I say. "It's okay."

He nods, taking that in, and color seems to creep slowly back into him. "I really couldn't move once I was down there. It wasn't until I heard the key and thought I'd be locked in, and . . ." He takes a deep breath, then stares up at me silently.

"Why are you even here?" I ask. "Did the blackmailers get back in touch?" Maybe with Donna dead, they had to move up their time line.

"No." He shakes his head. "It's just yesterday . . . you sounded so angry on the phone, and then I never heard from you. I called but no one picked up. I was afraid you'd dropped the case."

"No," I say, thinking of Donna slipping into the water. "I'm not dropping it now. Come on, get up, we'll get you a drink."

"No, no." He shakes his head, almost laughing. "I can't be seen here, Andy."

"Then why did you come back, really?"

"I didn't like that you were angry. So . . . I'm sorry." He looks back up, and his eyes are large. They're the color of the ocean at sunset—the parts farther from the sun, where the water isn't quite as dark as it gets at night. Where it's still turquoise but also navy. I used to love staring at that part of the ocean when the sun was low on the horizon. I'd go to the bow of the *Bell*, and smell the ocean and feel the wind and look into the parts that went dark first.

Sometimes he found me there. Like he's found me here. And he would just stand beside me and watch. Sometimes his hand would rest on mine. Death didn't feel farther away in those moments—on a warship, death is always just under your feet—but it felt less terrifying.

"Forget it," I say, more to myself.

"I don't want to forget it. I was rude on the phone, but that's not what I'm trying to apologize for." His voice is soft, misty. "I'm sorry for vanishing." The words run together so fast it takes me a moment to realize what he's said. "That was cruel of me. I was scared and I thought I was going to get picked up for sure, blue ticket, maybe worse."

I should feel happy, I think. But I just feel bad for him. "Worse?"

"You remember how it was. Either you felt free or you felt terrified or you felt both. The war made it feel like anything was possible all the time. You could die, you could kiss the man in the bunk next to you, you could get thrown in one of those prisons for the gay soldiers, interrogated until you gave up names, they'd tell your family, make sure you never got a job. All of it, any of it all at once." He intones his list of fears almost religiously, like it's something he repeats to himself before bed. Please don't let these evils befall me.

I sigh, leaning back on my desk. "Yeah, I remember that."

"When they offered me the promotion, to send me out to the Atlantic, I felt like . . . the possibilities were falling down. Like with the war ending, it was just a whirlpool, sucking out the good things. Or a bathtub, draining. I thought I'd be a fish on land, and you'd be one, too, and we'd just flop there together and die."

I smirk and look him in the eye. "Fish don't live in bathtubs."

"You know what I mean. It was a feeling. Like the one when I told you to check the sonar again. Or when I followed those guys who ended up being spies. Or when I went to one recruit-ment center and not the other. And this time, the feeling said if I didn't leave, I was going to get caught, and I was going to get you caught, too. Everything was about to change, and I loved who we were too much to change us. But if we didn't, we were goners, I knew it. So I just . . ." He stands up. He's closer than I thought he was.

"Left," I say. He's warm, so I turn away from him and go to the door. He follows me out into the hall, lets me lock the office as he talks.

"If I'd told you, I wouldn't be able to. And then we would have been caught, Andy. Everyone on the ship already knew. I think everyone on base knew."

"But you got the promotion," I say, turning and opening the door to my apartment, but lingering in the doorway.

"The brass didn't know, I guess. Can I maybe have a drink . . . in your place? Since I can't go downstairs." He glances down the hallway where some of the chorus boys are gathered, watching.

"Sure," I say, glaring at them. I open the door to my apart-ment. Inside, I'd left the window open, and the cool air shudders into the hall. I turn on the light and take off my hat and coat, hanging them up and watching James as he takes in my apart-ment. He smiles at the record player, at the photo of my mom and dad. Then he turns back to me.

"I just wanted to say sorry for all that."

"You risked coming here just to say that?"

"I had to. And I was careful. Made sure I wasn't followed, checked for tails in mirrors, walked the most meandering route. I've gotten good at this." He smirks, and it's sad. It reminds me of my old smiles, the ones that never fit. "If it weren't for that raid . . . but I hid well enough for that." His eyes flash for a mo-ment, proud of that.

I nod. "Okay. So you did all that just to apologize. But you wouldn't have done it differently, would you? You wouldn't have changed the way you left?"

"Maybe . . ." He shakes his head. "I don't know. What were the other options? We leave, get a place together, become, what . . . bartenders at some fairy bar? Bouncers? Would you have been happy?"

"Would you?"

We're both silent. He takes a few steps toward me, too many. We're close now.

The wind blows the door shut and I almost jump at the sound.

"I think I would have been happier," he says, and he moves his mouth toward mine. I pull my face back and he stops. "I'm sorry," he says, taking a step back. "I . . . it's late, and I'm remembering too much, seeing you, it's just all flooding me, again, I couldn't stop thinking about you. You probably have someone."

He doesn't move, and neither do I, but I can feel our bodies wanting to close the gap between us. The breeze from the window blows my hair into my eyes. I smell pine and the ocean.

The ocean. It makes me think of Donna, her body fading into the water. Like a sinking ship, black and white striped. What we almost were. I succeeded in protecting us then, the sonar, the mines. Tonight I failed.

I want to forget all of it.

I take a step toward him and kiss him. He kisses me back, hungry, his hands pulling me close.

"I've been remembering too much, too," I say. It's more and less than what I mean. We kiss again.

There's a rockiness to the ocean that takes getting used to. Being on a ship that sways and heaves feels unpredictable, and sometimes it is, but there's a rhythm to it. When you return to land, and you close your eyes, your body still feels the rocking of the ocean. You usually feel it as you're falling asleep, but it can happen whenever. Some guys get seasick on land. They explained it in the navy, had a fancy French term for it—*mal de debarquement*. That's what being with James again is like. We peel off our clothes, the kissing new and so familiar like maybe it's just my body remembering his, remembering being at sea. Ghosts overlap us like a photo with a long exposure. Maybe that's what I'm feeling.

He tastes different, his skin no longer rough from salt air, but smoother, and softer, maybe from age, too. His voice is lower and the noises he makes louder. The places that make him moan are sometimes the same, but sometimes gone, and sometimes moved just a little to the right. Or maybe that's my misremembering.

And I'm different, too. I see that now as he strokes a scar I didn't have before, or brushes my hair from my eyes in a different way. And from how it feels. I'm not about to die, I'm not alone on the ocean, I'm not trying to have as much fun as I can before the war claims me. And neither is he. That changes it all. The ghosts that overlap us aren't just about to die, they're long dead, but we're still hungry. Maybe for the memories more than each other, but what we have is good enough—was always good enough—it makes me forget everything else.

It's warm and familiar and feels better than I remember. And afterward, with him curled in my arms, like I always did when my body remembered the ocean on land, we fall asleep. And the ghosts do, too.

I wake in the middle of the night, the Ruby's neon sign outside casting everything pink. There's water running in the bathroom. James comes out a moment later, in his underwear, holding an empty glass.

"Sorry," he says. "I was thirsty. I didn't mean to wake you."

I sit up. "You leaving?"

"You want me to?"

I can't make out his expression, just a few contours of his face. I shake my head. "I won't hold it against you this time."

He sits on the edge of the bed, curling one leg up. "I can stay."

"Can you? No one's keeping tabs?"

"If they were, I'd have been done the moment I set foot in this place." He smiles, a little sad.

"How bad is it? Still being in the navy?"

His shoulders rise, like it's a big question, then they fall. "It's bad" is all he says.

He lies down, his head near my hand, and I stroke his hair while he stares at the ceiling. "I mean, you've heard the news. McCarthy, Bridges, the State Department, everyone looking for us, killing careers, ruining lives."

"That's why you didn't walk out when you saw it was me, you were desperate."

He turns over on his stomach. He's close enough now I can see him watching me. "When I saw it was you, I couldn't walk out."

I squeeze his hand in the dark. I'm not sure I believe him. Not the way he's making it sound, like a grand love. But I'm glad to have him again.

"But yeah, it's bad," he says. "So much worse than the war. Guys assigned to follow people who had a swish in their step once. Tailed everywhere. If they even make conversation with another man, some guy from the navy police will sit across from them, staring. And the interrogations aren't just demanding names. Asking things no man should ever have to answer. Details. What it felt like. Just to embarrass you. For hours. No food or water, no bathroom. Torture."

"You can quit," I tell him.

"I thought about it."

"So why didn't you?"

He curls into me, his head heavy on my chest. "In '48, after the Kinsey report, I thought for sure it would change things. A bestseller all over the country. More than a third of men had had some kind of homosexual sex. Everybody knew we were normal, finally!" He pauses, sighs. "But the navy just gave us lectures and pamphlets on how to look for limp wrists. I kept telling myself things get worse before they get better. Something had to happen." He shakes his head, his jaw pressing into my ribs. "Two years I told myself that. And then McCarthy." McCarthy. It had been commies first, but in 1950, in an open hearing, Peurifoy at the State Department reported ninety-one homosexuals had resigned, and the Republicans, led by Bridges, had pounced. McCarthy was a solo act, but Bridges led a chorus.

I'd felt safer than ever as a policeman then. The guys I worked with weren't hunting the halls for me.

"Reports, investigations. Thirty-seven hundred homosexual federal employees in DC, they said." He stares at the ceiling, eyes wide for a moment, as if remembering. "I was sure I was on a list. I knew I was in trouble, we were all in trouble then, but I couldn't just resign the day after they came looking. That would be obvious. I didn't want to be McCarthy's or Bridges's next poster boy. So I stayed, just a few months . . . and got assigned as East Coast secretary to Sam Marks, who was overseeing the hunt." He laughs, but it's sharp. "I didn't spy on anyone, but I compiled paperwork, went over the reports. I got to see all the ways they found out. All the things to avoid. Me! That was a sign, right? That I was safe . . ." He pauses, his tongue clicks on the roof of his mouth. "And it was fun. Getting away with it while watching everyone who didn't." He lets out a long breath. "I never told anyone that."

"It was like that for me, too. When I was a cop. I liked getting away with something."

"It's addictive, isn't it? Power."

I tilt my head. "Maybe. More . . . being better than anyone who was caught." Knowing I was superior. Every time the guys said they'd "caught some fags in the park" or "busted some fairies' heads" it had run through me—terror like fire, and then remembering they were telling me because they didn't suspect. That cool water put it out, and the steam it made in my mind was the most soothing hiss. It was a game I kept winning, so I kept playing, an addict at a slot machine.

"Did you help anyone, when you saw their paperwork?" I ask, thinking of my own regrets. "Warn them?"

He shifts again, his head so heavy on me it's almost painful. "I did my job."

"Me too," I say, the guilt like lead in my veins. "I did, I mean. I like this one better."

"I only did it for a year. Then they transferred me here to help run strategy for Korea." He takes a deep breath. "Maybe I should quit, but with this promotion in sight . . . imagine how proud my dad would be. And I haven't been caught yet, right? I keep going and it feels better and better." He rolls back, his head facing the ceiling now, almost in the crook of my arm. "But it gets harder and harder, too. I know how to avoid it but it's still like I'm being watched all the time. I wandered the whole city to get here. I stopped into bodegas, I looked at shop windows to see if I caught the reflection of anyone watching me."

"Then maybe you should—"

"I can't." He has a heavy sadness I remember from my own reflection, a year ago. "I can't . . . do what you do. Give up my life. My parents would be angry. The navy might—I wouldn't have anything to do, I'd just be . . . what . . . I mean, are you happy?"

I smile. "Yeah."

"And your mother? She like it?"

When I don't say anything, he lifts himself off me. "Sorry," he says. "I just—I couldn't do it, Andy. It's not a real life. It's a shadow."

"That's what I'd say of yours." I can't keep the pity out of my voice. He turns away from me. I light up a cigarette from the nightstand so I won't say anything else. After a moment, he turns back and takes it from my lips, claiming it as his own, so I light another.

"You feel bad, being in bed with me, when Danny's missing?"

He frowns. "You interrogating me?"

"Just trying to figure out if I'm butting in where I'm not wanted."

He laughs. "No. He's just a guy I see to handle things. He knows how to be discreet. He found the hotel, knew what room was safe. I was impressed."

"I thought you said you found it. Belltower, the good-luck charm?"

"Oh yeah, I liked the name, but Danny suggested it. I'm not naive, I know what he is. So I'm not broken up if he's holed up at the Belltower with somebody else for a weekend."

"How about if he's dead?"

James freezes and stares at me. "Are you kidding?"

I shake my head, trying to be serious, but don't tell him about Donna. "He's missing. There's blackmail. He pissed a lot of people off. From what I gather he doesn't like it when he doesn't get his way."

"That's true." James smiles a little. "I told him once I liked him in green, and he told me he'd wear whatever he wanted, and it didn't matter because it was coming off anyway and it was none of my business."

"I saw his photo. He's almost cute enough to make that sound worth it."

"Nowhere near as cute as you," he says, leaning up to brush some hair out of my eye. His cigarette trails smoke in the red light like spilled wine. He kisses me softly on the lips then sinks back down. "But Danny isn't blackmailing. He doesn't have the spine."

I don't correct him. Not now, not yet. He doesn't need to know about Donna, the photos she took, her body in the water. Maybe I can get the photos back and never tell him. Never let him know his thermometer is a lie.

He tilts his head. Says like he's trying to convince me, "Some guy, back in DC, got extorted by the navy police tailing him. Milked him dry, then turned him in. Lost his job and his savings. He still gave them ten names. Some guys just don't have it in 'em."

"Well, apparently guys like us run the State Department, maybe he got a job offer."

"Don't joke. Guys in the department now don't even finish telling you their names before they say they've got a wife and kid so nobody assumes they're a homo."

I laugh. "Really?"

"Only happened to me once. I'm starting to worry, though. Maybe I should get married. What's her name, who went with Helen for a bit? Suzanne something? She's secretary to an admiral. Widow. I could ask her."

"The one from the Farallones?" I ask.

He tenses up against me. "Yeah, I guess she was there. She might be up for it, right? Can't be easy for her, either."

I almost push him on what Helen told me about that night, but he sounds so sad imagining a sham marriage to protect his sham life. So he beat someone in self-defense. I would have done the same. "I should talk to her. It's so . . . the hearings and the newspapers. Moral weaklings, sex perverts. If Eisenhower wins, it's going to get even worse. I don't talk to people anymore. I haven't talked like this . . . since . . ." His breathing gets a little ragged, so I put out his cigarette, another husk in the ashtray next to mine, and hold him tightly. I remember feeling the way he did, in the police. He's right where I was, months ago.

His breathing turns deep again. Calm. He lays his head on my chest.

"I've been really lonely," he whispers.

"I know," I say. It hangs there; his loneliness and mine.

Soon he's asleep, but I stay awake, staring at the pink light, and thinking of Danny and Donna. They had each other, but then he vanished. Was she lonely, too? When I close my eyes, all I see is the water.

The next morning, he's gone when I wake up. For a moment, I lie there, and new ghosts rise up—these the ones of the day I woke up and he was gone. His bed empty, no note, like he was taken in the night. Fear seizes my body like it did then before I remember there's no one he can report me to, that he probably wasn't taken out in the middle of the night. That if he left, he just left.

Which is what he did last time, too. I just didn't know.

So then I turn angry, tearing the sheets off, and only then spotting the note on my nightstand. It's on the back of a scrap torn from who knows what. It says, "I had to go home to change before work. I'll call." Which is more than last time, and somehow that's enough.

He gave me an apology. The one I'd wanted for so long. Thinking of it now, I almost sob as I feel something leave me. My muscles shudder, different from how they did last night. It's like something that had been tight around me for years is suddenly loose, though if you asked me to name it, I'm not sure I could.

But I don't want to dwell on it. There's still the blackmail and Donna is still dead. So instead I brush my teeth and shower. I know James and I aren't back to how we were. I know this is confusing and probably not great for my case objectivity. But I'm glad it happened, in a way. I'll figure out James later. But if I want the chance to do that, then right now what I need to figure out is who's blackmailing him.

I'm going down the stairs to leave the building and meet Gene coming up them carrying a crate of bottles, his shirtsleeves rolled up to show his arms, bent, straining at the crate. He smiles at me and it's like a knife going in. Did he see James leaving? Have any of the performers told him James came into my apartment last night?

"Morning," he says. He seems cheerful. I can't read anything into it.

"Morning," I say. I know I don't owe him anything, that we weren't anything but a kiss and some mooning on my part, but I hadn't even thought of him last night. I hadn't thought of him this morning. "You're here early."

"Elsie asked me to be here to sign for a shipment." He nods at the crate in his hands. "You heading out on that case?"

"Yeah," I say.

"I'm glad you took it. Even if there's some history there. You're helping someone."

I nod. That part is true at least. Someone. Not Donna, but . . . someone. I won't let James end up like her, either, a body going into the water.

"Good luck. Stay safe." And he smiles again, and I smile back, and I think about that one kiss we shared and feel like I'm tumbling down the stairs as he walks up them.

I swallow down the cold air when I get outside, reminding myself that I don't owe Gene anything, and I'm not committing myself to James, either. Last night was a lot of things. Memories, but also both of us feeling lonely, me because of what we did to Donna and him because of his life. But today I'm going to fix all that. And then, after that, maybe I'll know what's going to happen between us. I don't think it can be much, though. Not if he wants to stay in the navy. He can't spend an hour losing a tail just to see me. That's not going to make any kind of relationship work. So it was probably just once.

Still, seeing Gene made me feel like an asshole.

Outside, I take out the key from Donna's collar and look at it again: 34. I flip it over in the light to see if there are any other markings, something to tell me where to start, but there's nothing. It could be to any locker at a train or bus station, a YMCA, a bathhouse, maybe even a cheap hotel. I take a deep breath and head out to a newsstand where I buy a tourist map of the city and circle every place with lockers I can think of. Then I stuff the map in my pocket and get to work.

When I was an inspector with the police, I had uniform cops I could send on errands like this. I could have had the key duplicated and given them out to a whole team who would then spread out across the city, and the first one to open the locker would radio in. It would take an hour, maybe. But I'm on my own now, so I'm hiking around the city and trying the key in every locker 34 I can find.

I don't mind it as much as I thought I would. There's a pleasantness to taking a bus or streetcar from one station to the next, getting off, walking to any nearby lockers, trying the key, marking it off on my map, and then taking another bus or streetcar to the next station. It's peaceful, watching the city go by, bronzed in fall colors. And it gives me time—to plan to try to get ahead of the blackmailer and murderer, if they're even the same person. Donna's an itch inside my skull that I can only scratch at by thinking of it. Who would kill her, and why?

Lee would point the finger at Helen, but Lee hadn't seen how Helen had looked yesterday. She likes playing games, but calling me would have been too much of a risk unless she were genuinely scared.

So if not Helen, then who? Danny, her own brother? Was Donna blackmailing her brother, or were they in on it together? I'm mostly sure the blackmail money was to improve the act, though, so not much point blackmailing half the talent. From what everyone said, Danny seemed high-strung. Maybe they argued over something, he got hysterical, hit her, or knocked her over into something. Or maybe it was someone else altogether. Maybe he's already dead and she found who killed him, got to join him for her trouble. If James wasn't the only one they were running this scheme on, maybe they blackmailed the wrong person. Still, it would take real trouble to figure out that it was Donna and Danny doing the blackmail. Sidney the hotel manager would have mentioned if someone else came by asking questions.

So maybe it was someone else, a lover of Donna's, or just an enemy, or someone who just hates gay women, who followed her home then dragged the body back to Cheaters to get it shut down. It's not hard to imagine. There are endless possibilities for murder if you're queer. Most people don't really think it's a crime to kill a criminal—and all of us are criminals to the rest of the world.

When I finally feel the key turn in the right locker 34, and hear the click, it's already past six. I'm at the YMCA in Presidio, where I'd come a few times during the war. It's a pretty little white stucco building with palm trees out front, across the street from the hospital. Inside, the lockers are in the basement, and it's not hard to get in and open it without any questions. No one looks at me, no one is watching, waiting for someone to open it. And inside is one large, sealed manila envelope. Big enough for a bunch of photos, and maybe some film, too.

Knowing what could be on those photos, though, I don't open it in public. I just take the envelope and leave.

The fog has rolled in and it's spiraling over the city, making the park dim and damp. I hold the envelope close to me and walk past the golf club and to a streetcar stop. I don't usually mind the fog. Before I worked over a club, and I was just going to them, I always thought the fog rolling in was lucky, that it would hide my face from anyone I happened to see as I slipped through doors I wasn't supposed to enter. But holding this envelope, knowing Donna is dead, I'm also very aware that the fog can hide other people, too. It can hide anything.

I make it back to the Ruby without anyone leaping out at me. And once in my office, with the door firmly shut, I slice the envelope open with a letter opener, and pour the contents on the table: photos, film. The top photo is of Danny, naked and enjoying himself with a man I don't recognize. I move it to the bottom of the pile, but there's another of them, then another, and then one of Danny and James. They're naked, kissing, touching each other. I swallow and flip the whole pile over. I don't know what last night was, and I haven't even heard from James, but this is part of the job. I don't know how we could be together. But I know that pictures remind me of what that night felt like. My neck tingles looking at them.

More importantly, the job is done. I have the photos, the film. The blackmail is over. All I need to do is tell James and get paid.

Except it doesn't feel done. There's none of that release from finishing a case, no sense of filing it away in the back of my mind, my body going loose for a moment. I still don't know why Donna is dead or where Danny is—if he's alive. But I'm not a cop anymore. My job is just to do what the client asks, no more, no less. But maybe I can still poke around and find some justice for Donna, somehow. First, the good part: I swallow and pick up the phone. Searching the lockers has taken me most of the day, so it's pretty late, but I try his office first. The same kid from last time picks up and transfers me.

"Hey." James's voice is soft. "I was going to call."

"Yeah," I say, leaning on the desk. "Listen—I have them. It's over."

There's a long pause. "Really?" he asks finally.

"Come get them yourself."

"Thank you," he whispers. He sounds like he might cry. "I'll come as soon as I can, okay?"

"Yeah, I'll be here," I say.

"And Andy, it's not over. Don't worry. It's never really over with us."

He hangs up before I can respond, and I wonder if he's right. It was so easy to get entangled with him again, so easy to fall back into bed. But it wasn't the same. And we're not the same.

I lock the photos away and go downstairs for a drink. Gene isn't there yet, it's one of the other bartenders, Eileen. Technically, she's a cocktail waitress, but as long as she's out from behind the bar when the police raid, Elsie doesn't mind her pouring drinks, so she gives me a shot of rye when I ask for it.

"Working a big case?" she asks. We barely talk, but she's polite. Wears a pencil skirt and blouse to work. She's got blond-red hair cut in a messy bob and lots of freckles. She was a nurse in the war, and my impression is that her bedside manner would be all business, not like Gene's.

"I think I cracked it," I say.

"So it's a celebration," she says, pouring herself a glass of soda and toasting me. "Here's to that."

I laugh and drink. "Thanks. Still a lot of questions, but I guess . . . I just leave them, right?"

"Do what you get paid to, that's what I say. More than that is borrowing trouble."

I nod and she goes over to pour a drink for someone else. Gene shows up about an hour later, smiling at me but not coming over to the small table at the edge of the room that I've moved to. I smile back, but he serves drinks, and only comes over after about half an hour, after getting back from bringing down some bottles from upstairs. He walks over to me, and his smile looks a little forced now.

"Hey, Andy, your, uh, friend, is in your office."

My eyes widen. James got here fast. I would have thought he'd have taken more time to lose any tails, but I guess he just wanted to get it over with.

"He's a client," I say.

Gene tilts his head. "He's handsome, I think, under the hat and scarf."

I want to say not as handsome as him, but it would come out forced. Handsome isn't the issue. James makes me feel something familiar is the problem. Gene makes me feel something new. And I want my future to be more than ghosts.

"I guess I'll go close this case then," I say. I hope I sound final. Gene raises his eyebrows then returns to the bar without looking back.

Upstairs, in my office, James takes off his hat and scarf and then takes me around the waist and kisses me. I let him. I do more than that, I kiss him back.

"That's for fixing this for me," he says.

I smile. "I'm going to need to get paid, too," I say. "But first—" I take out the envelope and put it on the desk. "There are others in there, too—I didn't sort them, I didn't like looking at the one photo of you I saw, felt intrusive." I almost laugh, because that's how different things are. Eight years ago, I would have been in the room watching, if not participating.

"Yeah." He licks his lips, maybe thinking the same thing, takes the envelope and opens it.

"Get the film, too," I say, more for him than me. I turn away from the desk, peeking my head out into the hall as I let him fish out his photos. Some male impersonators I only half know are all jostling one another as they arrive. Some wear suits like Elsie, but a few are in dresses, their hair down to their shoulders, not pinned up yet. To avoid suspicion, I guess.

"Sorry you had to come here," I say to James. "I just thought it was safest. I know you have to check for tails and make sure you're good before you get anywhere near this place."

"It's all right," he says. "And I got the photos."

I turn back into the office and he's smiling, bright and wider than I've seen him these past few days. He looks like the old James. He looks ready for mischief and fun. He takes out his wallet and fishes out a bunch of cash. More than the bill. He hands it to me.

"That enough?" he asks.

"I should give you change," I say, going through the money, but he shakes his head and closes my hand around the cash, his hand around my hand.

"It's a bonus," he says. "For doing it so well."

"I thought that's what last night was," I say with a laugh.

He laughs then shakes his head. "No, that was . . . things going back to how they should be. You and me again." His hand feels warm over mine.

"James . . ." I tilt my head away from him. "I don't know. How would that work? You have to spend an hour making sure you're not followed to come here. I'm a 'known homosexual'—who knows what the police have already told the navy? It's too dangerous for you."

"I'll make it work," he says.

"And we don't even really know each other," I say. "Not like we used to."

"So let's get to know each other again. Let's go downstairs. Have a drink." He takes his other hand and puts it on my shoulder, almost like we're dancing.

"You won't even show your face down there," I say, nodding at his hat and scarf on my coatrack. "How can we have a drink?"

He smiles. "It'll be fine. I wasn't followed. I promise."

I wonder if I should, or if this is just his optimism back, high on the case being solved. Having the photos back in his hand is like pouring cool water over the fire of panic. Another win, and another reason to keep playing the game. I take a step back. "Not tonight," I say. "But . . . if you still want this, if you want to go out sometime, see if we can make something work again . . . tell me again tomorrow. Right now, I think, you're just feeling too light from getting the photos back. You feel invincible. Tomorrow you'll remember you're not."

He opens his mouth, then closes it again and nods. "All right," he says. "Tomorrow I'll ask you again."

"The decommissioning ceremony is in three days," I say.

His eyebrows rise.

"Helen told me," I say. His face goes still for a moment, but then he nods, like this is the most natural thing in the world. "She's going to be there. I will, too. Take until then. If you don't come say hi, I'll understand."

He tilts his head. "I'll be sitting with the brass, but I promise we will talk after, and I will ask you to dinner with me. Maybe at my house. I'm still a great cook, you know."

"Some things don't change," I say.

"Like us," he says, and leans forward, kissing me lightly on the cheek. "I'll see you in a few days," he says, taking his hat and scarf off the stand and putting them back on. "We'll have dinner after that."

He leaves my office, and I sit back on the desk, smiling. I look at the cash and calculate Elsie's percentage of it, plus a little extra, as a thank-you. This is my first big payday. Maybe this will show her I was a good investment. If I can get more clients, anyway.

Lee knocks on the open door, then walks in. She's got her makeup, with lipstick, on, but is just in a robe, no wig.

"I saw that handsome man leaving your office looking very happy," she says. "You solve the case without me?"

"I'm afraid so," I say, pointing at the envelope on the desk. "I found a locker key on Donna's body, spent the day finding what it opened, and when I did, these were inside. James wasn't the only target."

"So who killed Donna, then?" she asks, going up to the desk and staring at the envelope but not opening it.

"Probably one of the other people in there," I say, pointing at the envelope. "Maybe someone else did some investigating themselves, figured out the scheme, tried to get the photos back from Donna, since Danny's vanished. But she hid the key well, sewn pocket in her collar. If I hadn't seen her use it the night before . . ."

"So just luck, then?"

"That's usually how it works," I say.

She shrugs, and lifts an edge of the envelope. "So what are you going to do with these?"

I pick up the envelope and empty it onto the table. Photos and film fall out in a pile. "I should destroy them, I guess," I say. "Give the victims peace of mind."

"They won't know, though," Lee says. "It'll be hanging over their heads like the sword of Damocles for the rest of their lives."

"So . . . I should find them?" I ask. "Give them back? Isn't that a little personal?"

"They don't have to know what you saw or didn't. You just say you found them while working on a case, they seem to belong to them, here's the photos and film, do what you want with them."

I glance at the top photo, focusing on the faces, not the rest of it. Maybe there's a clue to finding Donna's killer in there, too. "I don't even know this guy. How can I find them?"

She crosses her arms. "You're a detective, Andy." She glances down at the photos. "And that's Donald March, he's in here most nights. Big fan of Stan's, for some reason."

I smile. "Okay." I flip past Donald's photos to the next guy. "Know him?"

"Ralph O'Connell, he's a friend of Shelly's. Didn't know he was that flexible."

I flip to the next guy, but this one I recognize. "That's Bert," I say. "Danny's boss."

"Trust Bert to be hiding something," Lee says, frowning. "But he can't be blackmailed. He's queer, everyone knows it, he doesn't have a boyfriend. What does he have to lose? If these were taken at the bar they could get the place shut down, but this is just some hotel room. Why would they have these?"

"I don't know," I say, "but maybe we should ask him when we give these back."

"You think he killed Donna?"

"Could be," I say. "But you're right, there's not much you can do with these. His boss knows he's gay, so he won't get fired, and while the cops might harass him, put him on a list, he's not going to prison in California just for being queer. And that would get

Danny in as much trouble as Bert. Maybe they were insurance for something. Or just an empty threat."

"I like that you're still working the case," Lee says with a grin.

"I'm not," I say. "Just . . . old habits. Someone should try to find Donna's killer, and the cops won't, so . . ."

I flip to the next photo, who Lee doesn't know, and the one after that, who Lee does, but the one after that makes me drop the whole bunch. Danny isn't in this one. It's Donna. And she's with Helen.

SEVEN

"Told you," Lee says. "Helen killed her, and there's why."

I shake my head. "No. She can't be blackmailed same way Bert can't. Who do they show this to? She doesn't even have any family left, her parents died during the war."

"Well, they have the photos," she says, looking at them. "And that's not the hotel."

"No . . . it doesn't look like Cheaters either, though." I focus on the backdrop of the shot: it looks like a bedroom in someone's home. There are some shelves behind the bed, filled with pictures and knickknacks. "I don't know where this is."

"Someone's apartment, maybe?"

"Yeah, probably," I say. "Well, I can ask her about it, too."

"Be careful, Andy. I don't like her. She's the only one they didn't try to get revenge on, she found the body, she dresses like a man she knew seven years ago as some kind of vendetta. Seven years! That's a long time to hold a grudge."

"That's a joke," I say, shaking my head.

"It's strange," Lee says. "I've been in this business awhile, and trust me, it's strange, and I wouldn't trust her."

"I'll be careful."

"Good. I like this girl Friday thing and it doesn't work if you're dead."

I smile at her and she frowns back.

"So," I say, "you said one of these guys comes into the Ruby every night? I may as well test out how returning blackmail photos goes."

"I'll let you handle that on your own, but I'll be watching from the stage." She glances at my clock. "I'd better go finish getting ready. I'm on soon. And his name is Donald. He'll be in by nine, that's when Stan is on. I'll see you out there."

She turns and leaves and I start going through the photos, sorting them into piles with the film. I put each in a separate envelope and put all but Donald's back in my desk. I hope this gets me some goodwill, and then maybe some more clients, and doesn't just make everyone feel more sure about what they thought of me—that I'm still a cop, that I'm here to black-mail them.

I put Helen's envelope in a different drawer. I can ask her about it tomorrow. Clearly she's hiding something, but she seemed so scared yesterday, so broken seeing that body. Not like a murderer. More like someone whose lover had just been left dead at her door. Which makes me think Donna was killed to get at Helen more than anything else. But then why not tell me?

Downstairs, the crowd has grown, and people are dancing. One of the male impersonators I don't really know is on stage, singing "Someday You'll Want Me to Want You." I look around the room for Donald, but either I don't see him or don't recog-nize him from the photos. So I take a seat in the corner and keep scanning the room. Gene comes over, and sets a glass down in front of me.

"You looked thirsty," he says. No mint this time. It smells like lemons. I think he likes testing drinks on me. Or he likes trying to figure out what I need in the moment. "And Eileen says you closed a case."

"Yeah," I say, taking the drink and looking up at him. He's beautiful in the light, his skin catching it like streaks of makeup on his jaw and cheekbones. He's wearing a simple black shirt, but no tie, and it's unbuttoned at the collar. Elsie doesn't mind a ca-sual dress code. For some reason I can't take my eyes off the peek of skin at the open collar. "Thank you," I say. The drink tickles my mouth with fizz and citrus.

He sits down. "I have a break," he explains when I look surprised. "So that's the case with the ex that's over?"

"Yeah," I say, hiding my mouth by raising the drink to my lips again. It's sweet.

"That's good," he says, then looks around the room. "Are you looking for someone?"

I nod. "I came across some photos during the case. The kind people might want back. I know one of them is named Donald March and he's here a lot. I thought I'd . . . give them to him."

Gene grins. "Returning blackmail photos to people? That's . . . really kind, Andy."

He lays his hand on the table, and without thinking, I lay mine out, too, not over his, but the tips of our fingers touching. He looks at me and I see that this is the thing he's wanted from me. The thing I've wanted for myself, too—to help people. I can feel our hands wanting to interlock, like branches weaving together, but I hold back. I don't know if I deserve the look on his face, or for our fingers to weave into each other. Not with what happened to Donna. I take another sip, lift my hand away.

"I don't really know what to say. 'Hey, here are some compromising photos of you, have a great day'?"

Gene laughs, and then smiles at me, his lips wet. "Maybe something like that, but . . . subtler. Just be yourself, be honest. They'll respect that."

"Yeah, I'll try that."

"So you have anything else planned, besides this returning of photos?"

I look at him, wondering if this is a chance to ask him out.

"The ship I served on, the *Bell*, it's being decommissioned in a few days. I'm going to go to that."

"Ah." He frowns a little. "With the ex?"

"He'll be there," I say neutrally. "But I'm going with another old friend."

He nods. "The navy know why you left the force? You going to be safe?"

"I don't know," I say. "But . . . I hope so."

"Be careful then," he says. He glances behind me. "That's Donald who just came in, by the way."

I glance behind me and spot him, the guy from the photos up in my office. I look back at Gene, and I can feel the trepidation in my expression.

"You want me to come with you?" he asks. "Introduce you?"

I shake my head. "The more people who go over, the more people he thinks know what's in the photos, the more embarrassing it is for him. I gotta do this alone." I down the rest of my drink in one swallow. "Wish me luck."

"Just be honest. You want to help him, that's what's important."

"Let's hope," I say, and stand up, walking over to Donald.

He's sitting down at a table when I get to him, waving at Stan, who's about to go on. I sit down next to him. He looks over and smiles.

"You a fan of Stan's, too?" he asks.

"Yeah," I say. "But I'm here to see you, actually."

He looks me up and down and grins. "All right."

He thinks I'm flirting. I try to make my face professional. "I'm Evander Mills. The private detective with an office here."

"Oh," he says, his face falling. "The cop."

"Not anymore. I was working a case for another client and I found some photos and film that I believe have you in them."

He blushes crimson for a moment, but then his expression goes hard. "So now you're blackmailing me? I'm just a postman, okay? I don't have much money. It was one time, one outrageous expense because he was pretty. If you give those to my boss, I get fired, and then no one gets any money. So—"

"No," I say, putting my hands up. "I'm saying my client was being blackmailed by the same people. I found all their photos. I want you to have them so you can . . . do whatever you want with them. No money. I'm trying to help."

He looks confused. "You're just giving them to me?"

"It's the right thing to do," I say. "No one should be blackmailed."

He relaxes. "Okay . . . so where are they?"

"My office, upstairs." I glance at the stage. "You have five minutes before Stan starts. Just come up, look at them and take them. Or tell me to burn them. Or I can bring them down here, if you want, in an envelope. I'm just trying to do the right thing here."

It all rushes out of me, almost comically, and Donald gives me a little smile. "All right, all right, I believe you. Take me to your office."

I bring him upstairs and hand him the envelope with his photos. He takes them out and glances at them. "And the film," he says. "So . . . I don't have to pay them anymore?"

"I don't know if there were other copies somewhere," I say. "But I don't think so."

He smiles, wide and bright. Then he looks over at me. "You're okay, Mills. Thanks. This is . . . it's a relief."

"Hey, we all have to stick together, right?"

In answer, he tears the photos up into tiny bits over my wastebasket. He tries with the film, too, but it doesn't tear so well, and I hand him a pair of scissors out of my desk. He cuts it up into little pieces and rains them down over the torn photos like confetti.

When he's done, he looks different. Happier, sure, but relieved, and . . . younger, somehow. "Let me buy you a drink," he says.

"There's no need," I say. "I'm just glad I can help you out."

"I know there's no need. I want to, come on, I can hear Stan starting."

We head back downstairs and he buys me a beer and I sit with him, listening to Stan sing "Baby Please Don't Go," with a few of the other female impersonators doing backup. He's got a smoky kind of voice, not bad, really, certainly not as bad as Lee says he is. I buy the next round, and Donald and I watch him sing and the band play and then Lee comes on and sings, too, and there's more drinks, and more people join us, and Donald introduces me around and says I'm a real hero, and claps me on the shoulder like I'm his friend. At one point, I catch Gene's eye and he grins widely at me, and I'm filled with a warmth that's more than the alcohol.

I wonder if Donna ever had a night like this. The thought sucker-punches me, and I try to shrug it off, but I can feel the bruise.

After Lee is done singing, folks start heading home, but Donald gives me a hug and says thank you again before he leaves. I tell him he's welcome and he says he'll see me again tomorrow, like we're drinking buddies now. Maybe we are.

When he's gone, and there's a new male impersonator on stage, I head over to the bar for just some seltzer water before bed. Elsie is there already, grinning at me.

"Looks like you made some friends," she says.

"I just helped someone out."

"Gene told me," she says, nodding at him.

"So you know I closed the case," I say, and take out her cut of the pay and hand it to her.

"Wow, big case," she says, looking at the money before pocketing it.

"Trying to earn my keep," I say. "And thanks. I know it's been . . . hard keeping me on board."

"Where would you get that idea?" she asks. "It's a cinch."

I smile at the lie. "Can I get some seltzer?" I ask Gene. "Nothing in it."

He pours me the drink and hands it over. "How many more photos you have to return?"

I drink, suddenly thinking of Helen. "A few. Some I might have trouble finding. So I'm going to just scout some of the bars and see if anyone looks familiar."

"Someone is going to slug you, you know," Elsie says. "I mean, you're doing the right thing, but someone is definitely going to slug you."

I laugh. "Maybe."

She pats me on the shoulder. "It'll be worth it, though. This is a great way to build business. Make sure people know you're here to help."

"That's not why I—"

"I know. But it is." She shrugs. "Still, be careful. Don't want you to crack your skull open or anything. Gene's already patched you back together once."

"I don't mind doing it again," Gene says.

"Don't mind doing what again?" Lee asks. "Water, please."

"Patching up Andy," Gene says, pouring water and putting it down in front of her.

"He's gonna get slugged," Elsie says.

"Oh." Lee sips her water. "Probably yes. How'd the first one go?"

"Well enough," I say.

"You sure looked cozy. Be careful he doesn't think you want to reenact those photos with him."

I laugh. "I think it was just gratitude. But I'm headed to bed. Tomorrow I need to figure out how to find the rest of these guys."

"Not just guys," Lee says, her voice a warning.

"I know. I'll . . . deal with that."

"What?" Elsie asks, looking curious. "They were blackmailing women, too?"

"I don't know," I say. "I'll figure it out."

"All right. And thanks again for the cut. I like it when you make me money. Night, Andy."

"Night, everyone," I say, standing up, but I look at Gene when I say it.

Then I head upstairs and get into bed, the pink light from outside making everything feel rosy.

I'm not sure when Helen gets to the club, but I'm betting it's earlier than Bert, so I start there. I have all the photos in different envelopes in my bag, each marked with a few lines that help me remember whose photos they are, but nothing anyone else would understand. A song title reminds me of this guy, a squiggly line reminds me of another. Helen's is blank. Helen's the one I can't forget.

I wait out back, by the door I helped her move the body out of. She pulls in around four, parking her car near the alley and walking over to me with an amused expression.

"I don't think I've ever had a man waiting for me at the door." She turns to unlock it. "Except cops, of course."

"Helen, why'd you lie to me about you and Donna?"

She doesn't turn around but opens the door. "I didn't lie."

I take out her envelope and hand it to her. "I found the blackmail photos. I've been returning them. You're up."

She takes the envelope and lifts the photos out. Her eyebrows raise. "Not my best angle," she says.

"Don't tell me you've never seen them before," I say.

She puts the photos back and walks into the club. I follow her, the door slamming shut behind us. She opens another door, and we're out of the storeroom, in the hall leading to her dressing room. She walks down it silently and I follow. When she gets to that door she unlocks it, too. The place sounds empty. I know I should be afraid. She might have killed Donna. But I follow her anyway.

In her dressing room she sits down, putting the envelope on her vanity, then she looks up and meets my eyes in the mirror, like she did the first time I was in here. She looks more honest in a mirror. She's more comfortable talking in reflections.

"Yeah, I've seen them before. Donna showed up and dangled them in front of me. Said she'd send them to the cops. When I pointed out that she'd be getting herself in trouble, too, she made her eyes all big and did an impression for me. Soft voice."

"She used it on me, too," I say, thinking of when I first met her.

"She said, 'Officer, I didn't know what kind of club it was, but I just had one drink and then everything goes fuzzy. I just remember waking up and she was on top of me.'"

"She was going to say you were running a drug den and a porno shop?"

"Pretty much," Helen says with a sigh. "So I gave her what she wanted. But I swear, I didn't kill her."

"How much did you pay her?"

Helen laughs, low and sad. "She didn't want money. She just wanted to sing. Her and her brother. So I said I'd let them. But then Danny went missing and . . . that's why Donna was here every night, I think. She thought I had something to do with it. I told her I'd put her on alone, that she'd be good . . . but she said she was waiting for her brother. When I found her body . . . I thought someone knew, someone was trying to frame me, but I don't know who, Andy. That's what's so wild about it. I've been thinking since you left, and I have no idea who would have wanted me gone. And the cops never turned up that night. It doesn't make any sense."

"No jealous exes? People who vowed to put you out of business?"

"Nothing," she says. She turns around. "I'm sorry I lied, though. I'm trying to do that less with you. I think . . . well, I know I was scared. But also, the old days, the fun was the lying, you know. When you and I would hold hands and I'd bat my eyes at you in front of the brass, telling girls' husbands I was just an old school chum, or when I wrote the two of you letters and said I was writing to my boyfriends. The girls who didn't know me thought I was dating both of you—on the same ship. They were scandalized. It was so much fun."

"That's where James Bell comes from, isn't it?" I ask. "You just want to lie a little, cause some trouble?"

She turns back around to her mirror, her eyes down for a moment, examining her creams and brushes. Then she looks up, more at herself than at me. "I just want to have fun, Andy. That's all I ever want." She tilts her head and a loose lock of hair falls over her eye. She stares at me in the mirror and shakes her head, like I'm not understanding. "Life is cruel and miserable for us for no fucking reason. I'm going to milk out every bit of fun I can find. That's why I do the show, why I run a bar, why I let Donna bring me back to her apartment even though I knew something was off. Stupid, but—"

"That's her apartment in the photos?" I interrupt.

Helen looks confused and turns back around to meet my eyes. "Of course. You think that's my place?"

"I've been to Danny's place. It doesn't look like that."

"Well, this was Donna's place. Or she said it was."

"You remember an address?" I ask.

"Andy, you got the photos. Why does it matter?"

I pause. She's right, the case is closed.

"I don't know. But . . . someone should try to find out who killed her, do something about it."

She nods. "I'd like that, but I don't remember an address. It was a little apartment up by Nob Hill. Or maybe Pacific Heights . . . or Sea Cliff. North side of the city, for sure. I thought it was awful fancy for her, but I was drunk enough I didn't ask too many questions. Now that I think about it, she didn't seem to know where anything was, actually. And when she went to get us a drink all she had was rum, and I've never seen her drink anything but gin. It probably wasn't her place."

"But she had a key?"

"Yeah. But Andy—"

"I know." More questions keep bubbling up from this muck—if Danny finally had blackmailed his way into a show, why vanish? What scared him? Donna seemed sure he was still alive, but was that just wishful thinking? They could both be dead, some other john having taken them out. Someone like Helen.

"What could you do if you did find out who killed her?" Helen asks. "If I were to confess right here and now, what could you do?"

I raise my eyebrows. "Are you?"

She frowns and turns back to the mirror. "No, Andy. I already told you. I wouldn't . . . I liked her, even with the blackmail. She was cold, but ambitious, and I admired that. Blackmailing me to get a shot at singing?" She smiles, almost wistful. "That's something special. If it hadn't been me she was blackmailing I would have bragged about knowing her."

I snort a laugh.

"I did have one idea of who could have done it, though." She stands up and walks past me, opening the door. I follow her out. "You won't like it."

"Who?" I ask.

"James," she says.

I shake my head. "He doesn't even know Donna."

"No, but he knows you. He follows you, he sees you talking to her, he figures it out . . ."

"When?" I ask.

We walk into the bar. There's another woman behind it already, cleaning glasses. Helen gets up on the small stage then turns around, towering over me.

"Don't underestimate him, Andy," she says. "He's smart, and he figures things out. Not like you do, but enough. And if there's one person who would want her dead"—she whispers the last word—"and who would leave her on my doorstep . . . that's who I think of. It would almost be like a joke to him. The way I'm James Bell."

"He's not like that," I say.

"He's . . ." She looks like she's going to say something, but stops herself, goes behind the curtain. I follow her. She's organizing some lights. Busywork.

"He's what?"

"You're screwing him again," she says instead. "I told you you would."

I don't say anything, and she glances up at me, then goes back to moving the stage lights into a neat little row.

"I don't want to say anything else," she says. "I'm probably wrong. And if I weren't, the only person I'd be saving is you. And you don't want to be saved. You and James just dove right back into each other."

"It's not like that," I say. "It was after I went to South City with you. It was . . ."

She looks up at me, sad. "Yeah. Well. I hope he knows that that's all it was."

"I don't know what it is."

"Well . . . just don't bring him around here, huh? You're always welcome, but I don't know if he'd like my act."

"He'll be there at the ceremony," I say. "You can try talking to him then if you want. I don't know if he will, in front of everybody, though."

"Sure," she says. "We'll see. I gotta get this place cleaned up now."

"And I have more photos to return to people."

"You're giving them all back?" she asks. "I thought I was special."

"I'm trying to do the right thing."

"That's nice," she says. "Be careful. And . . ." She takes a deep breath. "If you do find out who did that to Donna . . . I'd like to know. Especially if it was about me, if—"

"If someone tries to get the club shut down, I'll help you again."

"Thanks, but . . . I meant I wanted to know if it was my fault. If they did it to hurt me, or her."

I let that hang there, maybe too long. "It's the murderer's fault, Helen."

She laughs, low and sad. "Sure, Andy. Just let me know what you find out, all right? If you do, I mean. I'm not hiring you or anything."

"You can if you want," I say, putting my hands in my pockets. "I'll give you a discount."

"No . . . I don't want you to get more caught up in this. Just if you hear anything, okay? But don't go looking. Like I said, I want fun, not trouble. For you, too."

"Yeah." I smile. "Okay. But if I hear anything."

"Thanks."

"See you soon."

"I hope not too soon," she says, a joke that doesn't land right. Neither of us are in the mood for it.

I force a chuckle anyway and walk back to the front of the stage and look out at the club. With the lights up, it feels dirtier, less shadow and mystique, more of just a small room with some heavy curtains that hasn't had the walls cleaned in a while. I let myself out the way I came in.

I pause in the alleyway and take a cigarette from the case in my jacket pocket. Maybe Lee is right, my past is making my vision blurry. Like the *Bell*'s dazzle camouflage; it's all messed up and I don't know what's the horizon and what's the sea. What's real and what's just a memory. And I don't know if I should go after Donna's killer. No, I know I shouldn't. Everything Helen said is right. There's nothing I can do, and no one is paying me. If they come for Helen again, maybe then . . . but I don't think this was about her. It was about Donna, the photos. And that's done now. Or will be, once I give them back.

I smoke the cigarette down to the nub and crush it out with my heel on the way to the Silver Jay. It's open, so Bert will be there by now.

Without Lee, I can go in the front, and once I do, I remember why I didn't come here much. The place smells like stale smoke and wet leather. It's a long, narrow room with windows only at the front, the cracks of light from between the curtains barely making a dent in the length of darkness. The bar is on one side, and there are tables on the other, with a stage at the end of the room and a jukebox next to it for when no one is singing, even though there's no room to dance. It's just after work, so it's mostly empty. A few guys in suits are at the bar, and three men in leather motorcycle jackets sit at a table. They all look up when I come in, evaluating, deciding if I'm someone to go home with. That reminds me of why I did come here, when I did. It was easier to find what I needed.

I walk up to the bar. Behind it, among bottles of liquor, is a sign that reads WARNING: YOU ARE SUBJECT TO A RAID AT ANY TIME. The bartender looks me up and down and smiles.

"What'll it be, handsome?" he asks.

"I'm looking for Bert," I say.

The bartender frowns and motions behind him with his thumb at a door.

Inside is barely an office, more of a storeroom with a desk. The walls are lined with shelves filled with crates of booze, and on the desk in the center is a small green shaded desk lamp. Everything else is dark. It reminds me of the interrogation room at the police station. Bert is sitting at the desk, going over some papers, but he looks up at me and narrows his eyes, not quite remembering. Then he nods.

"The detective, Lee's friend."

"Yep," I say.

"You need something else?"

"I want to know why you didn't tell me the whole truth."

"Huh?" He looks genuinely perplexed, so I take out his envelope and put it down on the desk. He opens it up and takes out the photos and grins wide like a cat.

"These are nice pictures," he says, eyes still on them, flipping to the next. "I look good here. You want to be Danny's role? That what you're asking?" He looks up at me. "As you can see, I've got a lot to like."

"I'm asking why you didn't mention Danny was blackmailing you," I say.

He shrugs, turns back to the photos, and grins again. "Because he wasn't. I mean, he tried, he flashed them, said I better give him and his sister a chance, but I asked him who he was going to show these to, and he had nothing. All bluster and drama. That's all that kid is. Oh, he didn't show me this one. I like what his mouth is doing." He shows me the photo. "You think you can do that?"

"So he just gave up?"

"Well, he robbed the place, like I said. You catch him yet? If you know where he is, I'll pay you to tell me, just so I can get my money back."

"And there's really no one to show those photos to that would hurt you?" I ask, ignoring the offer.

"It's not at the bar; the cops know what kind of place this is and we pay them to leave us alone, and my bitch of a mother kicked me out decades ago when she found me with one of the boys from down the street. These photos are just for fun, now. I can keep 'em?"

"They're yours," I say with a shrug. "Hey, you ever see his sister again? Donna?"

He shakes his head and glances up at me. "Honestly, not sure I'd know her from Adam. Sorry, fella. Hope you find them, though."

"Thanks," I say. "Let me know if you think of anything else."

"And you let me know if you want to try making our own photo album."

I turn around and leave, rolling my eyes. Bert could be lying same as Helen could, but he didn't even blink when I mentioned Donna. If he knew she was part of the scheme, he didn't show it, and if he didn't, he'd have no reason to kill her. Except maybe to get to Danny. That might fit—Donna's injury could have been someone knocking her down, an accident. But Bert seems too lazy to go out looking for Danny, even if he did steal from the till. He asked me to do it, and even then, it was an afterthought.

So I still have no leads. Which is fine, because the case is over, I remind myself, as I leave the bar. It might still be walking around in my head, but out here, there's no one paying me to ask Bert or Helen anything, and no justice even if I figure it out. It still claws at me, though. Donna's body sinking into the water.

So I try to focus on the rest of the envelopes. One of the sets of photos is a friend of Shelly's, and Lee says he's there most nights. The guy in the other, Lee says, goes all over town, and the last guy he didn't know, but we agreed he looked familiar, so I'll probably spot him eventually. Three left, and then I'm done. I head to Shelly's. If I'm lucky, all three of them will be there tonight.

When I get there, it's starting to fill up. There's a singer on stage, a female impersonator dressed like Betty Grable in the blue dress, singing "My Blue Heaven." I spot Shelly, who nods at me, but doesn't look like he wants company, so I take a seat at the bar, order a rye on ice, and sit down to wait until I see any of the guys from the photos. The singer isn't so bad and I tap my feet, looking around at the crowd as I sip my drink. I spot one of the guys when he comes in, the one neither Lee nor I knew, but who looks familiar. He's alone, which makes this easier. I wait until he's got himself a drink at the bar, then go sit next to him. He looks me up and down and smiles.

"Hi," I say. "I'm Evander Mills. I'm the PI who works over the Ruby." I smile so he doesn't run.

"Yeah?" he asks. "But you pick up guys here?"

"Sometimes." I laugh. "But actually I'm just returning things today. I was working a case and found some photos of a few guys I thought they might want back. You're one of them."

He looks a little pale, then shakes his head. "Don't know what you're talking about," he says, staring at his drink. "Wrong guy."

"I'm not going to charge you anything. I only wanted to give them to you, then I'll leave. Just so you know that they're destroyed . . . or whatever you want to do with them," I add, thinking of Bert.

He looks up from his drink. "So they were blackmailing other men?" he asks softly. "They kept asking for more . . ."

I nod, and fish out his envelope and put it down in front of him. "Yours now. That's all I wanted to do."

"I have a wife," he says, looking at the envelope. "What do I do? Trash them here?"

"Sure," I say, pulling over an ashtray and a box of matches. SHELLY's is written on the box in red letters. "Or take them outside. Burn them."

He looks at the matches, then the envelope, his eyes skipping back and forth like a tennis ball before he nods, and opens the envelope and looks inside, pulling the film negatives out and putting them in the ashtray.

"Well," I say, "those might smell—"

But before I can finish, he's struck a match and lit the film on fire. The smoke and smell are awful, and I have to turn away, coughing, eyes watering.

The bartender comes over and dumps some water on the ashtray before the film is done burning. "What the hell are you doing?" he asks.

The guy whose photos they are is laughing. "Sorry, sorry," he says.

I feel a clap on the back and turn around to see Shelly. "Starting fires?" he asks.

"I didn't think he'd do it in here," I say.

Shelly looks at the ashtray and envelope. "Ah," he says. "Well . . . here." He grabs the ashtray and envelope and walks away. Me and the blackmail victim follow him. He takes us outside, then around back, and dumps everything in a trash can, lights a match, and throws it in.

"I don't mind you doing what you have to do," he says to us. "But next time, take it outside, all right?"

"Sorry," the guy says. "I just knew I had to get rid of them, and . . ."

"I get it." Shelly claps the guy on the shoulder, then me, too. "Good to see you helping folks out, Andy." He goes back inside. "I'll make sure your drinks are kept cold."

We watch the photos and film burn down to ash, the smell less offensive out here.

"I love my wife," he says softly. "But . . ."

"You don't have to explain anything to me," I say. "I just came across them and wanted to make sure you got them back."

"Thanks," he says, turning to the door and walking back inside. I follow him. At the bar, I grab my drink, but the guy doesn't want to talk, and that's fine by me, so I scoot a few chairs away, and watch the act. Shelly comes and sits down next to me.

"You waiting for anything?" he asks. "Looks like you did your job."

"Oh, that wasn't the job," I say. "I finished that. Just came across these photos while doing it. So I'm returning them. Got a few more."

Shelly whistles, softly. "All right. No more fires inside, though, okay? Use the can out back."

"Sure thing, Shelly," I say. "Sorry for the trouble."

He shrugs. "Not so much trouble." He turns to walk away, but I find myself calling him back.

"Hey, Shelly?"

He turns to me and raises an eyebrow.

"You ever see Donna again, after that audition?"

"I told you already, I didn't."

"You know if there was anyone angry with her? Jealous ex or—"

He holds up his hands. "I barely knew the woman. If she was even in here before her audition, I never noticed. I'm sorry, but she was a stranger."

"Yeah, sure. Thanks."

He shakes his head and goes back to his booth, watching the crowd, like I do. But Shelly has friends coming in, sitting with him, laughing, drinking, and I sit alone, watching the door and wondering about a dead woman.

About an hour later, another of the guys comes in. I approach him and start my pitch, but at the mention of the photos, he takes a swing and runs. Shelly meets him at the door, tells him it's okay, and we go to the trash can out back, and light the whole envelope on fire without even looking in it. I rub my jaw, but he doesn't apologize for the sucker punch. A little after that, the last guy comes in, and when I give him his envelope, he hugs me and kisses me full on the mouth, then starts crying about how he's an astronomer, and he'd be sure to get fired if these got out. He doesn't just burn them, he pours his drink over the ashes.

It's a night of small fires of joy, chains burned. When I'm done I decide to have one more drink to celebrate, but when I walk back in with the astronomer, Shelly waves me over. I carefully sit down at his booth and he smiles at me.

"How many more?" he asks.

"That's it," I tell him. "At least for tonight. If I find any more, though, maybe we can make this a regular thing."

Shelly laughs. "I hope not. You smell like a burnt building."

I smell my collar. The chemical smoke has definitely woven itself between the threads. "I should get back and shower."

"No, no, sorry," Shelly says. "I didn't mean to make it sound like that. You're welcome here whenever you want, Andy."

"Thanks," I say. "I'm gonna have one more drink, then."

Shelly nods, and I get up and walk back to the bar.

"Detective," comes a polite voice as I sit down. I look over to see Sidney, the hotel manager. "I suppose I should have known I'd run into you sooner or later."

I smile and nod at him. "It's a small town. How are you? Get those holes filled in?"

"Yes, and discreetly," he says, sitting on the stool next to mine. "So embarrassing. How about you? Did you find the boy?"

"No," I sigh, shaking my head. There's the other part of the case I need to leave alone. Danny is still gone. Though if Donna's fate is tied to his, he's probably been dead the whole time.

Especially if they had their shot to sing and he never showed up. "That girl who came at the same time—she never talked to you, did she? Mention her brother maybe? Or some enemy?"

Sidney looks at his drink, then shakes his head. "No, no. Just that one time. Said the room had been where she'd honeymooned. Then the next time, I recognized her, she didn't have to ask."

"You're good at your job," I say.

"Not really." He laughs. "Then I would have seen through her sob story." He pauses. "Is she missing, too?"

I nod. "But the case is closed. I've taken care of it, even if they're in the wind."

"Well, that's good news," Sidney says with a grin. "Here, let me buy you a drink." He waves the bartender over. "What are you having?" he asks me.

"Rye, on the rocks."

"So manly," Sidney says, turning to the bartender. "Another for him and a mai tai for me," he says, then turns to me. "I guess I'm just a fancier drinker." He grins, a little proud, a little sheepish. The bartender brings us our drinks and he raises his, so I raise mine and he taps his glass against it. "To the end of both our problems," he says. "Your case, and my holes." He laughs and sips, then turns back to me, interested. "Can you tell me anything about it? What you found out?"

I shake my head. "Sorry, client confidentiality. But everything is sorted."

He nods, but sighs, disappointed. "Well, I'm glad, and if either that boy or young woman comes back, I'm going to tell them absolutely not. Maybe give them the bill for the repairs. Wallpaper patching is very expensive. My employer wasn't thrilled, but he couldn't say it was my fault specifically, so he chalked it up to the cost of business. The maids are now under instructions to look behind every painting when cleaning the rooms. You think that'll be enough?"

I shrug. "Maybe," I say. "Might be too late at that point, though. But if you find one, give me a call, maybe I can track down the client if they've only just checked out."

"We're not really big enough to have an in-house detective . . . but one on call isn't a bad idea. I'll run it by my employer. He doesn't have to know how I know you."

I smile. "Thanks, that'd be great," I say, wondering if I can work straight cases without getting caught.

"How did you get into the business anyway?" he asks, sipping his drink, pinkie extended. "It seems such an odd line of work for our kind of people."

"I was a cop before," I say with a laugh. "Even stranger."

"Then why did you join up?"

"I was navy before, during the war. I guess I just thought between that, and my dad being an insurance investigator . . . it felt like a good fit." I laugh. "That sounds crazy to say, I know."

"No, no." Sidney shakes his head. "I understand. I was navy too—years before you, of course. I was court-martialed in '19."

"Oh," I say, trying to keep my face straight.

"You don't have to ask. It's what you think. They found me out. I'd been in the navy a decade—this is back in Rhode Island—joined up because it felt like a good fit, as you say. My father was a fisherman, I grew up on boats, I wanted to serve my country . . ." He smiles, a little lost in the memory of idealism, then turns back to me. "And speaking frankly, it was fun, too. I was . . . not as careful as I should have been, as it turned out. I took a man home one night, and the next week I was standing in front of a military tribunal listening to him tell everyone in cold, specific detail about everything we'd done. Apparently he was a . . . spy. He went out, had sex with navy men, then reported back about each of us. Mortifying, hearing it all recounted like that. And it's not as though he hadn't enjoyed himself!" He takes another, longer sip of his drink.

I nod. "There were rumors of guys like that even when I was in the navy. The idea was if they gave rather than received, they weren't really gay, so it was allowed." I take a long drink myself. "Sometimes I'm shocked I wasn't found out. I took a lot of risks. Though during a war, I guess, they don't feel as much that way."

Sidney smiles sadly. "You're lucky. It was awful when they brought me in. They asked me to name names . . . and I'm ashamed to say I did, and then they court-martialed me anyway. Me and a bunch more. We did about a year in prison, and when I got out, I ran across the country to get away from what everyone knew by then. I wrote my ma when I got here, gave her my address. She never wrote back." He sighs. "And all that was overseen by FDR, you know. I did not vote for him when he ran for president, oh no; I'm glad that man is dead." He takes another long drink.

"I'm sorry to bring up bad memories."

He shakes his head. "Don't be, Mr. Mills. Really. Bad memories lead to good. I met my Joseph here, we have a nice life. He had to leave his job a little while back, but we make do, you know? I imagine you must, your line of work."

"I do," I say, smiling a little. "It's a better life than I thought it would be."

"Exactly. Oh." He looks over my shoulder. "Here's my Joseph now." He waves and I turn to see a man his age waving back, with salt-and-pepper hair and a kind-looking face. Sidney puts down his drink. "In fact, I'm going to go dance with him. It was nice talking with you, Mr. Mills."

"You too, and please, call me Andy. Have a good night. I'm just going to finish my drink and head home. It's been a long day."

"Well, get some rest then, Andy."

"Thanks, you too, Sidney." He smiles and walks over to his boyfriend and takes his hand, and the two of them are soon on the floor dancing, looking deep into each other's eyes and smiling. I watch them for a while, finishing my drink. Last time I was here, I was thinking of James, but now I haven't really thought of him once. Watching Sidney and his man dancing, two older men, still clearly in love, I wonder if that could be my future with James. Or Gene. Or someone else entirely. It could, I realize. I could have a real life, a future, helping folks out like I did today.

A future Donna won't get. Maybe she deserved it. She bought that ticket to trouble herself, after all. Maybe I should just drop it, like I keep telling myself to.

I finish my drink, nod once at Shelly from across the room, and go out into the night. The air has gone from cool to cold, that metallic smell of approaching winter suddenly prickling my nose. Or maybe that's the smoke from the film.

But still, I'm feeling good, so good that when a dark car starts tailing me on my walk back to the Ruby, I don't give it much thought. Not until it speeds up and screeches to a halt next to me. I turn to look at it, but that's when the guy on foot I didn't notice comes up behind me. I feel the whack to the back of my head just as the car door starts to open, and hear someone say, "Put him in here," just as the world goes black.

EIGHT

When I come to, I'm in the car, and it's moving. Outside I see neon lights, but my vision is blurry. I don't think I've been out for more than a few minutes. I blink and look around the rest of the car. I'm lying on the floor in what I think is a limo, or at least is a big enough car I can lie on the floor and the man sitting in front of me doesn't have his feet on me, though the toes of his black oxfords are banging against my knee with every bump. I look up, there's a screen between here and the driver. I can't see him. I don't know if he could hear me, but he probably saw me getting shoved in the back, so calling for help won't do much.

"Ah, you're awake. Sorry about that, didn't mean to be so rough," the man says with a chuckle. I look up at him. He's big, tall; massive really, with broad shoulders crammed into a dark suit—I can't tell in this light if it's black, gray, or navy. White shirt, dark tie. Very well put together. Too put together to just be the muscle for someone else, even if he's got enough of it.

He's smoking, a window rolled down slightly to let the smoke escape. He looks down at me, and his face is surprisingly gentle for a man who just knocked me out and threw me in the back of a car.

I sit up. My hands aren't tied, so I rub the back of my head where I got smacked. No blood.

"If you didn't mean to be so rough, what did you mean?" I ask.

"Honestly, I was just going to shove you in here with me, but . . . old habits." He shrugs. "Instincts took over. I've thrown a lot of men into the back seat of cars, if I'm being honest." He chuckles again. It's a sound that would be sweet under different circumstances. It's got the low depth of molasses. "I don't mean that romantically," he says. "Though . . ." He shrugs again, and inhales on his cigarette. He focuses his eyes on me, and we roll by a white neon sign that shines on him like a spotlight for a moment. Clean-shaven, green eyes, fifties, with some gray in his hair, and very handsome.

"I really am sorry," he says. "I mean for this to be polite."

"All right," I say. "I'm not sure all is forgiven, but why don't you tell me, politely, what you want."

"Oh, I thought you knew," he says, with a big smile. "I wanted to give you the opportunity to give me my pictures back."

I rub the back of my head again. I don't know this guy from the photos I found in the locker. "Pictures?" I ask.

"I heard you were giving them back tonight, and then you put on quite a show, lighting some film on fire at Shelly's. I can't go to Shelly's, of course, but I have people who do, who tell me things."

"Why do they do that?"

He chuckles again. "So, I assume you have them all, and you're giving them back to everyone. A good Samaritan. You don't see it every day. I admire it, Mr. Mills. Truly. I already went through your briefcase. You don't have the photos on you, so should I take you back to the Ruby? I can't go in with you, but I can wait out here while you bring them down."

I shake my head. "I don't have your pictures."

We pass under another neon light just as his expression flickers, so fast I'm not sure if it's real or the lights and my head. It's like he goes from pleasant, affable, to something much more dangerous, like one of those elegant housecats when he suddenly tears the head off a bird.

"How did you come across the other photos you returned today?"

"I was working a case, stumbled on them."

"They were all photos of Danny Geller with various men, correct?"

"How would you know that?" I ask.

"I've been doing my own little investigation. Not nearly as successful as yours, though. I didn't find anything."

"Who are you?" I ask.

He leans forward a little. "I'm someone who'd like his pictures back," he says. "Now, do you have them? Or have you not looked at all the photos you recovered? If so, you can go up to your office at the Ruby and find mine, and everything will be just swell."

"I've seen all the photos. I've returned them all. You weren't in them."

His face goes dangerous again, and this time I know it's not a trick of the light. He reaches out, and slaps me, hard, across the face, so fast I can't stop him.

He sighs and shakes his head. "I really did want to keep this polite."

My hand raises to my face, rubbing at the red mark he certainly left there. "Did you?" I ask.

"I did. I just wanted you to give me my photos. I know Danny took them. I know you have Danny's photos. Therefore, you must have my photo. I'm not sure why you'd keep it from me when you're giving the others back. But if you killed Danny for his photos—and I don't mind that, we've all had to kill at some point—and you plan on using them on me the same way, I'll tell you what I told him: I can't be blackmailed. If you try, it won't end well for you."

He says it so matter-of-fact that my throat goes dry.

"Then why are you so keen to get them back?"

"You misunderstand me. You can try to blackmail me. But anyone you sent those photos to, even if you knew where to send them—I could intercept them. The only thing I'm trying to prevent is the exertion it would take me. And of course, if you tried, I'd find you, and I'd make sure you stopped. But that's the annoying way. So much energy spent by both of us, for nothing. You're already giving back the photos, Andy. Just keep doing that. For me."

"I'm really sorry," I say, trying to sound as genuine as I am. "I don't have your photos."

This time, when he reaches out, his hand is closed. I raise my own hands to stop him, but he's fast and I'm still woozy. His fist hits me like a brick in the face, knocking my teeth back over my tongue.

"Don't you dare spit your blood in this car," he says. He hands me a plain handkerchief, and I wipe my face with it, then spit the blood in my mouth into it. It smells slightly of lemons and oranges, faint memories of cologne.

"I'm sorry," I say. "I really just don't—"

He hits me with a backhand this time. I taste blood again, and now I'm angry enough to try fighting back, to lunge at him, but he catches me around the throat with his other hand, dropping the cigarette out the window and pinning me to the floor in one movement, his face going angry again, twisted. He seems to feel it, though, and it settles back into a polite smile.

"I understand why you want to fight back," he says, squeezing my throat enough I start wheezing. "But this would be much easier if you just stopped lying."

"But I'm not," I say, though my throat is so tight now that the words come out of it like knives. "I didn't kill Danny." I wonder if this is the man who killed Donna, asking her about her brother, trying to find him.

He uses his free hand to punch my side now, harder than he did my face.

"Mr. Mills, that's not an acceptable answer. If you don't have my photos, then who does? Who did you give them to?"

"I've never seen them," I say.

He punches the other side. My body feels hot, already swelling up, and I can't get enough air.

"Mr. Mills, do you see where this is going? Again, where are my photos?"

I stare at him, his face so passive, still wearing that polite smile, as he crouches over me, cutting off my air.

"I'll get them," I say, to buy myself some time. At least I'll be alive. And maybe I can find them.

His grip releases and he sits back in the seat. "Good."

"It'll take me a few days," I say.

He raises an eyebrow, then takes out a cigarette case. He offers me one, but I shake my head, touching my mouth where he split my lip.

"Four days," he says, lighting his cigarette and putting the case away. "I'll be in this car, outside the Ruby, in four days, at midnight exactly. You will come downstairs and hand me the envelope with the photos through the window. You'll wait as I confirm that the film is with them, and then my car will drive away. Then we'll be done. If you ever see me again, you'll pretend you don't know me. Which is a shame, because under different circumstances, I think we could have had some good times. You're an attractive man, Mr. Mills." He pauses and looks at me. "Or you were before you insisted on lying."

The handkerchief he gave me is on the floor where I dropped it when he strangled me. He leans forward and picks it up and offers it to me. "If you fail to do any of these things, I will find you, and kill you, and then I'll destroy whatever is in my way to find the photos. That would start with the Ruby, of course, as I assume that's where you've hidden them. I'll burn the whole building down."

I swallow, thinking of Elsie, Gene, Lee, everyone in the building who dances and laughs.

"I'll get them," I say, wiping my face again with the handkerchief.

"Excellent," he says. He leans forward and knocks on the panel between us and the driver, then gazes out the window. "It's a lovely night, isn't it? I love when it's so late everyone has gone to bed, even the revelers. When the neon is the only sound."

I glance at my watch—it's late. Past midnight. I must have been out longer than I thought. And he was just driving around, smoking and taking in the scenery as I lay at his feet, unconscious.

"What's your name, anyway?" I ask, blotting my lip with the handkerchief again, smelling the way the lemon of the cologne mixes with the iron of my blood.

"No, no, Mr. Mills. I'm not foolish. If you want, you can call me Jonathan, though that isn't my name."

"Jonathan," I say, lifting myself up and sitting next to him. "How'd you even end up with a guy like Danny?"

He looks over at me, and I can tell he's deciding if he's offended or amused.

"How does anybody end up with anybody? I was drinking with friends, they went home, Danny was there. He was young, attractive. It's not like I was new to this. This isn't even the first time anyone has tried blackmail. But it's never worked. It's a shame. I liked Danny. He was arrogant and had a smart mouth, and I like that in someone who's about to service me. He gave me what I wanted, I gave him what he wanted. If he'd wanted more, he could have asked. But he had to go and take pictures. And now you're bleeding. It's a shame how these things happen, one thing leading to another, to another, and someone perfectly innocent like you ends up hurt. Well." He shrugs, inhales on his cigarette, and blows the smoke out the window. The car comes to a stop and I look outside. There's the neon sign for the Ruby, glowing directly in front of me.

"Maybe once I have my pictures I'll change my mind," he says to me. "If you'd like, of course. I don't force myself on anyone. But you'll be attractive again in four days, I think. I pay better than any of your cases do, I'm sure. You should consider it."

"Sure," I say, opening the door. "But you're already fucking me and I don't love it, so I don't see myself saying yes." I turn to close the door, but almost fall as the pain from his beating hits me. I grunt.

"Smart mouth," he says, smiling. "That'll get you in trouble."

"Always does." I resist the urge to clutch my side where it's throbbing.

"Four days," he says, pulling the door closed before the car drives off. I watch it, but the plates are covered. Once he's out of sight, I take a deep breath, feeling every bruise that's forming on my sides and face, the red-hot marks that'll be purple tomorrow, especially the ones around my throat. He left my legs alone, so standing isn't so bad, it's just having working organs that's making me ache.

I need ice, to make everything numb and keep it from swelling too bad. So I take the elevator to the second floor, where the Ruby is, instead of the third, where I live. Inside, the place is calm, just a small group dancing to the band, someone passed out at the bar, and Gene, who looks up when the door opens and starts running the moment he sees my face.

"I'm okay," I tell him, walking toward the bar. "It's worse than it looks."

"It looks pretty bad," he says, taking me under the arm.

"I can walk fine, he left my legs alone," I say, but he doesn't stop, and I lean into him a little. He feels nice, pressing into my side. Warm.

"He?" Gene asks. "One guy?"

"One real big guy." We get to the bar and I sit down on one of the stools. "Really, though, I just need some ice." I can deal with who he is later.

"Take off your shirt," he says, going to the bar and filling a towel with ice. "Everyone else, we're closing up, time to head home."

The sleeping woman at the bar shakes herself awake and leaves some money on the bar as she and the other stragglers leave. The band on stage starts to pack up. I unbutton my shirt and look down at my torso—bright red bursts on either side of me, like I've run through fire. Gene looks at me and gasps, then makes another ice pack. He comes back holding them both.

"You hold these against the bruises," he says, handing them to me. "I'll get another for your face." I take the wrapped ice and hold it on the developing bruises, where it makes me shiver but also eases the burning pain a little. Gene comes back with another pack of ice and presses it against my eye. "What the hell happened?"

"Apparently, word is out I'm returning pictures, and someone thinks I'm still holding on to his," I say, my voice rough, and I cough.

"What? How can that be? Did you give them back to him?"

"I don't have them." I look up at him with my one good eye. "I went through all of them, and this guy wasn't in any."

"So he beat you up?"

"Every time I tried to tell him the truth."

"How'd you get away?"

"I lied," I say, swallowing, then flinching at the pain. Gene's eyes flicker down to my throat.

"He strangled you, too?" he says, reaching out and gently touching my neck. His fingers feel like fire.

"Yeah," I say, and try to swallow again. It's like trying to force a rock down.

"Did you fall unconscious from it?"

"No," I say. "Though I did earlier when he greeted me with a smack on the back of my head."

Gene frowns and moves his hand to the back of my head. He touches a tender spot, then takes the ice and moves it there. He looks down at me, still holding two bundles of ice against my sides, my shirt open, and sighs.

"I'm going to need to wrap everything up," he says. "And you might have a concussion."

"Sorry," I say.

He laughs. "Why are you sorry?" he says, going back behind the bar and getting more ice and the first aid kit he keeps down there. He comes back around and puts some ointment on my lip and starts wrapping the ice in place on my sides. "Hold this one to your eye." He hands me another bundle of ice while he presses a fourth against the back of my head, and a fifth he gently moves against my neck. "You're going to be purple all over tomorrow."

"Not my most flattering color."

"And you'll need someone to watch you sleep tonight, make sure you don't stop breathing."

We're quiet. He did that for me before. Lay next to me in bed.

"Maybe Elsie," I say softly.

"She's gone for the night. You don't want to ask me?"

"I didn't want to presume."

"I don't mind," he says. "I'm not working until late tomorrow. Plus I haven't seen your apartment yet. This is a good excuse."

"That an accusation?" I ask, smiling.

"Just a fact," he says, moving the ice around my throat.

"I thought it would be a little too forward."

"To invite a friend over?"

"Well . . ." I tilt my head, which makes my throat ache, and I hiss in pain.

"Andy, you're way too beat up to be flirting," he says, amused.

"I'm best at flirting when I'm nursing bruises, makes me mysterious."

He laughs. "Are you okay, though? Aside from the bruises?"

"I was feeling amazing, honestly," I say. "Right before I got knocked out. I gave all those guys their photos back, and they were all so happy. Burned them, too. I probably still smell like smoke."

He puts his nose in my hair and sniffs. "A little. Blood, mostly. And exhaust."

"I was in a car when the guy started smacking me around. Back seat of a limo. A very classy and scenic beating." I cough again, and Gene laughs.

"Well, I'm glad you got rid of all those photos."

"Me too," I say, taking the ice off my eye for a moment. "It was really . . . good."

"I wish someone had done that for me, y'know?" Gene says, eyeing the bruise on the back of my skull again. "When I was in med school, I mean. If some stranger had just shown up, handed me the photos, and said, 'Someone was going to blackmail you with these, but I found them, so you can do whatever you want with them . . .'" He pauses, sighs. "I would have had a whole different life. I would never have been able to thank that guy enough."

"One guy bought me a drink," I say.

"That's not enough, you ask me."

"It was more than enough, really," I say, putting the ice back on my eye. "After everything I could have done before, and didn't . . . it was enough."

The last of the band has packed up and left, waving as they headed out. We're alone in the club. Some voices drift down from upstairs, male and female impersonators changing, maybe one of the stockboys moving stuff around.

"We only get these quiet moments together when you've been beat up," Gene says softly.

I nod. He's right.

"I guess I didn't know you liked them," I say. "When I talk to you at the bar, I'm sharing you with everyone, y'know? And so I don't know . . ." I shake my head, flinch at the pain. "Elsie says I should just ask you out to get a drink. I guess I didn't know if you'd say yes. Why you'd say yes."

He smiles. "I'd say yes . . . but . . ."

"But?"

"But I know you had that ex of yours spend the night. Stan saw you two go into your room together, said the door was still closed when he left. I don't want to intrude on something, if you're . . . rekindling or . . ."

I sigh. "I don't know," I say. "That's the truth. I didn't think it was anything more than . . . memories, y'know? A moment. But then I gave him back his photos and he said he was going to make sure we were in each other's lives. I think he was just giddy with relief, though."

"Do you want him?" Gene asks, looking down at me. "In that way?"

"No," I say. The word comes out without me even having time to process the question, before I have time to know if it's a lie. Want him? Maybe, some part of him—some memory of him, our bodies. But who he is now? I don't even really know him. Gene I know. Gene I want. Maybe I want them both.

He laughs. "You sure you mean that, and it's not just that I'm in front of you, nursing your wounds? I know you get romantic after someone's knocked you out."

I smile; I don't know if he's right. "I can't promise that, no. But . . . I don't even know James anymore. It's been seven years." That at least is true. "Maybe I never really knew him. I'm not sure. The war made all of us different. Made us work. I don't see us working without it."

"Do you want to, though?" Gene asks, taking the ice away. "That's the question."

I take the ice away from my eye. Gene is smiling, but it's sad. He knows I don't know the answer, even if I want to.

"C'mon," he says, putting his arm under mine and lifting me up. "Let's get you upstairs."

"I can walk fine, really." Still, he doesn't move away, helping me over to the elevator.

"So what did you lie about to make him stop hitting you?" Gene asks, as we ride it up a floor.

"I told him I'd get his photos."

"But you don't have them. What happens when you don't give them to him?"

"He kills me and burns this building down."

I feel Gene go slack. It's a good thing I wasn't lying about my legs being fine.

"Don't worry," I tell him. "I'll find the pictures."

"Andy . . ."

"I'll find them," I say firmly. The elevator doors open and I walk out with his support to my apartment. A few folks are in the hallway and they stare at me, shirt still open, black eye, and bandages around my sides.

"Tony, can you clean up downstairs?" Gene asks one of the stockboys. He nods.

I unlock my door and go inside, Gene following. My bed is made at least—years of navy training made that a habit. It doesn't look too messy. It's not really big enough for mess.

"Lie down," Gene says, pointing at the bed. I slip off my shoes and do as he ordered. Then he starts poking around, looking at stuff. He focuses on my record collection first, flipping through it. "Good taste," he says. He chooses a record and puts it on. "Linda" by Buddy Clark.

Then he starts poking around the rest of my room, looking at the photo of my parents, and then my bookshelves.

"You have *Prince Caspian*, but not *The Lion, the Witch and the Wardrobe*," he says. "You have to read that one first."

"Oh," I say, blushing a little. "I didn't know. I only got it 'cause I saw you reading it. But I haven't cracked it open yet."

He looks over at me and smiles, then shakes his head. "I'll lend you mine. Now lie back. Rest. I'll monitor your breathing."

"You going to snoop while I sleep?"

"Absolutely. How often does a guy get to play detective in the home of a real detective?"

"Fair enough," I say, lying back and closing my eyes. "Don't judge me too harshly. I'm still moving in."

He comes over and sits down on the edge of the bed, next to me. "You're going to find the pictures, right? I don't want you to die, and I'd rather not have my place of employment burn down."

"Yeah," I say, going through where they could be in my mind. I searched the locker as much as you can search a locker, so I'm sure I didn't leave anything behind. The only people who saw the photos besides me were Lee and James, and there's no reason either of them would want pictures of a guy they didn't know. Which means they were probably kept separate from the others. Special. Maybe because they knew how dangerous this "Jonathan" was. With Danny missing and Donna dead, I don't have many leads. I searched Danny's apartment and didn't find any-thing. The only thing I can think of is the mystery apartment Donna brought Helen to. I need to find Danny or figure out who killed Donna, and if they did it for Jonathan's photos.

Gene brushes my hair back, then runs his hand down my arm. "Relax. Your brain needs to rest now. If you start thinking too much you're just gonna hurt yourself."

"Gene . . ." I can feel myself drifting off.

"You gonna ask to kiss me again?" he asks. "Because I already told you—"

"Just hold my hand until I'm asleep," I say, my eyes closed. "Please."

He doesn't say anything, but I feel his fingers weave between mine. I squeeze his hand, feeling grateful he's here, and knowing if I don't find these new photos, then he and this apartment, and everything else is going to burn away like the film in the ashtray—with a bad smell and a lot of smoke, but forgotten just hours later.

NINE

I open my eyes and the light stings, but not as badly as the rest of my body. I really thought I was done. I'd gone above and beyond—returning photos to people who hadn't paid me, trying to make things right for us, our community. I thought it was going to be good now, easier. Instead my body feels like a sack of flour that's on fire, and I only have a few days to fix everything.

Maybe this is my punishment, I think. Not just for what I didn't do as a cop, but for what I didn't do on the case—I didn't find Donna's killer. So he found me instead. It has to have been him who killed Donna, looking for the photos. She wasn't battered like I was, but I bet she tried to push back, run. He swatted her like a fly, didn't know she'd fall so hard. That's why he was so careful with me—getting me in his limo, aiming for my sides, not my head. He doesn't seem like someone who minds killing—I'm sure he would have easily murdered me last night if I'd kept telling him the truth—but he would mind killing before he got what he wanted.

I look at my clock, and it's later than I normally wake up, which means I've already lost hours I should have spent looking for the photos. Gene is asleep in my kitchen chair, which he's pulled up next to my bed. I let him keep sleeping as I peel the soggy bandages off me and go into the bathroom to look at the damage. I have a shiner like a black smudge around my eye, my lip is swollen but healing, and both my sides are blooming lavender. I ache around my waist, but it's not as bad as I thought it would be. I realize after I shower that all my clothes are in the rest of the apartment and all I have to cover me now is a towel.

Well, Gene was training to be a doctor; I'm sure I'm just a patient to him right now.

I look at myself in the mirror again and wrap the towel tight around my waist before opening the bathroom door. Gene is still in the chair, but his eyes are open.

"Did you piss blood?" he asks, definitely not at all interested in the fact that I'm just in a towel.

"No," I say, going to my closet and taking out some clothes.

"I think you'll be fine, then. Your bruises look better than I thought they would. Does it hurt to swallow?"

"Yeah," I say, "but less than last night."

"Drink lots of water, it'll help."

"Will do, doc." I go back into the bathroom and change, talking to him through the door. "Do you want to get breakfast with me? There's a diner down the street."

"I should get home," Gene says. "I only got a few hours of sleep, I was watching you, remember?"

I open the bathroom door. He's standing. I shake my head. "Stay here," I say. "You're just going to be back here tonight. Use my bed."

"Andy . . ."

"I'm not in it, I'm not making a move, Gene. I'm just trying to take care of you the way you did me, okay? Sleep here."

"It's all right," he says. "I have clothes at home."

I look him over. He rubs his eye and yawns, groggy. "I'll lift you up and put you in the bed if I need to," I say. "You won't even make it home without passing out."

He raises his eyebrows. "You'll pick me up? In your condition?"

"Yes," I say.

He smiles. "I almost want to see you try, but you'll just hurt yourself, so . . . okay." He slips off his shoes and sits down on the bed, then lies back and closes his eyes.

"You want music?" I ask, but he's already asleep. I take a spare key out and leave it on the table with a note thanking him and asking him to lock up, then lock the door behind me, and head out. I'm starving, but eat fast.

I know I already tossed Danny's place, but I take the streetcar again, and break in again, this time tear the place apart, looking for more photos, for another locker key, anything. I go through jars of Sanka and salt, open up cushions. I take pictures out of frames to see if there's anything written on the backs and knock every wall and floorboard for a secret compartment. I tear through the place like the fire that will tear through the Ruby if I can't fix this. Still nothing. They left no trace—or someone beat me to it. All I find is photos of Danny and Donna, in an album at the back of a drawer. Them as kids, Donna in Danny's lap, though they're both the same size. Them singing together in a choir. Them singing together in high school maybe, for a talent show. He's in a bow tie and she has a high-collared dress. Then just shots of them together, in San Francisco, in front of tourist traps. Hugging, laughing. They loved each other. And now one is definitely dead, and the other probably is. All that affection gone—easy as burning negatives.

The only other lead I have is the mystery apartment, so I make my way back to Cheaters and go bang on the door in the alley until someone lets me in—one of the women from behind the bar.

"Helen here yet?" I ask.

"She's in the main room," the woman says, and I march by her down the hall to the bar, where Helen is counting liquor bottles and making notes in a pad. She glances over and frowns when I come in.

"What happened to you?" she asks. "Pick up the wrong guy?"

"He picked me up," I say. "Then he pinned me down by the neck."

"I hate it when a trick goes wrong," she says with a grin. "But I hear you've been returning photos to everyone. Folks are calling you a hero."

"Well, I'm not feeling real heroic right now. Apparently there are some other photos I didn't find, and now I need to."

"James wasn't happy?"

"Not James," I say. "The guy who gave me this." I point at my eye. "He didn't love being left out of my heroics. Gave me four days to make it up to him. Any chance you know him? Big guy, real big, short hair, blue eyes . . ." I try to remember more about Jonathan's face, but the memory is blurry, his face striped in shadow and neon.

"That could be a lot of guys. You have a photo? Can you draw him?"

I shake my head. I was never good at suspect sketches, always left those to the professionals. And besides, I can't quite hold his face in my mind. I know I'd recognize it again, the eyes are still pressing into me, rough as his fists, but describing the rest of him is like holding water.

"Andy, if I don't know what he looks like, I can't help."

"Yeah." I nod. "I get it. But then I have to find him the photos. And the only lead I have is you."

"Me?" Helen's eyebrows raise. "I'll help however I can, but I don't know about any photos aside from the ones you gave back to me."

"Tell me more about the house Donna brought you to. If that was their other picture location, maybe it's where they developed the film and kept other photos. I haven't found a key or address or anything that points to it, though."

Helen sighs. "It was an apartment near Nob Hill, maybe Pacific Heights," she says. She closes her eyes, trying to remember. "A house, not an apartment, pretty big. I remember it was nice, like nicer than I thought Donna would have, but not fancy. Just . . .

well put together. Tasteful, I guess. There were doilies on the table, that kind of thing." She opens her eyes. "That's it."

"Can we look at the pictures? They might help you remember, or I might see something."

She wiggles her eyebrows. "If you want another peek, I can strip down right now, but just to look. You're not really my type."

"Helen," I say, my voice wearier than I realized, "he threatened more than just me. He threatened a lot of people, and it wasn't a bluff. You didn't burn them, did you?"

"Nah," she says with a smile. "I liked them, actually. They're in my office, come on." She tries a wry smile, but we both know if she kept them, it was sentimental, that she misses Donna.

She walks me back to her dressing room, which I guess is also her office, and goes behind the changing screen. This time I follow her. There's a wardrobe back there but also a few filing cabinets. She goes into one and pulls out the envelope I'd given her.

"No commenting on me in them, please," she says, and she hands it over.

"I'll be a gentleman, promise," I say, sitting down at her vanity and opening them up. She stands behind me, looking over my shoulder. I study the photos carefully this time instead of looking away in respect. I evaluate them as evidence now, not naughty photos of a friend. I examine the sheets—floral—the shelves behind them—one large oak wardrobe and a cabinet with some books and picture frames, but I can't make out any titles or photos. There's a bookend shaped like a woman, and what looks like a snow globe with a flower in it.

"A flower?" I ask.

"Oh . . . yeah," she says, remembering. "Pink ones. There were a bunch of them around the house. I only really saw the entry, and then she took me into the kitchen to make a drink, but could only find rum, so I started kissing her instead, and we fell on the sofa and I remember laughing because the sofa was patterned blue covered in pink flowers like that one. Then we were in the bedroom." She shrugs. "Not so weird, though, right? There are pink flower things all over the city."

"But a snow globe could be a souvenir from some place. Or a gift from a company. Did you see what it said?"

She shakes her head. "Sorry, wasn't so focused on it, as you can see."

I smirk. "How about when you left? Did you poke around any?"

She shakes her head. "It was late, I was embarrassed—I'd been drunk. I just left. Donna was still asleep. So the only poking I did—"

"Where would these photos have been taken from?" I interrupt.

"Out the window, actually," she says. "How perverted, someone out there with a camera."

"What was out the window? It wasn't the street, right? Someone would have seen the photographer."

"Yeah . . ." She moves her hand over the photo, like she's trying to turn the room around in her mind. "Outside was a little garden. Not large. There was a tree in it, some flowers, tall white fence."

"You know what kind of tree?"

"A tree's a tree," she says with a shrug. "It was one of the ones with long droopy vines instead of leaves, like a tent."

"A willow," I say. "That's good, that's helpful. Anything else?"

I look up at her as she stares at the photos. She picks them up and flips through them again, but then shakes her head. "I'm sorry."

"That's okay. A willow tree in a backyard in Pacific Heights or Nob Hill . . . that's somewhere to start."

"And flowers," she says. "Pink, yellow, red."

"If they're still blooming," I say.

I swivel in the seat, looking up at her. "Anything else you can tell me about Donna? Where she might have hid things, if not at this house?"

Helen frowns; she looks genuinely sad. "I honestly didn't know her too well. The one night we . . . well, that those photos were taken, we'd just been chatting at the bar about singing. I know she liked singing. She wasn't trained, she just sang along with the radio. But she loved it. Danny was more about the being on stage part, she said. But she'd do anything for him. I feel bad we didn't talk more, just flirting at the bar, really. She was good at that. Razor tongue, but then she'd kiss away any insults. I should have done more than flirt, actually gotten to know her."

"It wouldn't have stopped what happened," I tell her, standing up and putting my hands on her shoulders, trying to reassure her.

She stares up at me, her eyes like moss on shore rocks. "You can't know that. We don't know what would have changed if I'd been . . . a little kinder."

"Helen . . ."

She shakes her head. "I'm fine. And I'll ask around tonight. Some of the girls were closer with her, maybe they'll know something."

I nod. "Thanks. I guess in the meantime, I'll try to find that house. Hopefully it'll tell me something." I stand up.

"What about Danny?" she asks. "Can't you find him?"

"At this point, I think . . ." I stare at the floor. The rug is worn so thin in one place you can see the wood grain through it.

"Oh," she says, her voice soft.

"If I could find his body, I'm sure . . . but I've got no leads there. Could be he's at the house, but more likely he's in the water, with his sister, or buried in some patch of dirt in the middle of nowhere."

"Right. Well. Good luck with the house, at least." I turn to go but she stands up behind me and I turn. "You still coming to the decommissioning tomorrow?" she asks. She looks down at her hands as she speaks, like a shy boy asking a girl on a date.

"Yeah," I tell her, and she smiles. "James will be there, too." The smile fades. "He said he'd say hi after, but I don't know if he can; you and me, we're not someone he should be seen with."

She laughs. "How'd we end up the ones with the bad reputation and he's still a saint?" she asks. "Doesn't seem right."

"Luck, I guess. Well, choice, in your case."

"More of a calling," she says. "You have to want to put together an act, you know. Clothes, wigs . . ." She stares at me a minute. "They had new wigs. Well, Danny did."

"What?" I ask.

"When they auditioned for me. The wigs were pretty new looking. You can tell, the hair is too clean looking, and they hadn't really styled it much. I bet they'd just bought it. Maybe that's a lead?"

"Maybe," I say. "Can't be many folks who'll sell wigs to a man. Who it was would have been one of the last people to see Danny before he vanished. But if he already had the wig when you saw him . . ."

"Yeah, probably a long shot."

"Well, aside from a willow tree, I don't have much else. You know where he bought the wig?"

She shakes her head. "I don't need one for my act, I just pin my hair up."

"I'll ask Lee," I say. "Thanks, Helen."

"Sure. I hope you find them fast, too. I'll tell you tomorrow if I remember anything else."

"That would be good. This guy is dangerous."

She points at my eye. "I can see. Just the face and neck?"

"My sides got the real action."

"You have a doctor look you over?"

I nod. "I'm okay. At least if I find these photos. So I'd better get going."

"Okay." She nods. "Good luck." She reaches out and gives me a soft hug. I flinch when she squeezes, the pain of the bruises right where her arms landed. "Be careful."

"I'll try," I say, hugging her back. And I mean it.

I walk back to the Ruby, stopping to get a few sandwiches to go. Gene is still asleep in my bed, curled up with his hands under his head. I lay the blanket over him and put the extra sandwich in the refrigerator and write him another note telling him it's there.

I eat mine alone in my office, then search it, too, just in case some photos slipped away somewhere, but as I expected, nothing. Looking for a willow tree behind a house in the north part of the city is going to be a long day. If the wigmaker is a lead on Danny, that might be the better trail to follow. Danny is probably dead, but could still answer some questions if he's not. Where was he holed up? Where's his body? Where's his hiding spot? The house might just be another dead end. So I wait in my office a few hours, door open so I can hear the hallway, and when Lee comes in.

After a little while, I hear the door to my apartment open, then close and lock, and Gene sticks his head in.

"Shouldn't you be out looking for something?" he says, stepping in. He's rumpled from sleep, just in an undershirt, hair askew. He's been sleeping in my bed, and even if I wasn't next to him, knowing that makes me feel warm, like we were holding hands the whole time. And he's got the brown bag lunch I left him. "Don't misunderstand me, I'm happy you're taking it easy, you need to, but I thought you'd be tracking things down, detective stuff."

I smile. "I was, but now I'm waiting for Lee. He's going to tell me where to go next. If that doesn't pan out, then tomorrow I start searching the city for a backyard with a willow tree."

Gene sits down in the chair across from me. "There are probably a lot of those, right?"

"Probably."

"So how do you know which one?"

I shrug. "You need to borrow clothes? You can shower at my place, too, you know. Sleep some more, if you need to."

"Thanks, but it's nearly three. I don't need any more sleep. I might take you up on that shower, though. I have some extra shirts in the storage room for when stuff spills on me." He puts his bag on the table and opens it. "And thanks for breakfast, too."

"Lunch," I say. "I didn't know what you liked, so I got you egg and cheese on rye, which is what I usually get. Seemed inoffensive."

"It's a classic," he says, smiling and unwrapping the sandwich. He bites into it and grins at me, chewing. I smile back without even thinking about it.

"I would have waited for you if I'd known you'd be up," I say, watching the muscles in his arms as he bends the sandwich away from his face. "We could eat together."

"You can sit there and watch me eat, that's mostly the same thing."

"Thanks again for last night. And, for what it's worth, today, not fuzzy-headed from a beating, I feel the same as I did last night. I want to take you out, Gene."

His eyes flash, a smile playing on his lips. I want to go over there and kiss him again. "Once you've told James it's done, we can talk about that. And if you do, I'm looking forward to it." His smile fades. "But . . . if you don't, that's all right, too, Andy. You don't owe me anything for patching you up."

"That's not why," I say.

He shrugs, not believing. "Actually, you do owe me this sandwich, because it is very good, so every time I put some ice on you, I'm going to expect this now."

"Deal," I say. I watch him eat for what feels like a solid minute more, my eyes lingering on his jaw, his neck, and him looking up at me strangely between bites.

"Are you just watching me eat?"

"I guess so," I say, laughing. But then I hear music starting from downstairs, and Lee's voice, and I stand up. Gene is done eating anyway. "I should go talk to Lee," I say. "He'll know which wig shops would sell women's hair to men."

"All right. And I'm going to shower at your place." I pause, the image of him in the shower—my shower—suddenly strong in my mind. I nod to shake it loose. He wants to wait. I'll wait.

"I only have the one towel," I say. "But you should use it. Use whatever you want."

"Toothbrush?"

"It's all yours."

Gene laughs.

"I have mouthwash, too," I add, wiggling my eyebrows.

"A gentleman with varied tastes," Gene says, standing up. He walks to the door and I follow but he pauses outside and turns around before unlocking it. "Thanks, Andy. Really. You don't have to do this."

"I kind of do," I say. "You're only here because you stayed up all night watching me."

He shrugs. "And because I wanted to finally see inside your apartment."

"Well, now you have all the time you want to poke around, and permission to take anything."

"Anything? You have some forty-fives I've been trying to find forever—"

"Those we can talk about," I say. I lay my hand on his shoulder, and he looks at me, and my thumb drifts over to his jaw, and I think about kissing him. His face is broad and strong and fits so well in my hand, it would be so easy to just bend forward. I like touching him, I want to sit here and kiss him and negotiate his stealing of my 45s for hours, to feel part of something, warm and wrapped in a blanket together. But I remember what he said about James, and he's right. I'm not going into the future with the past as an anchor. "I'll see you later," I say, pulling my hand back.

"I'll probably be down there soon, but if you're gone before I am, come find me when you get back. To check you're healing right, of course. That's why."

"You got it, doc," I say.

He smiles and turns back around, his back to me as he unlocks the door, and I watch him, then before he can look back at me, I turn to the stairs, trying to hide my grin. Talking with James didn't feel like this, like stamping your feet, getting ready to run a marathon, practically jumping up and down. It didn't even feel like the first time we met eyes and knew, him dancing in a towel, or him finding me in a dark corner later that night, and without saying anything, just kissing me. It felt like remembering those things, like trying to find that moment again and realizing I never will.

I open the stairwell door downstairs and walk out into the club. Lee is on stage with the band, rehearsing, but he looks over at me and stops singing mid-word and says, "Jesus Christ, Evander, what happened?"

He leaps off stage and comes over, peering at my face.

"There's been a twist in the case," I tell him.

"You don't say." He takes a sidestep, looking at my bruise from a different angle. "Your throat, too? Did Gene look at you?"

"Yeah," I say with a nod. "He iced everything for me, and he saw me just now, and says I'm probably fine."

"Just now? He's already here? I thought he was on late tonight."

"He stayed at my place."

Lee's eyes grow big with excitement.

"Not like that. It was to watch my breathing. I still . . . have to work things out with James. He . . . stayed the other night, too. Less innocently. Which Gene knows about because of Stan."

"God-damned Stan." Lee shakes his head, apparently unsurprised by my nightly activities. "Well, I'm glad you're okay—but what happened? Did someone not like the way you gave the pictures back?"

"No," I say, going over to the bar and sitting down. I glance over at the band. "You might want to tell them to take five, unless you want to save this for later. But I could use your help."

"You guys are perfect," Lee calls over to the band. "We'll be great tonight."

The band nods and starts rehearsing something else.

"So," I say. "After I returned all the photos, someone knocked me out." I tell him the rest of it—the car interrogation, the missing photos, talking to Helen, the house with the pink flowers inside and the willow outside. It doesn't take as long as I thought, but Lee stares transfixed the whole time.

"So if you don't find these new photos, this mystery giant, Jonathan, is going to burn this place down?"

"That's the idea."

Lee whistles. "All right. Well, what's the plan?"

"I only have two leads—the house is the better one for finding those photos, but I'd have to scour all of the north side, and that might take a while."

"Do you think whosever house it is is gay?" Lee asks.

"I . . ." I hadn't really considered it. "Probably. I mean, it could be another house Donna and Danny own, but Donna didn't seem to know the place. Could be there's someone else involved, I guess, but there's no evidence of that, and I have no idea who it could be. It could just be a friend of theirs. Or they broke in somehow, were squatting. Other than that . . ." I shrug. "That's why I'm hoping you can help me find the wigmaker."

"I can . . . but I'm not done with this house. If you think the owner is gay, I can find it."

I feel my brow furrowing. "How?"

"I'll ask around. Gay people all talk, Andy. We don't all know each other, but it's a small world . . . I'll just ask. Put it out there."

"Won't that alert whoever's house it is? If they find out I'm looking for it?"

Lee smiles widely and puts his hand down flat on the bar. "No. Because here's how it'll go." He pulls his hand up then lays one finger down on the bar. "I'll go up to Stan tonight—Stan's the biggest gossip—and I'll say, 'Hey, I've been trying to remember this house party I was at. They had this great blue sofa with pink flowers, and a garden out back, and I have looked all over for that flower fabric. And I can't remember whose house it was at. Do you know who it was? I want to ask them.'" He lays a second finger on the bar. "Then he'll start asking around. Not because he wants to help me, but because he wants to then go out and buy the fabric and make a pillow or something, and lord it over me that he has it now, too, even though the bitch probably doesn't even have a sofa to put it on. But," he says, laying a third finger down, "I can go to Willy, in the band, and ask him to find out for me. See, Stan likes Willy, and Willy likes me, which is why Stan hates me, but we can use it so the information will flow in my direction. And I can ask other people, too, and Stan will be asking, and people I ask will be asking and eventually, if whoever lives there is in fact one of us, we will find out who it is. I can promise you that." He lifts his hand off the bar then brings it down again, all the fingers spread out. "Everybody likes to talk."

I stare at his hand. "Well . . . it's worth a try. It would be better than just having me looking around the city for a willow tree."

"Then I'll do just that tonight."

"Meanwhile, can you tell me where Danny would buy a wig?"

"Oh, sure. There are only a few places in the city that do that. He'd go to Rosalia's in the Mission, I'm almost positive." He glances at his watch. "I can take you there if you want. I'm not on until nine. I just got off work—a whole crate of violin bows came in early and once they were unpacked, boss said I could go, so I decided to come rehearse."

"Sure, I'd appreciate it," I say, standing up.

The elevator door chimes and Gene comes in, in a fresh shirt, his hair wet.

Lee looks over at him, then me, grinning.

"Stop it," I whisper at Lee.

"Your shower had better pressure than mine does," Gene says. "And I'm wearing your deodorant. I keep smelling you."

"And do you like that?" Lee asks. I elbow him.

Gene laughs. "I'm sure he told you that I was just in his apartment to make sure he didn't stop breathing in his sleep after a probable concussion."

"I did," I say. "I said that's all you were there for."

"Don't worry," Lee says. "I'm not a gossip like Stan. But I will tease you both." He grins, then looks at his watch. "But later. I may go on at nine but I have to be back by seven to get ready, and I don't know how your questioning works, but it's past three."

"Come say hi when you're back," Gene says, looking at me.

"I will," I say. Lee and I get into the elevator and Gene turns to watch me as the doors close.

The sun is gold as we take the streetcar down to the Mission.

The fog is heavy, though, and it blurs the light, diffusing it like the sky is made of fire. When we get off, I follow Lee a few blocks around a corner until we stop in front of a small glass-front store with a big yellow sign reading ROSALIA'S LADIES' HAIRPIECES AND MEN'S TOUPEES in red. In the window are mannequin heads with pretty bobs and buns, in blond, red, and brown. When Lee opens the door, a bell jingles just inside. There are more heads inside, more hair on them, and several mirrors placed around the store. It smells a little like mildew. In the back is a door, which opens a moment after we come in. A woman of about forty with dark brown hair in a very large bun, and a pink skirt and jacket, comes out. She takes a pair of glasses that hang on a chain and lifts them to her eyes, looking at us.

"Can I help you?" she asks. "You both look like you have fine hair, but if there's a bald spot under that hat"—she nods at me—"I think I can make something for you."

"We met once," Lee says. "I was in here for a very particular kind of wig—straight, black. For a performance."

She smiles a little. "Oh, you're those boys. Well, come on in the back, then. It's not as fancy but you can try things on in peace." She heads back toward the door she came through and we follow. "I love the shows at Finnochio's, and Shelly's. I'm not like that, but I think they're just so fun, and . . . I don't understand the rest of it, but it's none of my business, you know? Judge not lest ye, etcetera." She leads us back into a smaller room, with shelves of wigs on heads, wigs in boxes. A storage room, but with a small mirror on one wall. She turns to look at us. "I don't have too many black ones," she says to Lee. "I can get one custom, though, if you like the shape of one of the others. Oh! And I have one that looks like Elizabeth Taylor . . . somewhere." She goes over to one of the shelves and starts looking through the boxes.

"Actually," I say, "we're not looking for hair. We're looking for someone who we think bought some."

She turns around and raises an eyebrow. "I'm not a gossip," she says.

"We're not trying to pry into his personal life," I say, fishing out a few bills and offering them to her. "We already know he bought a wig here. I'm just looking for him . . . I have to tell him his sister died."

Her expression goes from suspicious to the verge of tears. "Oh no," she says. "Who is it?"

"Danny Geller," I say.

"Donna died?" she says, her eyes widening in shock. "Oh, that's awful." She frowns deeper, then takes the bills from my hand. "I saw Danny three days ago."

"Three days?" I ask. I try not to sound too surprised. That means he's not dead—or at least he wasn't three days ago. That's the day I buried Donna. He could be in the same state as her by now, with Jonathan looking for him. Or maybe it was him who killed his sister, some fight gone terribly wrong. "What was he here for?"

"He came in, looking very mysterious—big sunglasses, trench coat, a hat with a brim that was far too wide. He looked a little like a cartoon, but you know Danny, he can pull off anything."

"Sure," I say. Lee nods.

"He's fussy about everything, though. He bought some cheap wigs first time he was in, and I thought they looked good, or would if he styled them a little. But then he came back a few weeks later, he wanted something more high-end. Had the money for it, so we picked out something glamorous. But this time he doesn't want a wig for an act. He wanted men's hairstyles. A few of them! In different colors. I have no idea what he wanted with them."

That sounds like Danny's idea of hiding, I think. Always a performance.

"So what did you sell him?" I ask.

"Oh, I didn't really have anything in stock like that. I carry some men's styles, but full wigs that would cover his hair are harder to find. Mostly I carry toupees, for if a guy doesn't have much on top already. We only had a red one I found in the very back here." She points at a shelf. "He tried it on, but it looked weird, he said it wouldn't work. So I told him I could get brown and blond, too. He just had to give me a few days. So he gave me a phone number and told me to call when I had them. I think they're getting in tomorrow."

"A phone number?" I ask. "Can I copy it down?"

She purses her lips, staring at me in silence, and I fish out a few more bills, which I hand to her.

"He'd want to know about Donna," she says, tucking the cash into her blouse. She walks over to a cabinet holding some wigs and gets a book out of a drawer there, and flips through some pages, then reads me the number, which I write down in my pad. "What happened to her?" she asks when I'm done writing it down.

"I probably shouldn't say before I tell him. Privacy and all that."

"Oh, sure." She looks disappointed. "Well, while you're here, you want a wig? You'd look swell in a dress as a redhead. Put some makeup on that shiner, plus some more makeup, you'd look a little like Gene Tierney."

"I'm all right, thank you," I say, putting my pad away. I look at Lee.

"I actually need to get back for a show at the Ruby," Lee says, "but I'll come back to try on that Liz Taylor one."

"I'll find it so it's ready," she says. "Nice meeting you both."

She opens the door and we leave the back room and then the store.

"That was easy," Lee says. "Is it always that easy?"

"It cost me five bucks," I say. "And this is a job I'm not getting paid for. It wasn't that easy."

"I thought you'd have to threaten her or something."

I laugh as we walk back to the streetcar stop. "No, no, most people don't need that. Just ask some questions, give them an excuse to answer. Like you said, people like to talk."

"I think I'd be pretty good at this."

"Yeah?" I ask. "You want to come do this next part with me?"

"What's the next part?"

"The library. I'm going to go through all the phone books until I find the address that matches the number she just gave me."

"Why not just call him?"

"He's been hiding for a while now, scared, buying disguises. He's not going to tell me where he is over the phone. He'll think I'm working for Jonathan and bolt. Better to just show up."

Lee frowns. "So how long will it take to find the address?"

"Shouldn't be too bad. There are directories. Just about finding the right one. Maybe an hour or two?"

His eyebrows go up. "I'll let you handle that part, Andy. You're good at it. I'm more of a people detective."

The library is as quiet as ever when I get there, and closing soon, so I don't stop to admire the murals. Instead I head right for the records room and start looking for the address. Second time I've been here, looking up Danny's number. And when, after an hour, I manage to find this one, I wonder if it's going to be just as useless, because it's for a hotel: Ocean Breeze Park, over in

Sunset. Far enough from the beach it's probably pretty cheap. I write down the address and leave the library.

I take the streetcar through the tunnel under Twin Peaks down Taraval and get out at the zoo. The sun is going down by now, and there are families walking around, probably leaving the zoo after it's closed, kids hooting like monkeys and roaring like lions. The fog is coming in, too, so I can't see all of them, I just hear their jungle noises as I walk to the hotel.

When I get to Ocean Breeze Park, I pause, my heart getting loud in my chest. It's familiar—one of those setups with a three-level main building and a few others scattered around the parking lot. Just like the Farallones. It's not an exact mirror—these buildings are pool blue, not the sand color of the Farallones, and the setup isn't quite the same, but it feels the same. That cheap anonymity, the blinds closed in every window. The parking lot is empty and the fog makes it feel emptier. I take a deep breath and walk toward the main building. The Farallones was a bad place, and suddenly it feels so similar, so much like another ghost, that I almost gag. Bad things happen in bad places, I think. Why is the memory of the Farallones so strong now, though, so bad? I think of Helen, asking if I remembered it, warning me, then stopping when I said I didn't remember it. Like she was scared.

Inside, the familiar feeling, like *mal de debarquement*, continues. The floor is tile with a navy rug over it, and the Farallones was wood with a red carpet, but it still shifts underfoot, the memory of the old rising up to meet me instead of what's actually there. I approach the desk unsteadily, like I might fall. The guy behind the desk looks up at me from a magazine, bored.

"Hourly or daily?" he asks.

I shake my head, to answer him and to shed the ghosts. "I'm a detective," I say, and take out my wallet. Guys at places like this

are usually easy. This isn't Sidney at the Belltower, where discretion is part of the service. "I'm looking for a guy; young, dark
hair, thin, maybe a little dramatic."

He snorts a laugh. "Sure, I know him." He eyes my wallet and I
take out a few bills and hand them over. "Had a nasty shiner when
he came in. He checked out last night, though," he says, pocketing the money. Last night. So he *is* still alive. I'm impressed.

"Any idea where he—" I stop, because he's already shaking his
head, looking back down at the magazine he was reading. Another dead end. "Do you know why he left?" I ask.

The guy looks up at me again, eyes my wallet, which I put
away. "Give me something good and maybe I'll give you something good," I say.

"He was out of money," he says, frowning. "Started paying in
loose change, then offered to blow me to spend another night. I
told him I'm not a fairy, to get the fuck out if he didn't have the
money. Those perverts are everywhere these days, just like the
papers say. And this is a family place, y'know?"

"Sure," I say, my hands curling up into fists. I don't take out my
wallet again, and the guy frowns, looks back at his magazine. I
start to leave, but halfway to the door, I turn back around and walk
up to him. "This place used to have another name?" I ask. "Like,
seven or eight years ago? With yellow paint on the walls outside?"

The guy looks up at me, tired of this now. "How the fuck
should I know?"

"Yeah, of course," I say. This time I leave for good. The ground
here sways too much, so I make my way back to the streetcar stop
quickly as I can. Memories are in the fog, though, and flashes
of things: bloody water in a bathtub, the woman in the window
yelling, "Dare me, dare me!" with a manic grin, Helen's look after we put Donna in the water.

I'm glad I was blackout drunk that night. Being someplace like this makes it come back, rocks me in a way I don't understand. Why does the ground swell underfoot if it was just a night I drank too much? Why does talking about it make Helen nervous? I can see the pieces of it, but I can't assemble them. Maybe I don't want to remember all of it. But something tells me I have to.

The streetcar shows up quickly, and it speeds me away from the hotel, but we can't outrun the fog.

TEN

There's a different bouncer at Cheaters, but she lets me in when I tell her I'm a friend of Helen's. Inside, there's a small crowd and a different male impersonator on stage. She's wearing a bow tie and tux with tails, face powdered bright white, hair slicked back, dancing around with a cane. I slip past the bar and into the back, walking the long hallway to Helen's dressing room. I knock, and there's a long pause.

"What is it?" Helen's voice comes out, annoyed.

"It's me."

Another pause. "Come in."

Inside, she's in a dressing gown and in front of the mirror again. Her face is mostly painted already, so James's reflection is what looks back at me.

"The wig thing pan out?" she asks. "Or did you come back to bring me flowers?"

"I think it's time you tell me about the Farallones. That night."

She sighs, staring at me in the mirror. I focus on her eyes, the part of her that doesn't look like James.

"You don't need to know," she says finally. "And you don't want to."

"I do need to know, Helen. I need to understand what's going on, and this case is cut through with too many memories, and too many blank spots where memories should be. I was just at a hotel where Danny was holed up. I could swear it was the same place. Different coat of paint, sign out front, but . . ."

"It's just coincidence," she says, taking a pencil and filling in her eyebrows. "If it was even the same place. They all look the same, you know."

"Helen. You owe me." My voice is pleading.

"That's why I don't want to tell you . . ."

I stare at her and she puts the pencil down, turns around so she's looking at me directly.

"All right," she says. "But remember, you asked for this. You can't be mad at me."

"I promise," I say.

"That night, the guy who tried to roll James . . ." Her eyes drift to a corner, her mouth sags to a frown. With the makeup she looks like a sad clown. "He killed him, Andy. James beat the guy to death."

"What?"

"He beat him to death. Then we took his body out to the car and drove it . . . to where . . ."

"Where we dumped Donna."

She nods. "It was awful, Andy. There was a lot of blood. We washed it all up, and . . . you were passed out cold. We decided not to tell you."

She hunches her shoulders, then folds her arms, like she's cold. She seems to realize what she's doing and straightens out again, but her head stays down, her eyes distant. I stand up and go to her vanity where the tumblers and rye are, and pour myself a drink, then down it. James the murderer.

"It bothered me for . . . months. Years. Still does," she says, her voice faraway. "But about a week after, I looked him up. I'd seen his ID in his wallet, when we . . . He had a widow. His body had washed up, banged up because of the rocks. They thought he'd fallen in. So we were safe, but I still felt . . . It was like something was eating me from the inside, that guilt. I tried talking to James about it but he vanished right after. You didn't know. I thought the best thing would be if I just decided to forget it all."

"And I was lucky enough to have never remembered it, and you . . . didn't want to remind me?"

"I thought maybe you'd remember eventually. I guess not." She takes out a cigarette and lights it, takes a long drag and blows out smoke like it's heavier than lead. I think of James, hands bloody, a body under him, and swallow. It was self-defense, I tell myself. Someone attacked him, he fought back. And it's not like we hadn't trained to kill during the war. Still, there's something cold in me, thinking of it. I pour another drink to melt it.

"I would have let you keep forgetting, if you'd let me," she says.

"Yeah," I say. But James is still James. It wasn't cold-blooded murder. It was a fight gone wrong. A mistake. We've all made mistakes. I've made more than I can count. And mine have gotten people killed, even if my hands were never bloody. I roll my tongue in my mouth, almost smiling. Maybe this just makes James and me closer. I finish the drink.

"Have a good show," I tell her.

"Andy." She says my name like a question.

"I'm all right," I say. "Self-defense, right? What else could he do. Could either of you do?"

She turns back toward the mirror; smoke from her cigarette clouds the reflection. "It's rough, this kind of life," she says. "I don't like that I've sent two bodies in the water now. I don't like that I know how to do it."

"Is that why you do . . ." I gesture at her reflection. "This? Dress up as James? Because you're angry? That he made you help him bury a body?"

"Yes." She says it almost laughing. "Yes, that's part of it. And him leaving the way he did. Like he could just do that to me—to us—and run from it."

I nod, realizing. He's been lying. He didn't run because he was going to get caught for . . . us. He ran to avoid being caught from this.

"Well," she says, "he can't run from me when I get to stare him down in the mirror every night. When I get to make fun of him on stage. When I get to wipe that smirk of his off after." She pauses, meets my eyes. "Is it petty?"

I shrug. "Next to what you've done with him—what you've done with me—everything seems petty."

"I made you do for me what I did for him," she says, nodding. "That was cruel, too. Ever since you came back, Andy, all I've done to you is be cruel."

"No," I say. "You've been scared is all. That's what happens when the past comes back like a ghost."

"Well, then it's all James's fault. Again." Outside, there's a swell of music, and her eyes dart to the door. "I need to get ready."

"Yeah," I say. "Have a good show. I'll see you at the decommissioning ceremony."

"A family reunion," she says, her voice cold.

"Let's try to play nice. Let's try to forget it all, if we can."

"If we can," she repeats, like an echo. She picks up her pencil again, and goes back to her eyebrows. "You should stay for the show."

I consider it, but I feel a rocking in my stomach that's more than the alcohol. I want to get outside. I want to do something.

"Not tonight," I say. "Still need to find those photos."

"Yeah," she says.

"Break a leg." I put the tumbler down on the vanity and suddenly, without knowing why, I bend and kiss the top of her head.

She smiles, looking up at me curiously, like she wants to say something, but instead she shakes her head. "Be careful."

"You too."

She goes back to her face, and I leave, wondering if all I've gotten for my time is a little nauseous. I try to remember that night again, but nothing comes back clearer, even now. I remember the pale-pink water in the sink. It was a lot.

Is that really why James left without saying goodbye? Not because he felt like the thermometer was full, but because he had broken it? We'd just talked about it, in bed. Another lie. So many lies, forgotten truths, heaving like a storm, but James is still floating on the ocean, and I know I can't float with him anymore. Just because he's not getting seasick doesn't mean I'm not.

Outside, the air is too warm and it clings to my throat. I need to focus on the case. Helen was right about one thing: knowing what I know now doesn't help—they're not related. Unless James mentioned the hotel as a place to hide out to Danny once, but with the name changed, I'm not even sure it was the same place. And James would have told me.

There's still the gossip that Lee promised to dig up, but I decide to head back to Danny's place one more time. I know he's alive now, or was last night, so maybe he's been back. I've been to his apartment enough I practically have the place memorized by now, but if he was kicked out of the hotel, he had to go somewhere. If he's smart, he headed to a YMCA or a park bench, or even the beach, but maybe he thought he had stuff he could sell at home. Or maybe he was hoping to meet Donna. He might not know she's dead, and realizing that makes my mouth taste sour and old. There was something so scared in her eyes the last time I saw her. I wonder if it was Jonathan she was seeing.

Night has grown heavy by the time I get to his place, like velvet curtains down every street. I can hear people murmuring behind the walls but no one steps out when I pick the lock again. Inside, it's still the mess I made last time I was here. But then I start looking around some more and some things are missing—the photo album, some nice clothes, socks, underwear. He came back here, grabbed some clean clothes and some stuff to sell, and he took off. If the album were still here I'd say the place was just robbed, but it was him. He's still alive. I nod a few times, confirming it to myself. I don't know how he's managed to survive so long.

I look around, trying to find some evidence of where he could have gone, but there's nothing left behind, only things missing. I could try every pawnshop in the city, see if I recognize anything missing from the apartment, ask when Danny sold it, but I don't think that'll get me far—pawnshops usually don't know where the folks who sold them stuff are sleeping. And it'll be just as hard as finding a willow tree in the backyard.

So I sigh and leave again, taking the streetcar back to the Ruby. When I get in, it's packed. Lee is on stage, singing her version of "The Glow-Worm," and Elsie is at the bar, not sitting on a stool, but actually sitting on the bar, legs crossed, in a red velvet suit, a black shirt and tie on underneath. She's bouncing her foot in time to the music, holding a highball in her hand, and smiling at the dancing crowd as she chats with Gene. She has reason to be happy—the joy here is infectious. But to me, it's just ash—a reminder of everything that could burn down if I don't find those photos.

I approach the bar. Gene is behind it, his hair a little messy, washing a glass as he talks to Elsie.

"Oh, but I hate Eustace," he says. "He's just too much."

"Oh, he's annoying all right," Elsie says, "but I bet he'll grow out of it. If not by the end of this book, then by the next one."

"You think he'll be in the next book?"

"Absolutely. Why bring him into Narnia if he's not coming back?"

Gene tilts his head, then spots me and smiles wide, big enough for me to know he's actually smiling at me, and not just for the bar.

"What are you two talking about?" I ask.

"Book club," Elsie says, hopping down off the bar. Her drink splashes a little, but she manages to open her mouth and catch the liquor that's gone flying.

"Neat trick," I say to her.

"When I tell people I'm an expert drinker, it's not just a turn of phrase. I practice."

I smirk.

"So who gave you that shiner? An admirer?"

"It's a long story."

"Does it have to do with why you look like a ball of gloom? You closed your case, you got paid, I got paid, everyone is having a great time, Gene is smiling at you more than usual and wearing the same trousers as yesterday, and yet you're over here looking like someone just told you you have days to live."

I glance at Gene, who blushes, then turns away.

I frown. "Not just me," I say, looking at the crowd.

"What?"

I take a deep breath, and tell her, quickly.

Elsie stares at her drink for a moment, then downs the rest of it in one swallow, then she smiles at me, but it's forced. "All right, so who is this guy? You think he can do all that?"

"I think he will, I don't know what would stop him."

Elsie pauses and I can see her face straining to keep its smirk, its nonchalance. She's practiced at it, but her eyes, for a moment, are far away, and scared. Then she looks at me and shrugs.

"Well, I can clear the place out, wait at the pay phone, call the fire department, minimize damage."

"I think he'd just keep coming back," I say. "He seems . . . determined." I put my hand to my neck and swallow. It still aches a little.

"Who is he, even?"

I shake my head. "I don't know. There was something familiar about him, but I didn't know him. I don't have a photo, and aside from his eyes, his face is kind of . . . blurry in my memory."

"That'll happen when someone introduces himself with a fist. Still, what do you remember?"

"Blue eyes, big, maybe fifties or sixties. He could be a crime boss or someone I crossed paths with when I was on the job. Mafia, something like that. They have a lot of internal fighting, and if it gets out one of them is gay, they could lose a lot of face, a lot of power." I frown. "I'm sorry, I wish I could draw him or something, ask around with his photo, but even if I could, who he is isn't as important as the clock he gave me ticking down."

Elsie frowns. "Well, then find the photos."

"I'm trying. I still don't know where Danny could be, if he's lived this long, though. So, tomorrow I'll start looking for the house with the tree in the backyard, the sofa."

"Peeping in windows, then?"

I nod. "That's the job, right? It's not as glamorous as bar owner, but . . ."

She cackles. "I spend my day managing bribes and beer payments. It's not glamorous. I just make it glamorous. We should try upgrading your wardrobe a bit more. Henry's old one-night-stand castoffs were an improvement, but we can do better."

I lift my fedora, which I'm holding. "You got me this," I say.

"Your hat shouldn't be the most fashionable thing you have on. But Hanukkah is coming up. I'll think of something."

"What?" I ask.

She grins, and puts her hand on my shoulder, looking me straight in the eyes. "Go get some sleep, Andy. Find the photos. I have faith in you."

"And if that faith is misplaced?"

"Then . . . this place burns down, but I make sure it's empty when it does, and no one gets hurt, and I rebuild. The building isn't important. The people are." She spreads her free arm, taking in the crowd. "I can manage rebuilding. What's important is keeping everyone safe." She brings her arm around to poke me in the chest. "But that means you, too. So solve this thing. I can't have my detective going into hiding and moving across the country or anything."

I nod. I hadn't thought of that. Running away. Just when I'm finally starting to have a life. I guess it's an option. But I still have three days. I don't know if that's enough time to check every yard on the north side of the city, but . . . I can try.

"I don't want that either," I say. "I'll figure it out. But I should get some rest. I have a lot of yards to check. And . . ." I swallow, remembering tomorrow is the decommissioning ceremony for the *Bell,* and it makes my throat burn. "Something else I have to do, too." If I'm going to have to run away from my new life, I may as well say goodbye to my old one, too.

"All right, get some sleep then. We'll be waiting for you to come celebrate with us when you've solved it."

"Thanks, Elsie," I say, but she's already turning away, and I'm not sure she's heard me until she turns back and winks, before slipping into the crowd, dancing with anyone who crosses her path. It's amazing how unconcerned she seems. But I guess she's right. A building can be rebuilt. Though I don't want to think how much it would cost her. I think back to the smile, the pep talk, the tone of her voice, the digression into fashion. She's worried, too. Hiding it best she can with bravado, but worried. She was encouraging me because she's scared I'll fail. So I can't. Not just for me, but for everyone here, dancing.

I look over at the bar. There's a space in the crowd and I slip in and Gene looks up and smiles.

"Any luck?"

I shake my head. "I'm going to have to do this the slow way. With only three days left, that's . . . worrying. I told Elsie. She seemed to brush it off, but . . ."

"Yeah, that's Elsie." He reaches out and puts his hand on my wrist. It's wet from rinsing glasses and pouring drinks. But then he pulls it back. He looks at me, and I can tell he's worried, too, and he wants to ask me to fix everything but he doesn't want to say it aloud, so I do.

"I'll fix it," I say. "I'll figure this all out."

He sighs, looks a little relieved. He believes me, which almost makes me believe me.

Someone calls Gene's name and he nods at them. "I have to . . ." he says.

"Yeah," I say.

"I'll come get my shirt tomorrow?" he asks. "I left it hanging in your closet."

"Whenever you want," I say.

"Good luck, and be safe," he says, then goes over to the patron to pour another drink.

I make my way upstairs and go into my apartment, locking the door behind me. In my closet is the shirt Gene wore yesterday, baby blue, and a white undershirt. They smell like him—like alcohol and cigarettes from the patrons, but also a bit like warm stone, like a kitchen about to start cooking. I try to hold on to that smell as I fall asleep, but when I do, all I dream about is fire.

In the morning, I get up to Nob Hill quickly as I can. The decommissioning ceremony isn't until noon so I have a few hours to look for willow trees. I spot four. I can only see the dining room through the window of one of them, but the sofa is green. The other three I mark on my map to try again at night, when everyone is asleep, and hopefully won't see me peeping in windows. Last thing I need are my old colleagues getting called out to find me as a Peeping Tom. Even without knowing who it was that would usually be a smack or two, but me—I'd be dead.

The decommissioning ceremony is at the naval docks down at Hunters Point. No streetcars stop there, so I head back to the Ruby and get out my old Buick sedan. Looking for parking is a surefire way to slow an investigation, so I've relied on the streetcars to get around, letting it sleep in the garage almost every day since I moved in, but it starts up with only a little rattle. I check my dog tags are still in my pocket from when I got them out of the closet this morning. After I've parked by the docks, I slip them around my neck, and under my shirt. The metal is cool and makes me shiver for a moment before I get out.

The docks are huge, big enough for aircraft carriers to station, like a trident of concrete reaching out into the ocean. I approach the guard at the entry gate and fish out the dog tags again. He salutes. He's young, maybe a new draftee for the fighting in Korea. If he thinks anything about my black eye, he doesn't show it on his face.

"I'm not sailing anymore," I say. "No need. But I'd love it if you could direct me to the decommissioning ceremony for the *Bell*?"

"Your invitation, sir?"

"Lost in the mail," I say. "I'm sort of between addresses." And also if I told the navy where I was living now, I might not get invited to anything.

"Sir, I'm sorry, but—"

"He's with me," says a voice behind me. I turn, and almost don't recognize Helen. She's in a gray-pink pencil skirt and matching jacket, her blond hair down and parted on one side, so it half covers one eye, like Veronica Lake. Pink heels. She's even in white gloves. She holds out her own invitation. The guard looks it over and nods.

"Dock seventeen," he says, pointing.

She holds out her arm for me and I take it. "C'mon, sailor," she says.

We walk through the gate and toward the dock.

"They would have let you in, I'm sure," she says. "What would you want with a decommissioned minesweeper nearly a decade old?"

I tilt my head and watch the sailors walking by, stare at the ships in port. It's a warm day for fall, and the sun shatters on the water's surface, glittering. I'm in one of my old suits, a black one, white shirt, black tie. Somber. It feels a little off now, but so do I, being back here.

"You miss it?" she asks.

And for a moment, I do. The smell of the ocean, the feel of cutting through it, the sunsets, the dark water under me that could swallow us all up at any moment, the quiet moments in the sonar room . . . I miss it all with a palpable longing. My mouth is dry with it.

And then I remember everything else, too—the eyes on me, the hiding, the sneaking, the stolen moments, James's empty bed.

"I think I miss the ocean," I say. "But no, not the navy. You?"

"Well, I was never on the water," she says, looking a little sad about it. "But sure, I miss . . . the war, I guess. Is that awful to say? I miss the wild nights where I felt like I could be myself sometimes. In bursts. Flashing it like a burlesque. This new one in Korea . . . I don't think it's like that."

"Well, now you get to perform as yourself all the time."

She laughs. "James Bell isn't myself. He's just a character I have more fun playing."

"And this getup, this the real Helen?"

She looks up at me, offended. "Evander."

I laugh. "Okay, okay."

"Though I do like playing this one, too."

"So when do you get to be yourself, Helen? Managing the bar after hours? Counting bottles?"

She smiles. "Exactly then. Knowing that place is mine, and safe. Keeping it safe. That's when I feel most free."

We walk in silence the rest of the way. I see the *Bell* before we get there, docked right up against the edge. It's smaller than I remember. And the black-and-white stripes on it have faded in the sun, less like prison bars and more like shadows on a sunny day, edges blurring, fading. It rocks and sways in the water, and I can feel my feet clinging to the dock through my shoes, rocking with it.

I take a breath as we step on the ramp up the deck, like I'm about to dive into the water. But nothing happens, and we just keep walking up. The ship feels familiar underfoot, like being home. Helen puts her arms out for a moment, like she's losing her balance.

"It's odd how this is new to me, even after years in WAVES," she says. I take her arm to help her balance and we walk forward. There are a few chairs set up at the end of the deck, and a few navy orchestra players are stringing out something somber. There's a

THE BELL IN THE FOG 195

crowd there already. Faces I recognize. My old captain, still in uniform, his face longer than last time I saw him. Helen stays on my arm, like she's my date, and I let people think that as I nod, shake hands, and say the usual things, like "Nice to see you again."

When people ask what I've been doing for the past seven years, I tell them I'm in law enforcement. They ask about the black eye, I say a bar fight. The half-truth comes easily. Just like the way both Helen and I let people think we're married, a couple, whatever. One of my old shipmates' wives asks about children, and Helen says, "Oh, we've got one at home with my mother. He's so young, I thought he'd make too much noise." I almost laugh at that one.

James is at the front of the crowd, and comes up to me when he sees me, shakes my hand, but lets his fingers stray on my palm as he does so.

"James," I say in a low voice, looking around to see if anyone noticed. "Careful." It's so easy to feel this way again, to feel the sidelong glances and wonder which are bullets. How does he not feel it? Maybe he's just so used to it at this point.

"I'm just glad to see you," he says, grinning so wide I can feel both of us glowing. "But what happened to your eye? And who is . . . oh," he says, looking at Helen. "Blond. I like it."

"Sort of an homage," she says, patting at her hair.

"To what?" he asks. His tone is heavy, an anchor dragging through sand. This isn't the good old times I remember. Not for them. The Farallones haunts them, and their ghosts aren't like the ones haunting me and James.

She grins, all teeth, and opens her mouth to reply, but the music swells a little louder and the chaplain steps up to the podium at the front of the deck. We all take our seats as the orchestra plays. The sailors currently stationed aboard the *Bell* are manning the rails, like a white picket fence along the outside of the deck, staring out at the ocean. We all sit down and the current captain boards the ship. The sailors turn to salute as he enters and walks down the aisle between the chairs like a funeral. Which, maybe on some level, it is.

One of the members of the navy orchestra stands and we all follow suit, hands on hearts as he sings the national anthem. Then the chaplain comes forward to say an invocation. But I'm not paying much attention. Instead, I'm staring at the little details of the ship, the small marks I remember that are still there, and those that are gone, too.

There's a slight divot in one of the rails; it was there when the ship was brand new, too, just a quirk of its building, that I used to rub my thumb over when I was staring at the ocean. I have to resist the urge to go over to it and touch it now. It always felt cool, like a small area I could hide, even just the pad of my finger.

I look up, away from it, and spot James, a few rows in front of us, staring at the same thing. Knowing we both remember it makes me feel warm, like I'm floating on calm water. But memories aren't enough for a relationship, even if they keep pulling me back, like undertow. Not when there are so many other complications, too. Someone from the shore patrol or navy intelligence could be watching us right now, could know about me, or Helen, and see James's friendliness with us as a sign of something more. They could send men to watch him, follow him, and then report back if he does anything that suggests the truth, from visiting me over at the Ruby to extending his pinkie finger while drinking. Everything is suspect to them. Anything can become a case to get rid of us. I don't know how James can stand it, but I'm not going to deal with it again. Not after today. And today isn't for him. It's for the ship I'm standing on.

The captain is talking now, about the history of the ship, how she used to be out in the water, searching for mines. That was me, but no one thinks of it like that. It was the ship. It was all of us.

The *Bell*. Most ships get nicknames, but the *Bell* never had one that stuck. Sometimes people called her the *Alarm Bell*, because when she turned too sharply, she made a high-pitched creak that sounds like an emergency, but wasn't. But even that would always get shortened back down to the *Bell*. That's what she was. A clear ringing across the ocean. And now she's gone silent.

The captain finishes his speech, and all the sailors salute, then march off the ship. Other sailors, not from the *Bell*, march on, and start pulling down the flags and pennants. When they finish, they fold them up and hand them over to the captain, with a bow. They march off, and we follow, standing behind the original sailors, still waiting, facing the ship from the dock. We all give the *Bell* one more salute, and the captain pronounces the ship decommissioned. She'll go live in a dry dock somewhere. Maybe get scrapped after a while. It's amazing she was kept in the water so long.

The sailors and captain march away, and the only people left are my old shipmates and me. We all start to part, to say goodbye in recited memories. One man gets weepy and hugs me. But eventually, it's just the three of us again: me, James, Helen, all standing in the shadow of the *Bell*.

"So, want to get out of here?" James asks me. "Go back to your place? I was allowed to take the rest of the day off, to honor the *Bell*. I can think of several ways to do that." He grins.

"James, people might hear," I say. I know he's the one who knows the boundaries of things better than I do, but it feels like he's practically holding a gun to his head now, daring me to ask him to squeeze.

"Let's just get a drink," Helen says. "The three of us, old times. No reason for you two to start that up again."

"You never liked me and Andy together," James says, not with defensiveness, but like it's funny to him. He starts walking away from the *Bell*. "First time I see you in seven years and you're right back at keeping us apart."

She rolls her eyes. "I loved you two together. I also loved trouble. I'm trying to find it in new ways now. All the fun, none of the consequences."

James snorts. "You've gone blond and boring?"

"At least I hung around."

"Did you? Because Andy says he hadn't seen you in years until just the other day."

"Both of you, stop," I say. They glare at each other. "We all have history. You've gotten past it with me. And I know all of it now." I look at Helen, who glances away. "So let's just try to move on. No need to be nasty."

"Oh, she didn't tell you?" James asks. "We have a little more history, her and I. Or is that all of it that she told you? That she tracked me down after I left. To say goodbye. She was the nasty one then, but left before I had a chance to reply. Sorry if I'm doing it now."

I feel my body shake. She knew he hadn't been caught? I turn to look at Helen. "You knew why he'd left?" She was with me, after. She saw me, terrified, and she could have told me at anytime. Even as I ran to join the cops and she told me not to, she never said I was safe. Never said where he'd gone.

She won't meet my eye. "One of the yeomanettes was doing secretarial work for the admiral, dictated the promotion and orders to her," she says softly, too fast. "She thought James and I were going steady so asked if I was moving, and when I asked why, she was horrified I didn't know, so she told me: the promotion, the move, what train he was leaving on . . . so I met him at the station." It rushes out of her like a confession. I feel cold all over.

"I was convinced he'd been found out," I say, my voice low. "I told you how terrified I was. And you knew?"

"Let's get outside," Helen says, her voice calm.

I'm boiling with fury, but she's right. We're quiet the rest of the walk down the dock, and through the gate. Outside, we walk away from the docks and around a corner, out of sight. We stand in the shadow of a squat brick building, the three of us facing one another, waiting for something to start, but no one speaking.

Helen takes out a cigarette and lights it, then leans against the wall, folding her free arm under the one that holds the cigarette.

"I'm sorry I didn't tell you," she says after a minute, looking at me. "I thought it would just be worse. You would have gone after him."

"And I was leaving to protect you," James says. "We were getting too reckless. People were staring, and it wasn't the war anymore. I knew . . ."

"It was changing," I say. My voice feels like steel coming out of me, and lands that way, too. They both flinch. "You told me. So you vanished. But she was with me, she watched me, scared. She could have told me everything and I would have known, at least. I wouldn't have been looking over my shoulder, I wouldn't have left the navy . . ." I shake my head. "I deserved to know."

"If I'd told you, you would have gone after him," Helen says. "And I wanted you far away from him." She turns to stare at James, still smoking, talking about him like he's not there. "He's dangerous, Andy. I've been trying to tell you that."

"Oh, come off it, Helen, you're no better than me."

They look away from each other then, like one of them has accidentally set off a bomb, their eyes down to hide from the brightness of the explosion, the pain of it searing their eyes. Something I can't see, some new old secret from me that keeps shattering them both.

"The Farallones," I say, realizing it. My body tingles. I look at Helen. "There was more you wanted to say when you told me . . ."

She won't look up. But James does. "It was right before you left," I say to him. He walks to me and puts his hand on my shoulder, standing close. I glance around. We're still close enough to the port that someone could see, so I shake him off. And because I hate having to wonder if someone can see.

"Andy, I love you," James says softly. "You know that, you've always known that. And what I've done . . . I've always done for us."

Helen scoffs. "You did it for you, James."

"Helen, mind your own business for once in your life," he hisses back.

"It's my business, too," Helen says, pulling up from the wall and walking toward him.

"Tell me the truth," I say, my voice final as I can make it. "What happened?"

They're quiet, so I start to walk away, wondering if I'll get dragged back in by their undertow.

No, I realize, a few steps later. I can leave all this behind, the fighting, the good memories. It'll make me sad, but I can do it.

"Andy, wait." James grabs my wrist.

"Tell him," Helen says to James. "Tell him the whole story. I'm giving you the chance to tell it first, so he knows what you were running from."

James stares at her, and shakes his head. Then he looks back at me. "Come on, we can go back to my place. She just likes drama, you remember, right? Chasing the married women. That's all this is. Trying to cause more drama, but between us. You said to take a day, and I took three, and I know I want to be with you, Andy."

I pull my hand back, glaring.

"Don't," Helen says. She drops her cigarette and crushes it under the toe of her high heel. "Listen. If he won't tell you, I will. Just . . ."

"Helen," James says, like a warning.

"What are you going to do, James?" Helen asks, sticking her chin out. "Kill me?"

They stare, silently, and finally, Helen turns to me.

"The Farallones," she says. "You're right. I didn't tell you the whole story."

My heart is racing. What now? What's worse than murder? "So tell it."

"I thought you remembered at least that he was dead, the self-defense story . . . the lie."

"What lie?" I ask. The world feels so small, the alleyway closing in.

"You were so lucky. We were so lucky. You didn't remember it all. Not even . . ." She swallows and forces the words out. "It wasn't self-defense," Helen says.

"It was," James says, but he turns away, walks a few steps.

"It wasn't," she says at him. "I've had a long time to go over it in my head. Couldn't stop, really. And all the reasons you gave then, everything you said to convince me—they don't hold up. Maybe it was self-defense, of a kind . . . but there were a lot of other ways to defend ourselves, you just chose—no, we chose— the one that made our lives easiest." She spits out the words, then turns back to me. "The guy you brought back to the hotel that night was navy intelligence. He'd been following you for a few weeks. Both of you. All of us, really. You hadn't noticed, or if you had, you hadn't said anything. And honestly, we didn't know for sure he was intelligence, but it made us suspicious."

I try to remember the man's face, a feeling of seeing him before, but I come up with nothing. I don't even know who he was.

"So James came up with a plan. We'd all heard those stories— the navy intelligence officers who went home with men, then turned them in. Spies who infiltrated gay circles just to ruin our lives, get us locked up. James knew if he was watching you two, you were already in his crosshairs. The best thing to do would have been to cool down for a while, to stay at the base."

"But we were finished," James says, his voice soft. "The war was over. Things were going to change, but we could have kept them going a little longer. I knew it. And we deserved it, Andy. You and me—and you too, Helen. We deserved a good time for what we'd done for our country. And here was this man, and he was going to . . . he . . ." His face is pink and he takes a breath, staring at the sidewalk.

"What did you do?" I ask, but I can feel the answer already. I can feel it creeping into my body and weighing it down like an anchor, dragging it to the darkest part of the ocean.

"We invited him back to a hotel, one out of the way," James says softly. "If he was intelligence, it would be the best way to get him alone—seduce him with the promise of getting to turn in a couple of faggots." He stares at the ground. "Helen brought Suzanne. She was wild, easy to create a distraction."

"I just dared her to lean out the window and she screamed. You came running, like we knew you would," Helen says. "You were always looking out for us, protecting us. But you were too good for what we had planned. You . . . would never have agreed, if you'd known. You would have behaved, or dropped out, or . . ."

"Or left me," James says softly.

"Both of us," Helen agrees.

"So what did you do?" I ask. My voice is calm. I need to hear it.

"I told the guy to get in the shower, that we'd join him in a sec," James says. "Then I went through his pockets—found his badge. He was intelligence, for sure. He was going to turn us in. And I didn't want that for you, Andy."

"Or for you," Helen says to him.

"Or for me," James concedes. "So . . . I took care of it."

"You committed premeditated murder?" I ask.

They're both silent, neither of them looking me in the eye. Helen takes out another cigarette and lights it. I swallow and it aches. I want to sit on the sidewalk, just get down and feel the hot stone under me, but instead I walk to the wall and lean against it. Something needs to hold me up.

"You don't even know if he was really going to turn us in," I say. "He could have just been looking for a good time. Could have been like you were, lucky enough to be part of the people hunting us. Hunting him." I take a deep breath. "He could have been one of us."

They're silent. I grab the brick wall so hard I can feel it gouging blood out of my fingers.

"A week later," James says, "his body turned up. It looked like a fall, but people were asking questions. So when they offered me the promotion, I asked them if I could go east, where my German might be more useful. I needed to get away, to make sure you were in the clear. You didn't remember anything, your hands weren't on anything, and Suzanne could alibi you during the murder. But not me. I was the one they could finger, if we weren't careful. And you weren't being careful, Andy. You tried kissing me on base one night."

"The war was over," I say. "I was happy."

"I was scared," he says.

"Because you killed someone," I say.

"I regret it every day," Helen says softly, lighting another cigarette.

"I did it to protect you. Protect us," James says. "Because I love you, Andy. I thought going east, we could forget about each other, but the moment I saw you in your office, I knew there was no one else like you. There'd never be anyone like you."

I shake my head. "No, James. Those are all just memories. I'm not the same guy I was." I laugh. "Or maybe I nearly am again. After seven years, after you left like that, and you lied to me." I look at both of them. "I thought it was me, you know? I got so scared. I thought I was too much, too obvious, too dangerous. I left the navy. I became a cop because it seemed like a great cover. I killed myself a little every day until I wasn't happy anymore. I wasn't anything."

"Andy, I tried to talk you out of being a cop," Helen says. "I warned you."

"No," I say. "You didn't know why I became a cop. I didn't know until James showed up again and all the memories started twisting up inside."

"So let's go back to the way things were," James says. "We can be happy again."

"No, we can't," I say, angry again now. "It's the same—there're still people watching you, James. More than ever. Even if you haven't murdered any of them recently."

He turns away like I've slapped him.

"I don't want that life again," I tell him. I turn to Helen, but her eyes are on the ground. She leans against the wall, one leg against it, bracing herself, smoke spiraling off her cigarette like a plane going down. She saw all this coming. She was scared, and ran away from it. Now she can't.

I straighten myself out and start to walk away. At least they'll see me go. They'll know what I'm choosing. That's more than they ever gave me.

"Andy," he says. "I did it for us."

"I don't want you doing anything for us anymore," I say without looking back. "There is no us." I hear them follow me for a few steps, but then they stop. I get to my car and get in, driving past the alleyway to make sure they're not murdering each other.

James is gone, but Helen is there, smoking. She spots me and nods, like she's letting me go, and I drive away.

It's hard to focus the rest of the day, knowing about the murder. Knowing about the lies, the way the past wasn't what I thought it was. Nostalgia's a killer. It makes things seem uniform, easy. The past was days of hiding, and nights of pleasure, and then it all just ended. But it was more than that. It was complicated, and there was light in the dark parts, and dark in the light parts, and it was messy. So, so messy.

And James is a murderer. I understand what he meant about it being self-defense, but it wasn't. Helen knows it, that's why it's haunted her for years. It's why she dresses as a ghost every night, to exorcise it. We could have just stayed away from the clubs. We could have just behaved. But James saw another solution. A cold, dark one I didn't see, even though I was there. I feel like an idiot. I feel broken.

My past has shattered, I need to make sure my future—the Ruby, my life—stays intact. So I drive up to the north side and start looking for willow trees again.

Over the next few hours I find four more trees, and check countless yards. I manage to get a look inside two of the houses— no blue sofas with pink flowers. I feel myself getting tired and hungry as the sun sets and people come home. When I get my third curious glance I decide to head back to the office. I can come back later, in the dead of night, when everyone is asleep.

I park under the Ruby and take the elevator up to the club. I need a drink. It's only starting to fill up, so there's room at the bar and I feel myself get lighter when I see Gene behind it.

"Hi," I say to him, even though so much more is bubbling under me.

"Hi," he says. "You look like you need something strong."

"I do," I say. He makes a drink with whisky and bitters and puts it down in front of me. I take a long sip of it before looking back up at him. "I ended it with James. For real. So . . . I'd like to take you out."

He smiles. "How'd he take it?"

I shake my head. "I'm not even sure," I say, and take another sip. "I was so angry. We were fighting. Or . . . they were fighting."

"Sounds confusing," Gene says, frowning a little.

"It was a lot of stuff bubbling up from the past. But I don't want that anymore."

"Because it's getting messy?" Gene asks.

I frown, confused. He should be happy. "Because I want to look forward."

He sighs. "Andy, are you really done? Or is it just . . . confused right now?"

"We're done," I say quickly. "I promise. Even if you weren't in the picture, we'd be done."

He nods, but I'm not sure he believes me. He takes out a glass, and starts washing it.

"So . . . next week?" I ask. "If I'm still alive?"

"Sure," Gene says, his tone a shrug. "If you still want to."

"Gene . . ." I sigh. "I'm done with him, really. You have to believe me."

He looks up and smiles. "I want to. But I think giving it a week will make it all clearer. So yeah." He grins, but it feels forced. "Next week."

Another patron orders a drink, and he turns away, working. I finish mine and go upstairs to take a quick nap before I go out again to peep in windows. The door to my office is ajar, though, so I go inside, in case a new client is waiting. The chair is empty, but the moment I take a step inside, the door slams behind me. I spin. In front of the closed door is Danny Geller.

It's the first time I've seen him in person. He's handsomer than in his photos—his hair curls over a fading bruise under his eye. His lips are soft looking. He's dressed a little outlandishly, in a long tan trench coat over an undershirt and oversized pants. The coat is falling off one of his shoulders slightly, and he has a purple scarf tied loosely around his neck. It's a lot, but somehow it makes him more alluring, like I've caught him in the act of getting dressed. He's striking, good-looking; I can see why so many men wanted to be with him. But maybe the most noticeable thing about him is the gun he's holding in both his hands, pointed at me.

"Where the fuck are my pictures?"

ELEVEN

"What?" I ask, looking at the gun. It's a revolver, an old .38 special, I think. But the way he's holding it, I don't think he's ever pointed a gun at anyone before. His arms are bent, both of them holding the handle. He has a finger on the trigger, though. That's all that matters.

"My pictures," he says, moving forward, the gun shaking. I put my hands up, back away, toward my desk. "I know you've been giving them out. I heard about it. But there are some important ones I need back. So where are they?"

"Jonathan?" I ask. He flinches. "He give you that bruise?" I point at my own eye. "Me too. I don't have his photos."

"Liar," he says, lifting the gun a little. I shift to my left, off-center.

"They're all in that cabinet," I say, pointing at a cabinet that holds old case files, and so is mostly empty. "Check for yourself."

He narrows his eyes. "You think I'm stupid, don't you? Just some pretty boy in over his head?" His voice is rising; he gives each of his words a fullness like he's on stage and is expecting applause at the end of the line. Every syllable is a meal.

"I don't think that at all, Danny," I say. "Well, aside from the pretty."

He smirks. "Go get them out." He motions with the gun to the file cabinet. I take my chance and duck low. I rise with the palm of my fist, knocking the gun up. I hear his hands loosen and I grab, but so does he, and it fires. It shoots up, away from us, but with enough force to knock Danny's hand back. I grab the gun and immediately open the chamber, dumping the bullets out. Danny frowns at me, trying to swipe the gun back, but I hold it out of reach.

"You bitch," he says.

"I'm trying to help you out, Danny. I really don't have the photos. Jonathan, or whatever his name is, he gave me four days to find them or he's killing me and burning this place down. I have two days left, after tonight. I've been looking all over for them. Is that why you want them? Why you went into hiding? He threaten you, too?"

Danny sighs, his body going slack, and swaying, like he's going to fall. He lifts his hand to his forehead.

"I need a drink," he moans, the words long in his mouth.

"Fine," I say, putting the gun in my pocket. "Let's go downstairs, I'll buy you a drink, and you can tell me all about your little blackmail scheme."

He rolls his eyes, but walks to the door. I follow him out and lock it behind me.

"So you've seen my photos?" he asks, as we walk to the stairs and down them.

"I have," I say.

"You like them?" He grins, cat-like. "We could do some of our own, y'know?"

"I don't have enough money to be worth blackmailing," I tell him. "Plus, who would you show them to? My employer? She's probably here tonight, and she'd have a good time making fun of me, but not enough I'd pay to stop it."

"Well then, how about we just do it for fun?" he asks, turning around. He's a step below me and his face is level to my chest, but he looks up, then starts to kneel.

"Get up," I say, shaking my head. "This isn't working on me, Danny. Come on. We can help each other out."

"I just think I'm entitled to a good time before I die," he says, his voice haughty, as he turns back around. "I deserve it, after everything I've been through."

"Well, after we talk everything through, you can try picking someone up. I'm sure you'll have no problem."

He smiles at that. "That's nice of you to say." He opens the stairwell door into the Ruby. We go to the bar, where Gene raises an eyebrow and I just shake my head, but order myself a drink and one for Danny, who asks for a pink squirrel, making Gene get out an old bottle of crème de noyaux from the bottom shelf. He hands the drink over, frothy pale pink, and I lead Danny to an out-of-the-way table, where he drinks his pink squirrel and I sip at whatever Gene mixed up for me, which tastes like if an orange spent the night in Vegas. I look at him, bringing the pale-pink glass to his lips, his eyes darting around the room, taking in the crowd. His expression goes a mile a minute, frowning, then looking sly, then licking his lips. I wonder if he knows his sister is dead. I wonder if I have to tell him.

Eventually, his expression seems to grow steadier and he looks back at me.

"So what do you want?" he asks.

"I want to know who else had access to the locker where the photos were kept," I say. "Who even knew about them, besides you and Donna?"

He frowns. "So you found her? Where is she? She was supposed to meet me two days ago."

I sigh and look at my drink. "Danny . . . your sister . . . she's dead."

"What?" he says, narrowing his eyes and crossing his arms. "Absolutely not. You're trying to trick me."

"I only got into the locker because I found the key on her body," I say.

"But . . ." He pauses, swallows, his hand rising to his throat as the drink shakes in his other hand. "Then . . ."

"I assume it was Jonathan, looking for you."

"No, no, no," he says. "I don't believe you. You stole it off her. Or she gave it to you. She thought you could protect her maybe."

"Danny, I'm sorry, but she's gone."

"Someone would have told me!" He slams his drink down. "Stop lying!"

A few people are looking over at us, so I lean back, try to relax. "Who else could have taken the photos?" I ask. "Who else knew about them?"

"But . . ." Danny's eyes go far away, like he's trying to figure something out. When they finally come back, he starts to cry. "Who killed her?"

"I don't know," I say. "Jonathan?"

"He didn't know . . . no one knew about any of it. They guessed it was me, which I should have known . . ." He dabs at his eyes with the napkin from his drink. I take out a handkerchief and hand it to him. He blows his nose. "We just wanted more money for our act," he says, his eyes pleading. He's quiet now, his voice shaky and sad. "The act is spectacular. *We're* spectacular! We were going to be famous. Our whole lives we knew it. We could sing in perfect harmony since we were four. We didn't look so alike, but makeup, a dress . . . it was fun. And funny, but in a clever way, and still so good. We just needed more money. They kept saying that—that our dresses were old-fashioned, our makeup was cheap. We just needed . . ." He starts to cry again, covering his face with both his hands. "I turned tricks to make ends meet, you know, but it wasn't enough. So I thought we could cash out. What's a little blackmail if it made us famous like we were supposed to be . . ." His voice dissolves into heavy sobs. Real ones, not acting.

"I'm really sorry, kid," I say. I want to tell him he should never have done what he did, that blackmail is dangerous, not to mention the people he was blackmailing. But he knows all that now. He knows it the way you know a knife through the chest—with a sudden, awful awareness.

He cries some more, and I sip my drink until he blows his nose. He looks at me, his eyes red.

"Where is she?" he asks.

"The water," I tell him. I don't have to explain why I moved her body, not now. "The police weren't going to do anything but cause problems, so I gave her a burial I thought was most peaceful."

"She liked the water," he says, sniffing. "I'll put up a stone by the beach or something. I'll say goodbye there . . ." He drifts off, his eyes red and distant. Then he takes a long sip of his drink.

"So if Jonathan didn't know about her," I say, hoping to get some answers, "who did? Who would have killed her? Who would have taken the photos?"

His eyes go away again, but come back quickly, his face going cold then cracking into a sneer.

"That bitch," he whispers.

"Helen?" I ask, but he's not looking at me. I grab his wrist. "Danny, who?"

Suddenly the lights flicker. No, no, not another raid, not now.

The music stops, Danny looks confused. I glance up at Gene, who motions at the stairwell with his head, but then the elevator doors open with a chime, and the cops pour in.

I glance over at Danny, to see if he's going to cause a scene, but he's just as used to this as the rest of us—why wouldn't he be? His face goes calm, almost demure, as the cops spread out through the people who aren't dancing anymore, among the tables, into the bathrooms.

"What is this?" Elsie asks, striding forward. She must have been in the crowd before and I didn't see her. "I just paid up, and I paid well."

"Yeah," says the lead cop, "but we were thinking about the last raid here, and your bartender. He was a little mouthy. Gave us some backtalk." He glances over at Gene and my whole body goes cold.

A cop grabs Gene from behind the bar and pulls him out to stand next to Elsie.

"You don't get to do that," the lead cop says to Gene. "Not without paying some price. You gotta remember your place, especially a fairy like you. Where you from, China?"

Gene keeps his eyes on the ground, but I can see the slight shake in his shoulders.

"Oh, now you're not talking back?" the cop says. "That's fine. Sometimes to teach a lesson, no one needs to talk much." He raises his fist and without thinking I'm out of my chair and across the room. I catch the fist, midair. I manage not to punch the cop back, but I take the fist and guide it, gently, into my shoulder, taking the hit instead of Gene. It knocks me back a little. I hear a few people in the crowd gasp, watching us.

"Andy," Gene says in a whisper. "No, if—"

"What are you, his boyfriend?" the cop asks. "You just assaulted an officer, you know. That's how you get arrested around here."

I swallow. If I'm arrested, I'm dead. And then no one can save the Ruby from being burned down.

"Oh, quit it," Elsie says, exasperated. "We paid up. You're not supposed to be here. You want me to start going around town telling all the other bars that we paid up and you raided anyway?

How much do you all make off our bribes, hm? All of them combined, I mean? There are a lot of our kind of bars in this town, Officer, and I know for a fact that you're not the top of the food chain. I can tell the bars not to pay, tell them it was all because you broke the rules. How's the pension fund going to look without our donations, hm?"

The cop glares at her, his tongue licking his teeth. "You're a mouthy broad, too."

"I am," Elsie says with a smile. "And I own this place, and I give money to fundraisers and mingle with the elite, your bosses. Because I am the elite. I am one of your bosses." She takes a step forward. "There's a tax for being like us in this town, sure. But we paid it. You don't get to drag people in just because you want to anymore. We can sue you, same as the Black Cat did."

"He assaulted me," the officer says, spitting a little.

"Did he?" Elsie says. "I didn't see it. Did you?" she asks a woman next to her, who shakes her head. "You?" she asks another guy, who shakes his head. "Seems like a lot of people didn't see that, Officer. Now leave." Another cop steps forward as if to argue but she glares at him, too. "Get the fuck out or I'll tell every other bar in town to stop paying those bribes. We'll unionize. How about that?"

"Bitch," the cop says. Elsie yawns. The cop whistles, and the rest of them head for the elevator, marching out, looking angry and glum. When the elevator door closes, the whole room breathes together, relieved.

"It's going to be worse next time," I say. "You should have let them take me."

She pats me on the cheek. "No chance," she says. She turns to the band. "Play! Let's get this place alive again!"

The band starts up and people start dancing. Someone taps me on the shoulder, and I turn around, and it's Gene, looking at me with something like wonder.

"You could have gone to prison," he says. "Even just a night in lockup, and you'd be dead. We both know it. You should have let them hit me."

"I . . . didn't know how," I say.

He smiles, and then suddenly launches himself at me and we're kissing. Not like last time, when I was kissing because I was alive and I wanted to kiss someone. This time I'm kissing Gene because he's Gene. And it's not like kissing anyone else. There's no fancy French word for it—or, there probably is, but I don't know it. My body feels like Christmas tinsel, shaking in the breeze, tinging and shining and ringing, and all I can feel is Gene, my arms around his waist, his around my shoulders, our lips, our tongues, our bodies. Something new. Something so much steadier than the ocean ever was.

"All right, you two, you have a room upstairs, take it there," Elsie says, and we break apart, grinning like schoolboys who just got caught pulling a prank.

"I should get back behind the bar," Gene says, still grinning.

"And I was interrogating a suspect to find out where those photos are, so this place doesn't get burned down."

We're still holding each other; people dance around us. We don't move. But then the weight of what I just said hits me, and I start to pull away and he nods.

"Go," he says, still smiling. I turn away and head back to the table where I left Danny. He's gone, his drink still half-finished. I frown and look around. He could be dancing, so I go to the bar and stand on it for a sec, looking out over the crowd. A few people near me applaud, but I don't see Danny. I hop down and run upstairs, check my office, the dressing rooms. Not there either. So I run downstairs to the street, and look out both ways. He's gone.

I've gone to Danny's apartment so often at this point, people probably think I'm his roommate, but he's not there again this time. It's the same as the last. Which means he's in the wind again. For someone who so clearly likes a scene, he's real good at waiting in the wings. And without him, I'm out of leads again, aside from willow trees.

And, I realize, putting my hands in my pockets, the gun. I fish it out and look at it in the light of the floor lamp in Danny's apartment. The thing must be twenty years old. There's no tag or anything to show where it came from, but if Danny did pawn some stuff to buy it, then it shouldn't be hard to find where—only a few places in the city deal with guns. I glance at my watch. It's too late to go to any of them now, but it might be a stronger lead than the trees. And I still have to go peek in some windows.

I head to the willow-tree houses I marked and creep around outside them. It takes a few hours, but I don't see any blue-and-pink sofas, and I'm only nearly caught once, when I let out a groan after climbing over a fence, because I hit the ground on one of my bruised sides. It's not much, but it's a handful of houses I know aren't the ones from Helen and Donna's photos.

By the time I get back to the Ruby, it's after eleven, and the place is still dancing, but not as full as it was before. Gene smiles at me when I walk up to the bar. Lee is already sitting at it, her hair a short bob, in a red sequin dress.

"I hear you made a scene," she says to me. Then she looks at Gene. "Both of you."

Gene blushes furiously and looks down.

"It was a gut reaction," I say, though I feel my own cheeks color, too.

"What body parts are you counting as your gut these days?" she says, grinning and sipping her drink through a straw.

"All right," I say, blushing even more. "Any luck with gossiping your way into a lead?"

"Give it time," she says. "I've only just sent out feelers last night."

"I don't know how much time we have," I say. "Danny got away."

"Was that my fault?" Gene asks, looking shocked.

"No, he was going to give me the slip any way he could. The cops are what gave him the distraction he needed. But he did leave me his gun, so I'm going to check around some pawnshops, see if I can get a lead that way. I used to have good relationships with most of the guys pawning in town."

"Used to?" Lee asks.

"When I was on the force. Not sure how they'll respond to me now. Or what they've heard about why I left."

"Be careful," Gene says.

"I will," I say.

Lee finishes her drink and puts it down on the bar, then stands. "I'm on in a few minutes. You sticking around, Gene, or you and Andy going to go upstairs? I'll sing real loud if you need me to cover moaning."

Gene blushes again, but then looks at me, questioning. And I want to, I really want to bring him up to my room and make him moan.

"Well, that's a decision I'm not a part of. Night, boys," she says, getting up and walking to the stage.

"I mean, I am off in a few minutes," Gene says, putting his hand on the bar.

I look at his hand, then put mine over it and weave my fingers through his.

"I did something kind of heroic today," I say.

He laughs. "Yeah, you did."

"And I don't want you making a decision because of that," I say. "I didn't do it because I wanted you to come to my room tonight. I did it because I couldn't not do it."

"So, no," he says, disappointed. I feel his fingers go slack.

"Not tonight," I say. "You told me to wait a week, remember? You didn't believe I was done with James. Although . . . I am," I say, suddenly remembering everything today has been. "I really, really am. Today has been a lot."

"How about," he says, squeezing my hand again, "we just go upstairs and talk about it? Your day, I mean. You're right, waiting is a good idea. I mean . . . I know I want to go upstairs with you. I've wanted to for months."

I laugh. "I still can't believe that. I felt like you were just being nice."

"We don't have quiet moments," he says. "Like I said. So either we go upstairs and talk, or you go out and get beat up again."

I laugh. "Well, your shirt is up there anyway."

He takes my hand as we go upstairs. I unlock the door to my apartment nervously, aware of the showgirls and -boys staring, cackling.

"I pour your drinks, remember," Gene says to them. "Show some respect."

They laugh at that, but go into their dressing rooms. In my apartment, he grabs my collar and kisses me, hard, and I kiss him back, our bodies close. He pushes me against the door, with enough force I drop my hat on the floor, and we don't stop kissing for what seems like an hour.

"I thought we said—" I start, panting.

"Just that," Gene says. "We didn't really get to finish before. Elsie interrupted. But now we can talk."

I laugh. "Now I don't want to."

He laughs. "Nope," he says simply, sitting down in the chair he was in the other night, watching me sleep. "You were right. So . . . tell me about your day."

I sigh, sitting down across from him at my tiny table. "Mine was long," I say. "Tell me about yours?"

"Well, I volunteer at a soup kitchen once a week, so I served some soup at lunch, looked at a few bruises on a homeless woman. I'm more there to try to help out folks who can't afford a doctor. The shelter knows I used to be in medical school, they don't ask why I'm not anymore."

"What do you think would happen if they knew?"

"Oh, I'd be fired for sure," he says with a shrug. "Well, not fired, 'cause I'm not paid. But banned. They don't need the reputation of having a pervert inspecting homeless people's bodies. Newspapers would love that story. And I don't want to be a poster boy for what people hate. I'm not white, I'm not rich, I can't protect myself the way Elsie does. Plus, there's a chance folks would just start beating up random guys who they thought were me—and that could mean Chinese, Japanese, Mexican. People mistake Filipino for all of them."

"Sorry, I shouldn't have asked."

He smiles. "It's okay. If we can't talk about that with other people like us, what are we supposed to do? Bottle it all up? That's why I like being a bartender, honestly. People tell me their problems—and at a gay bar, it's always gay problems. And I can say 'Yeah, I get it,' and they know it's not just them feeling it."

I smile, and our eyes meet and we're quiet for a moment.

"You're so busy, I'm surprised you have time for that," I say. "You never have time to talk to me."

He glares. "I always have time for you. You just always take your drink and sit at a table instead of hanging around."

"I don't want to bother you, you're working. Plus I don't want to take up space at the bar, take money out of Elsie's pockets."

He shakes his head. "Andy, you need to get this through your brain or I'm going to worry you've taken one too many concussions—you belong here as much as any of us. You're one of us. You don't need to sit off to the side or make room for someone else. You get your place, too. Elsie has been telling you this for months. She literally gave you rooms."

I look around at my little studio, my home, that she gave me. Pale-pink light comes in off the sign, but with the lights on, it just makes everything feel warmer.

"I suppose you're right," I say. My eyes fall back down to the table. I put my hand on it and he immediately reaches across and takes it. "Tell me about the rest of your day?"

"Not much else," he says with a shrug. "After the soup kitchen, I came here, tended bar, got saved by a handsome detective, then served some more drinks."

"Tell me more about this handsome detective," I say, serious. "Do I need to beat him up?"

Gene laughs for longer than I think the joke deserves. "You already do," he says finally. "Constantly."

I laugh at that too. "Well, I hope you like watching men fight over you."

"Not usually, but I don't mind it in this case." He squeezes my hand. "Now how about you? Your day?"

I sigh and take out a cigarette and light it. "You want one?"

He shakes his head.

"You want me to put mine out?"

He shakes his head again. I take a long drag and tell him about my day. About the fight, about the past, about the murder.

"I hate that they think they did it to protect me. Killing someone. Making me so scared I ran away from life."

"People do things to protect people they love," Gene says. "If Elsie hadn't stepped in and that cop arrested you, you'd . . .'"

I grin. "You think I love you?"

He smiles, coy. "I think you like me, we'll see." He shrugs, still grinning, then squeezes my hand again. "But I'm sorry about your day, the raid, the fight with your friends."

"At least it's ending well," I say. "And maybe the fight was a long time coming. I look back at the war, at all of us, and it's like it was so good until it all stopped suddenly. And that scared me, I think, so I locked it all up, the past, tried not to think about the good times if they could end so suddenly. But it wasn't all good, it turns out. It was good and bad. And I sort of just want to lock it all up again. I just want the future now."

"It wasn't all bad though, Andy. You can remember the good."

"Maybe. But the past is a ball of string, tangled and knotted. I can't pull on one happy memory now without getting a bunch of others."

"That's how I feel about medical school," he says with a nod. "But now I can look back at it like it's . . . through glass, y'know. I can remember the good stuff, and smile, and the bad stuff comes with it, but it's all under glass, a diorama. It can't do anything to me now. I pick what happens next."

"That's what I want to do, too," I say. "I want to pick what happens next, and not keep getting tangled in that knot."

"So what do you want, then?"

"I like what I'm doing, so I'd like to keep doing it—being a detective here. Which means the place can't go up in flames."

"What else?"

"Well, I'd like a fella," I say. "Maybe. Not like it was with James, where it was so many things at once I don't know what we were. I want a man of my own."

"Of your own?"

I nod.

"Have anyone in mind?" he asks, arching an eyebrow.

"Well, I do remember someone saying they wanted to come up here, shoving me against the door, and kissing me."

"Do you?" he asks. His skin looks soft in the light. "I really am going to worry about those concussions."

"All right, so what kind of man do you think I should go for?"

He takes a big, fake sigh. "Well, I don't know. But I can tell you what I like in men."

"All right." I lean back, watching him.

"Well, I like a man who never gets into any trouble. One with a nice, safe job. Like an accountant. Are you an accountant?"

I laugh. "I could be."

"Well, that's a good start. I also like a man who doesn't drink or smoke too much. A little is all right, but too much seems to me to be a want of moral character."

"A want?"

"Yes," he says, very serious. "A want."

"Well, I like a man who likes alcohol so much he gives it out," I say. "And tests his bartending skills on me when he's practicing."

"I'm not testing—"

I raise an eyebrow and he blushes for a moment, then laughs.

"Well, if you like being tested on, sounds like a good match."

"I do. And I like a guy who knows how to take good care of me."

"Good care?"

"Very good care."

"You have a thing for being nursed back to health?"

"I didn't before, but the past few months, I seem to have developed one."

"How peculiar."

"Isn't it?"

He stands up, and comes over to my side of the table, then sits down on my knee, looking down at me. His thighs are soft on my leg, and I wrap my arm around his waist, feeling the muscles of his torso through his shirt.

"I have no idea where you're going to find a man like that," he says.

"Me neither, but I guess you'll do in the meanwhile," I say, stretching my neck up and kissing him. He tastes like mint, somehow, with a hint of gin underneath, like he might evaporate off my tongue. He kisses me back, and we kiss for a while, his arms on my shoulders, then my neck and face, my hands pulling him close and warm. Our bodies press together, still clothed, like kids making out in the back seat of a car. My body aches but it sings, too, loud enough to cancel out any pain. He stands up. He's smiling, his skin flushed. Somehow, my body is still singing, looking at him.

"I'm going home now," he says, still smiling. "But I'll see you tomorrow."

"See you tomorrow," I say.

He walks out the door, and I lie down in bed, feeling like a waning fire. I fall asleep in my clothes.

TWELVE

The next morning, Gene still on my lips, I shower and dress. I only get to go on a date with him if I survive, after all, and I need to find those photos to survive.

I spend the morning scouring more of the north side for willow trees. I only find two by noon, neither of which are attached to houses with blue-and-pink sofas. At noon, it's time to go to the pawnshops. Most of them open later in the day, and the owners are cranky when they do, so after noon I'm more likely to get answers from them. I try Mac down in the Mission first. The day is cold and I button my coat to the neck on the streetcar riding down there.

Mac's pawnshop just has a small neon light out front that says PAWNSHOP—no fancy name, no other signs trying to lure people in for hidden treasures. He does good enough business without that, because most people know about Mac. He'll buy anything, sell anything. Legalities don't bother him at all. He's got no scruples and follows no rules aside from trying not to get caught. But as a policeman, I found him useful. He was easy to threaten, with all his obviously illegal activity, and easy to flip, telling us who sold him what—weapons, usually. Everyone knew if they had a gun to unload, they could sell it to Mac. If they got caught after, that wasn't his problem. He had his money. And to keep him in business we would always say we found the gun on someone else.

I walk into the pawnshop with my collar still turned up and my hands in my pockets. It's a small shop, narrow, all glass display cases filled haphazardly with watches, jewelry, random knick-knacks. It always smells like stale cigar smoke, too, which makes sense since Mac is always smoking. He's behind the counter now, a pair of large glasses, a bad comb-over, and a cheap suit that hangs off his scrawny frame. He grins at me when I walk in.

"I heard you left the force," he says.

"Yeah," I say, approaching him.

"I heard you're a fag now, too."

"Always was," I say, keeping my face even.

He laughs, a loud, hoarse noise. "My sister's a fag. She lives with some other broad in Sacramento. Tell people they're room-mates, but I know they're trying to figure out how to fuck every night."

Mac isn't pleasant to be around, but this is about how I thought it would go: a few jokes, a little hassling. He doesn't really care, though. He doesn't care about anything aside from cash, near as I can tell.

"How do two women do it?" he asks. "I mean, I get how two guys do it, we all got assholes. Must stink, though."

I take out Danny's gun and lay it on the counter.

"You sell this?" I ask.

He laughs. "What? You still playing at cop? What do you care who bought a gun or who sold it?"

This is the part I knew would get harder. I don't have anything to threaten him with. I can't look over his wares and cite six vio-lations that would require closing the store. But when there's no stick, there's a carrot, and I did overcharge James. I fish out my wallet and lay a few bucks on the table. Mac eyes them.

"Oh, I like this," he says. "I like this much more than you being a cop."

"You sold it?" I ask, keeping my hand on the bills.

"Maybe."

"Tell me about who you sold it to," I say.

"Why? You clearly took it off him, you know who he is."

"So I know you're telling the truth. Then we can get to the real questions and you can have all this"—I tap the money—"for answering those."

He snorts a laugh. "Admit it, Mills, you always had a thing for me, didn't you? I always knew it, the way you stared at me."

"Sure, Mac, what guy doesn't like a man with a voice like a grunting pig and lips cracked and dry as Death Valley. It's what I dream of coming home to."

He laughs again. "I knew it."

"The gun?" I ask again.

"Oh, sure. He was clearly one of you. Loafers were so light his heels were over his head, you know? Dramatic type. Wore big sunglasses the whole time, had a scarf wrapped around him, and kept looking over his shoulder. Whispered he wanted a gun, but loud enough people could hear. Dark hair."

I nod. That sounds like Danny. "Good," I say, "you did sell it. So tell me more about this kid. I'm looking for him."

"I thought I was your type," he says, snorting again.

"I like to play the field."

"You're breakin' my heart. But I got nothing for ya, Mills. I sold him the cheapest gun I had, some bullets, and he took off with it."

"Really?" I say. "You got nothing else off him?"

He sucks in through his teeth and eyes the bills. "Nothing that comes to mind."

I add another dollar.

He smiles. "Well . . . maybe he didn't come in alone."

"Who was with him?" I ask.

"Some college kid. I see him in the neighborhood. They didn't seem too chummy, more like distant acquaintances. But I don't know how your kind interact. Could have just had bad sex or something."

"What did this college kid look like?"

"He's blond, glasses, fat. Wears the City College sweatshirt. Kinda vibe you can't tell if he's a kook or a genius, y'know?"

"And you said you see him around a lot?"

"Yeah, at that soda shop at the edge of campus. I go there for a burger at lunch sometimes. The food's not great, but there's this waitress with . . ." He cups his hands in front of his chest. "But I guess you don't appreciate that."

"I'm guessing she doesn't either," I say, looking at his hands, which drop. "The college kid?"

"Yeah, he's usually there with a lot of books all spread out, hogging a booth."

"All right," I say, lifting my hand off the cash. His hand snakes out and grabs it like a frog's tongue catching a fly. "Thanks, Mac."

"Anytime, faggot," he says. I turn around and leave. It wasn't fun, all the verbal abuse, but from Mac it's not so bad. He's awful to everyone. And I'd take the insults over another beating from Jonathan any day.

I walk a few blocks west, toward City College, looking for a soda shop. I spot it on the outskirts of campus, a flashing neon sign with bubbles announcing it in blue. Inside, the blue continues on the walls, over a black-and-white linoleum floor. There's a waitress behind the counter, and little red stools. A jukebox at the end of the room plays Doris Day's "A Guy Is a Guy," and in one of the booths by the window is a blond kid in glasses and a red cardigan with the white *SF* on it, tapping his foot to the music. There's a milkshake and a bunch of books spread out in front of him.

I sit down across from him and he looks up at me and blinks a few times. He's cute, maybe twenty, with broad shoulders and a soft figure. He's familiar, too. I think I've seen him around.

"Hi, I'm Andy," I say.

"You're the detective," he says, his eyes widening. "Oh gosh, I saw you last night." He leans in and whispers. "With the police. That was so nifty."

"You were there?" I ask. Maybe I'm getting famous.

"Sure," he says. "I mean, not if anyone asks, but for you, sure, yeah. Everyone was talking about it after. I wanted to shake your hand but you were gone. Maybe with that bartender you were . . ." He blushes a little. "You know. Oh, I'm Alfie, by the way."

I reach out a hand and he smiles excitedly and shakes it too hard.

"Nice to meet you," I say with a sugary smile. "So were you at the Ruby with a friend?" I ask, trying to sound sweet.

"Um, yeah. I mean, a few."

"Was one of them Danny Geller?" I ask, my voice still sweet, but his eyes narrow slightly at Danny's name. "I'm working a case."

"Oh wow," he says, his eyes widening again. "What case?"

"Well, I can't tell you that. I have to keep that secret," I say, conspiratorial.

"Oh, sure. But it has to do with Danny?"

"Yeah," I say. "He could be in trouble. I'm looking for him."

His eyes narrow. "I'm not stupid, mister," he says, gesturing at the books in front of him. "I'm not slick the way Danny is, but I'm not stupid either. When I told Danny about the stories, about you returning blackmail photos to people, he got real interested. And now you're looking for him. But I don't think anyone could blackmail Danny, so . . ." His expression shimmers, then falls as he puts it together. "Oh. I didn't know." He suddenly looks scared. "You don't think I did, do you?"

"No, no," I say. "I don't think that. I just need to find Danny, is all. He was there to see me last night, wasn't he?"

"Well, yeah, but I saw him leave during the raid. I was afraid to move, so I . . . Oh, this is so wild. I'm like figuring it out now. Did he try to get the photos back? Blackmail you?"

"Sort of. But I don't have them anymore. I need to know who does, and Danny can tell me. So . . . how do you know him? Are you friends?"

"I mean, kind of." He shrugs. "I see him around the clubs and stuff, and I . . . like him, so I tried talking to him. And he talks to me. But more like I'm an audience, y'know? I don't think he'd say we're friends, really." He frowns. "He took me once on what I thought was . . . but it was just he wanted my help picking out a gun at a pawnshop. He remembered me saying I'd gone hunting with my dad. I told him the guns weren't the same and he got all huffy with me, so . . . I like him, though."

"You're sweet on him?" I whisper.

He turns red, then nods. "But . . ."

"It's okay, kid. And you could do better. He's not that nice a guy."

"But he's handsome," the kid says dreamily.

I nod, trying to play along, trying not to think about how much time is left before I have to find those photos before the Ruby burns down.

"So who else was friends with him? Who did he hang around with or talk about?"

He shrugs. "I don't know, not really. He talked about his sister and their act a lot, and then their job. Mostly he talked about the act. How good it was going to be. How famous they'd be."

"A job?" I ask. "As a waiter, you mean?"

"Oh, no. Some other job. He said they were going to get rich. Him, his sister, and some other person."

"What other person?" I ask, my fingers drumming on my thigh under the table. "Did Danny say a name?"

The kid pauses and scrunches up his eyes, but shakes his head. "I don't think so. He didn't seem to like whoever it was very much. Just called 'em 'that bitch.'"

Just like he'd said last night when he'd seemed to figure out who killed Donna. A third blackmailer—the one who killed Donna, and probably has the photos of Jonathan. He called me a bitch, too. Could be a woman or a man.

"Did he tell you anything else about this bitch? Man or woman? Where they lived, what they looked like?"

The kid shakes his head. "Oh, but one week, he said the bitch asked him to water her—I think her—plants while she was out of town. Gave him a key to her house. Danny said he was going to throw a wild party there." He looks down. "If he did, though, he didn't invite me."

"Like I said, you could do better."

He sighs. "Maybe. I just don't know anyone at the bars. I feel like everyone is looking past me."

"You know me," I say. "And you know that singer at the Ruby, Lee? You go up to her one night and say you helped me out on a case. She'll want to hear all about it, and she knows everyone in town. She's a real good friend. Cares about people."

He smiles a little. "I don't know if I could do that."

"Well, until you try, you won't know how it'll turn out." Alfie tilts his head at that, considering it. "Now, this woman, the bitch, you know anything else about her? Where her house is?"

The kid shakes his head. "Sorry. Like I said, I wasn't invited. And maybe it was a man. Danny was always coy with details."

"All right," I say, realizing I'm not getting anything more out of him. Another dead end. I take out a card and hand it to him. "If Danny calls you, you let me know, okay? It's to help him out." I mean that. If this third person was in on the blackmailing and owned the house, they could be the one who killed Donna. Which means if Danny goes after them, he's probably next.

"All right," he says, taking the card.

I stand up. "Thanks for your help, kid."

"Can I really talk to you at the bar?"

"Sure," I say. "I'm friendly."

"You're a hero," he says. I laugh at that, and turn my collar back up, then head outside. All I know for sure now is what I'd suspected—the owner of the house with the willow tree and flowered sofa was in on it, probably developing the film, helping them out somehow. Maybe picking targets for Danny. Someone who would know who was worth blackmailing.

The wind picks up, right into my eyes as I walk to the streetcar stop. I've met plenty of people on this case who know everyone else: all the club owners; Shelly, Bert, Helen. Shelly was the only one not being blackmailed, but he seemed to enjoy the burning film, too, didn't try to stop it. Bert doesn't seem smart enough to pull any of this off, more likely to keep the photos for his personal pleasure than blackmail anyone with them. And Helen's photos were at a house, maybe in there to throw me off, if she got to the photos before I did and took the ones of Jonathan. She could have planted her own to throw me off the scent. Donna's body was found at her club. And I know she's capable of planning a murder. Hell, maybe burning down the Ruby would be a bonus for her—less competition. My body feels cold by the time I'm at the streetcar station, and I have to wait a while longer before it shows up.

I don't know what to think about Helen or James. I keep pushing them out of my mind. It was easy to say all the right things with Gene, to say they're the past and I'm moving forward. But Helen is my friend. Was my friend. James was . . . something else. Something messier, and because of that, it's easier to pry myself away from him and know I shouldn't go back. Being with him again was never what it was. And it was never enough to be something new, either.

But Helen . . . Helen was new, and the best parts of the old.

But that doesn't mean she's not still a killer. When the streetcar shows up, I ride it to the library. It's only midafternoon, still wide open, and I go to the records room again. This time, I don't look up addresses by phone number, I look them up by name: Shelly, Helen, and even Bert for good measure. If any of them have a willow tree, then I've done my job. Shelly and Bert's last names I don't know, but with Shelly I just look up the ownership records of the building, and for Bert, I call the bar itself and ask him.

"You want to see how it'll sound next to your name?" he asks.

"Just checking if you're a murderer," I say, and hang up before he can respond.

I look them all up, find addresses, and head out into the city. Bert's place I walk by and can eliminate without even stopping, it's an apartment building, no garden. Shelly's over in Forest Hill, which sounds promising. Even has a yard, but no willow tree. I peek in through the windows anyway, just in case, but the sofa is white. Which leaves only Helen's place. If it is her, she put on quite a show—photos of her and Donna in her own bed, lies about the apartment, a whole web to make me think it couldn't be her.

But, she's done it before. Of course, if it is her, then she could have lied about everything—the tree, the sofa. The thing I'd need to check would be the bedroom. All I really know now is that those photos were taken in someone's house, and someone was part of the blackmail ring. What's real and a lie crumbles when I look too close at it, blends together, like a boat on the horizon.

Her address is in Potrero, not too far from Danny's place. It's a narrow building against a steep slope with some steps up to the door that are at an angle to the sidewalk that makes me dizzy. A few stories tall, but there's a garden out back. No willow tree.

She's listed as being the ground floor. Someone could take photos through the window easily. I'm just about to jump the fence when I hear a car door slam behind me, and turn.

There's Helen, staring.

"What are you doing here?" I ask.

"Forgot my sailor hat here," she says. "I brought it home at the request of . . . a guest."

"Sure," I say.

"But if you weren't expecting me, what are you here for?" Her tone isn't angry. If anything, it's sad. "Leaving me a Dear John letter?"

"No," I say. "Checking out your bedroom. Trying to make sure those photos of you weren't taken here."

"Ah, I'm a suspect again." She puts her hands in her pockets, and nods. "That makes sense. Well, come in, I'll give you the tour."

She unlocks the front door and then another door inside, and I follow her in. I'm not sure what I was expecting, but this isn't it—it's not grand and flashy, like her show, or dark and mysterious, like Cheaters. It's just . . . an apartment. One bedroom, with white carpeting and pale-green walls, a little eat-in kitchen, and an old brown sofa. She goes into the bedroom and I follow. It's not the one from the photos. It's got a small bed with purple sheets and a rattan nightstand. The walls are white, and there's a framed poster of Greta Garbo on one. A dresser to the side has a bunch of photos on it—photos of Helen with other women, smiling at the camera, of her parents . . . and one of the three of us, standing in front of the *Bell*. James and I are in our sailor suits, Helen between us in the WAVES uniform, our arms all around one another. This must have been taken early on, maybe nine years ago. We look so much younger. I pick it up and stare at it. We're all smiling so wide. We were so happy.

"Suzanne took that, if you can believe it," Helen says. "She was always hanging around, wanting a good time. I think maybe she wanted more with me, but I didn't realize that until years later."

"I don't remember her much," I say.

"She was fun," Helen says. She studies the photo with me. "We were so young. Who'd have guessed what it would come to?"

"Yeah," I say, putting it back.

"It wasn't all bad times, though, Andy. I mean, I know James and I messed it up in the end, and I know I'm probably not going to see you again, except maybe on the street, and you won't meet my eye."

"Helen—" I start, not sure if she's right.

"But I want you to remember that: it wasn't all bad times. There were a lot of good times, too. And if this world would just let us be who we are, I think it would have been good the whole time. All the time after. Not that I'm trying to blame the world for what I did, but he was going to rat us out, Andy, our lives would be over, and we knew we had to stop that, so—"

"Helen." I interrupt her this time. "I didn't come here for this. I came here because I'm still trying to find a man who threatened to kill me and burn down my home tomorrow night. I don't have time to do this. Later, okay?"

"So there'll be a later?" she asks, surprised, her eyes looking hopeful.

"Maybe," I say, my body feeling a little relief as it comes out of me. "I hate what you did but . . . you were scared."

"It was James's idea, I just—"

"You chose to go along with it. And the lies. But look, I can't do this now, Helen. And it still hurts."

"Yeah, you're right," she says. "And I've hated it every day. I think it's why . . . When you joined the cops, I hated it, but it gave me an excuse. To run from you, the way James had run, too. I regret that the most, more than everything else. I shouldn't have lied to you, and then I shouldn't have run because of the lie."

I nod. I don't have time to do this now, but it's good to hear. I squeeze her shoulder.

"I . . . appreciate that, but I really can't—"

She nods, grabbing a sailor hat that's on the bedpost. "Yeah, you need to go find those pictures. You're in a hurry. Let's go." We walk out, and she locks the door behind us. Outside she stops in front of her car. "Any way I can help?" she asks. "You need a lift?"

"You remember anything else about the house?" I ask.

She shakes her head. "I'm sorry. Except . . . the rum."

"You told me that already. Rum, but Donna only drank gin."

"There were two kinds," she says with a shrug. "Like in fancier drinks."

"Fancier?"

"Well, complicated. Like those tiki ones. You know, like zombies or mai tais."

I swallow and it burns. I've only ever seen one person order a mai tai.

"Can you drive me to the Ruby?" I ask.

"Sure," she says, "hop in."

She doesn't try to apologize again as she drives, which I appreciate, and when she pulls up in front of the Ruby, she waits until I'm outside and leans out the window.

"Maybe I'll see you around, Andy. But if I don't, I . . ." She pauses and the moment hangs there, her trying to say goodbye. "I get it, and . . ." She smiles, trying to be charming, flippant, but looking too sad. "Have a good one."

The corner of my mouth tips up and I nod at her before going inside. Upstairs, as I'd hoped, Lee is rehearsing with the band. He waves when he sees me, and I motion for him to come talk to me. He stops singing, and tells the band to take five before stepping down.

"The rumors have started pouring in. Apparently pink floral sofas are very trendy," he says. "I have a half dozen suspects already."

"Are any of them named Sidney?" I ask.

He raises an eyebrow. "Yes, in fact. A couple in Russian Hill. Blue sofa with pink hibiscus pattern. Joseph Cook and Sidney Cardwell."

It hits me hard, but it makes sense, too. It's why he let them get away with the blackmail—because he was part of it. His involvement would have made the whole experience so much easier, so much smoother.

"Do you have an address?" I ask.

THIRTEEN

Sidney's house is what a real estate salesman would call charming: white picket fence, willow tree in the backyard, and in a nice quiet neighborhood. Idyllic.

I pull up across the street from it and kill the engine. I drove there, in case I need to bring him with me to wherever the photos are, and I have Danny's gun, too, in case I need to threaten him. I look at the house for a while, the windows shining bright light onto the sidewalk. It's pretty big. Room enough for a darkroom to develop the photos. Why did he hold on to Jonathan's, though? Or were they just in a different batch he'd never handed over? But then why didn't Danny come here first to get them?

There's a lot that still isn't adding up, but I think Sidney will be happy to fill in the blanks for me.

I get out of my car and walk across the street to the house. The doorbell buzzer is shaped like a pineapple, and I press it once. I peek into the yard from the doorstep. Flowerbeds, a few flowers still blooming. Some look just planted. There's a few footsteps and then the door opens. Sidney is standing in front of me in an apron over his shirt and pants.

"Mr. Mills!" he says, surprised, but happy. "Or, Andy, I mean."

"Hi, Sidney," I say, trying to keep my tone light. "Mind if I come in for a second? I have a few questions."

"Well, certainly. Joseph isn't home from his new job yet. Sometimes he takes a while, depending on where he's working, you know. The exciting and fast-paced life of a temp bookkeeper."

He laughs, so I laugh too, and he beckons me inside, arms wide.

"That's great he found a new gig," I say, keeping my hand in my coat pocket, on the gun. He might have killed Donna, and I don't know what happened with Danny. Inside it smells warm, like garlic and olive oil. I can't remember the last time I had a home-cooked meal, and not something from a greasy spoon. It reminds me of my mother. She always used to cook for me.

"Well . . . he was almost found out at his last one. People were asking questions. Temp jobs don't pay as much, but no one knows you enough to ask, so . . ." He sighs and I nod as we walk through a little foyer into the rest of the house.

It's a nice house. There's an open dining room, a pass-through to the kitchen on one wall, an archway to a living room on the other. In there, I can see the sofa—blue, pink hibiscus on it. It looks comfortable, and there are divots from two people sitting on it, close together. It's home.

"Isn't it adorable?" Sidney says, seeing me. "We found that fabric in Hawaii a few years ago and bought enough for two sofas. We love Hawaii. Have you been? It's just amazing. If we could retire there . . ." He sighs, happy, and walks into the kitchen. I follow him. There's a cutting board with a large knife and some chopped onions. He picks up the knife. Then he starts chopping again.

"I hope you don't mind," he says. "But if I don't get everything right, it'll burn."

"It's fine," I say.

"So, you had more questions? I thought the case was over."

"It was," I say. "But turns out I didn't have all the photos." He looks down at the board, chopping, his hands moving quickly.

"You think there are more?" he asks. "What do you want from me?"

"I want to know where they are," I say.

"Ow," he says, the knife slipping, a line of blood on his hand. He sticks it in his mouth, then ducks under the sink and takes out some Band-Aids and puts one on. "Clumsy," he says, but he knows now. It's a weak excuse, and he doesn't put much energy into it.

"Sidney," I say. "I know you were part of it."

His eyes look at the knife, left on the cutting board, so I take out my gun, just to show him.

"Now, now, Andy," he says, his hands up in front of him. "Please. I would never."

"Why don't you tell me how you got involved?" I say. I can ease it out of him, then.

He sighs and unties the apron.

"Can I sit down at least?" he asks, nodding past me to the dining room.

"Sure," I say, backing out of the way. He walks past me like a funeral march and sits down in one of the chairs.

"I knew what they were doing," he says. "And I told them to stop. That was the good thing to do. The right thing. But then they said they'd cut me in. Only twenty percent, but it was a lot of money and . . ." He taps the table runner with his bandaged finger. "We want to retire, go live in Hawaii. They don't care about two old men living together there. And the water is so beautiful . . . Joseph doesn't know about it, of course. He thinks I got a raise." He laughs. "It seemed harmless, you know?"

I don't say anything, and he holds my eyes for a moment, then looks down again, resting his head on his hand.

"It worked for a while. They took the photos, they blackmailed, they paid me. And they were very polite about it, honestly."

"How nice," I say, sitting down next to him. "So how did it go wrong?"

"There was a new john Danny brought in . . . I recognized him. Dangerous guy."

"Tall, fifties, huge?" I ask.

He looks at me and nods. His face goes pale. "I guess you met him. He give you that?" He nods at my black eye.

"And more," I say.

He laughs, sadly.

"What's funny?" I ask.

"I thought you were working for him," he says. I let that hang for a moment, not sure what to make of it. "This is what I didn't want, you know. I told them he was off-limits, that I knew him, it was too dangerous, they couldn't blackmail him. I told them to not even develop the film. The moment I saw his face . . . it was like everything was different. Like I knew everything I'd been do-ing wrong all at once. It slammed down on me. So I told them not him. We argued, they said they wouldn't. But they lied. They de-veloped the photos here, but I never checked . . . I didn't know . . ."

He's starting to cry now, but quietly, tears brimming at his eyes as he talks.

"I thought they were my friends. Even introduced them to Joseph—said I'd met them at Shelly's one night. They came over for dinner, they watered my plants when we were away . . . but they didn't listen. They blackmailed him. And then he came for them."

"That's when Danny disappeared?" I ask.

He nods. "He came to me, with Donna, black eye, split lip, beaten rougher than I'd ever seen him. He said I was right, and he had to hide, that we all had to end it. Which was fine by me. Danny could vanish, and I'd never see either of them again. Or him. And for a few days, that's how it went.

"But Donna didn't like that. Danny was in hiding and she was drinking every night. She called me. She was drunk. She said Danny was waiting because he knew the guy would pay up eventually, but she was getting worried. I told her she had to go to him, beg him to just give him his photos back. She laughed and hung up. And then the next day, you showed up."

He swallows. "Like I said, I thought he hired you. And if you were working the case, if you'd met me . . . I had to make sure no one could connect us. I called Donna. Got her to meet with me in my car, told her I knew how to fix it. I asked her to tell me where Danny was, but she didn't know. And then, I . . ." He starts to sob, puts his face in his hands. I let him for a while. "It was an accident. She was getting out, and I went after her, in this alley by her house. She pushed me off, called me a bitch. So I pushed her back. She fell, hit her head. But then . . . She was alive. I could have done something. I watched her eyes flutter. It was awful. I watched all of it. I never saw a man die. Not when I was in the navy. I was on the water all of the first war. I just saw ships go down. Little sinking stars. It's so different, watching eyelashes flutter, hearing that breath fade away."

He swallows. "But I let it happen. And then I dumped her in the alley behind that bar you said she was at every night, so someone who knew her would find her. I thought it was over," he says, offering me a weak smile. "You even said you'd solved the case. I knew that man was gone, out of my life again, for good."

"What's his name, anyway? The big guy?"

"He told me it was Jonathan. But that was just the middle name. Sam. His name was Samuel. Still is, I guess."

"So what happened next?" I ask.

"I thought it was done . . . until Danny showed up at my door last night. He said he knew what I'd done, that I'd killed Donna. He was screaming, fumbling in his pockets for something, and then he tried to strangle me. Joseph was out again. I guess that was . . . lucky. We struggled, and . . ." He looks away.

"Where is he?" I ask.

There's a long pause. "Under the begonias," he says softly. "It was the best thing I could think of. It was dark and Joseph would be home soon."

I keep my body still, but it wants to shiver. "So then, the final question, Sidney—Where are the photos?"

"What photos?"

"Of Jonathan, or Sam, or whatever his name is. He didn't hire me, he threatened me, and if I don't get them back, I'm giving him your name."

He freezes at that, his eyes going wide as he pivots slowly toward me. Then he falls on his knees. "Please no, Andy. You can't, please."

I shake him off and stand. "Where are the photos?"

"I don't know!" he shouts, and starts sobbing again, collapsing on the floor. "If I had them, don't you think I'd give them to you?"

He's right. It's just another dead end. Everything is a dead end.

"So who else could have taken them?" I ask. "Who would even want them? Who is this guy Sam? How do you know him?"

Sidney sniffs, then starts to laugh, his face still buried in the rug, laughing and laughing.

"What's so funny?" I ask.

"I know him from giving him a blow job thirty years ago," he says.

"What?" I ask, my blood suddenly so loud in my ears his voice is muffled.

"He's navy intelligence. He was the one who reported on me. He seduced me, and screwed me, and then told the world about it so I'd get sent to prison. And now he's some big shot in navy intelligence. The top of it on the West Coast, from what I've heard. Bastard. You should kill him instead, Andy. Kill him, and then he won't kill me. And I know I'm bad, I've done bad things but he . . . He's a monster, Andy. Please, Andy." He grabs at my trench coat and I kick him off again.

Navy intelligence. Big shot. I shake my head, but it's the only thing that makes sense.

"Sam Marks," I say. James's old boss. The one he'd filed papers for.

Sidney nods. "Yes. That's him."

The photos had always all been together.

I turn and walk out of the house, but when I'm at the door, Sidney shouts out, "Wait!" still on his hands and knees.

"What?" I ask, turning around.

"What will happen to me?"

"I don't know," I say. "I could tell the cops about the body in your yard, but I don't know if they'd believe me, and if they did, Joseph would get roped into it, too."

"No, no, he wouldn't. I wouldn't let that happen," Sidney says quickly. "I'll turn myself in."

"You're queer, Sidney. They'll figure it out. They'll say it was a couples' murder, two older perverts getting their jollies with a younger guy. Like that Hitchcock movie."

Two young lives gone. And if I try to find them justice, a whole lot of other people will lose it. Donna and Danny were imperfect, but they deserve justice as much as anyone. They won't get it. It used to be, I would call the cops—I'd be one of the cops—and I'd arrest Sidney and probably Joseph, too, and I wouldn't care much about who knew what or why. The body in the yard would have been enough to turn over to the DA, and he would have easily gotten them the chair. But Joseph is innocent. And he's one of us. He's the kind of innocent I need to protect. So . . . no. Justice isn't worth that.

He sobs quietly from across the room. I turn away, and open the door.

"I just wanted to go back to Hawaii," he says as I leave. It's the saddest thing I've ever heard.

FOURTEEN

It's too late to finish this now. The library is closed, and I don't know his address. I already know how it ends, anyway, so I go back to the Ruby. I feel a strange calm over me. It reminds me of when we passed from waters we knew were safe into territory where the enemy could be, where mines could be. On a calm day, the ship would go quiet, the men would go rigid, and I, down in my sonar room, would perk up. The ship would move slowly, giving me quiet to let me hear the little pings that meant a mine. I would focus. Just me, the silence, the water, which I could feel, cold as ice, through the hull.

And when I spotted a mine, I would notify the captain. The ship would stop, the two disarming boats released to cut it from the chain holding it underwater. It would float to the surface, and then, from a safe distance, we'd shoot it. Water mines are like that, you can't go in and tinker from the ocean, disarm them with tools. It always has to end with an explosion.

It was still loud, from far away. It would still boom across the water, make the ship rock. But if it was just noise, we'd won.

I already know what his excuses will be, what he's going to say. I can already see the explosion that'll come, hear the noise.

At the Ruby, it's starting to fill up, a few people dancing in the crowd. Elsie is dancing with Gene up front, as Lee sings on stage. They all know that this place could go up in flames tomorrow night. They're all sure I'll save it. Or at least, they seem that way. Maybe they're really just dancing the night away, taking life while they can, like we did during the war. Maybe for people like us, it never ended.

Elsie sees me, and waves me over, and I walk toward her, smiling. I'm still in my coat and hat and she takes my hat off.

"You look like . . ." She tilts her head. "I don't know. Something odd. You all right?"

"You look like something sad happened," Gene says.

"It did," I say. "Just now, and a long time ago, and tomorrow. But I've solved the case. I'll get the photos back soon."

"So we won't go up in flames?" Elsie asks.

"I don't think so. I think this guy, even though he's a brute, I think he'll be true to his word. I know who he is now, why these photos are so dangerous, but once I give him the photos, he knows he'll be safe. If I tried to tell anyone, it would be my word against his. I wouldn't be able to do a thing. And I have no reason to go after him, anyway. Once he has the photos, he'll be safe, and he'll simply stop caring. So we'll be safe."

"Well, that sounds like a reason for another drink!" Elsie says, throwing up her arms. "You two dance, I'll get them," she says. She heads over to the bar, and Gene puts his hand on my shoulder, takes the other one, and starts dancing with me. I don't follow him very well.

"Oh no," he says. "Don't tell me you can't dance."

"It's been a while," I confess.

"Well, I'm going to have to teach you."

"I'm not sure I'll make a very good student."

"I'll make you a good student. We'll go over waltz, and foxtrot, Lindy Hop, rumba—"

"You know all those dances?" I ask, my feet finally catching up with the rhythm, our bodies swaying.

"Maybe," he says. "You won't know either way. I'll just teach you to move how I want you to."

I grin. "Then I look forward to learning."

I think about leaning in for a kiss, but Elsie is back, holding four glasses of champagne. Gene and I stop dancing, moving to the edge of the dance floor, and Lee finishes her set and comes down, taking a glass from Elsie as if she was expecting it to be there. She takes a deep swig and looks at me.

"So that information panned out? Sidney have those photos?"

"No," I say. "But I know who does. It was staring me right in the face the whole time, but . . . the past got in my eyes, I guess."

"Oh," Lee says. "Well, at least you know where they are. How about what happened to Donna?"

"That was Sidney. Danny, too. He's buried under that willow tree now."

"Oh," Gene says. We're all quiet as the band plays a jazz number, waiting for the next singer to come on.

"What are you going to do about it?" Elsie asks.

"His boyfriend wasn't in on it, but if I tip off the cops, he'll get roped in. We'll see headlines for months about perverted murderers, their trial will be awful . . . Sidney is broken up about what he did, and Danny and Donna were blackmailers. They had dreams, and were people, and it's terrible they're gone, but . . . I don't know how to find justice here."

Everyone is quiet. "People like us don't get justice," Elsie says after a while, shrugging. She raises her glass, toasting. "But here's to trying."

I clink her glass, and it makes a hollow noise. "To trying."

"I can do better than try," Lee says. "I'm going to spread word around about this to all the bars in town. By the time I'm done, people are going to treat Sidney worse than they were treating you a few weeks back, Andy. He's a murderer. We might not be able to send him to prison, but we can make sure everyone knows and he's treated like the monster he is."

I nod. "Worse than they treated me, huh? Maybe that's . . . a kind of justice."

"Well then," Elsie says, raising her glass again, "here's to a kind of justice."

Lee and Gene raise their glasses too, and we all drink.

"All right," Elsie says, handing her empty glass to Gene. "I know you're off tonight, but can you bring that back so I can dance with your boyfriend," she says, taking me by the arm. Gene smiles and nods, and doesn't say we're not boyfriends, instead meeting my eye, daring me to say something. I don't, and he walks away looking smug, while Elsie starts to dance with me.

"I need a refill, too," Lee says, following Gene to the bar.

"You've gotten a bit of a reputation since last night," she says.

"I've heard," I say. "Some college kid I had to talk to today called me a hero." I laugh.

"Don't knock it, it'll be good for business," she says. "If this place doesn't burn down, that is." She spins me, unexpectedly, then pulls me back. "But, that means no more risks. If word gets out about a gay detective, the cops are gonna want to shut you down. And if they find out it's you . . ."

"I know," I say.

"So no matter what you're feeling for Gene—no more picking fights with cops. I'm still shocked what I said worked. Maybe I really should think about organizing the bars into a guild or something."

"Maybe," I say.

We dance until the end of the song, and then I join Gene and Lee at the bar while Elsie starts dancing with one of the female impersonators.

"I think I am owed a drink," Lee says to me. "For being so instrumental in solving the case."

I laugh. "All right."

"And what's with some blond child coming up to me and telling me he helped you on a case and I'd want to know?"

"Well, didn't you?" I ask.

She smirks as I order her a drink. She takes it and sips. "He seemed like a nice boy, though. Lonely."

"I told him you were good people," I say. "A good friend. An excellent girl Friday."

"That I am," she says, sipping.

I lean against the bar and slip my hand around Gene. He leans into me.

"Are you going to be all right tomorrow? You said the past was . . ."

"Yeah," I say, watching Elsie dance. "It'll be okay."

Gene leans in closer, warm. The music gets louder as the song ends.

The next morning, I wake up early. I'd almost invited Gene to stay, but I promised myself not until the bar was safe. And that's what I'm going to do today. Make it safe. Make us safe.

I put on some old clothes: a black suit, a white shirt, a blue tie. I put on my hat and trench coat and go out in the city. I skip breakfast. The air smells like gasoline and dead leaves. I take a streetcar back down to Hunters Point. The naval offices are there, too. I stand outside the gate, a little out of the way so the guard doesn't look at me. And then I wait. People start pouring into work a little before nine. He's late, though. He was usually late.

"James," I say when I see him, my voice neutral. He turns to me. He's in uniform, and it looks good on him, tailored and professional. He turns at the sound of my voice and smiles, looks relieved. He walks over to me.

"I'm so glad to see you," he says in a whisper. "I tried calling, but you didn't pick up, and I wasn't sure if you wanted to see me yet. But I'm glad you're here. I want to say sorry again. I know I screwed things up."

I nod, letting him talk.

"I'm sorry," he says. "And I know we can make this work. I love you, you love me. That's what's important. I can get us through the rest of it."

I nod again, and stare at his hands. I've held them so many times, but when I think of what they feel like—calluses, smoothness, warmth—I can't remember anything.

"Andy?" he asks.

"I need the photos back, James," I say finally.

He blinks, a moment too long, then tilts his head, confused. "The ones I hired you to get? I burned them, Andy."

"Not those. The other ones you took with yours," I say. "The ones of Danny and Sam Marks, your old boss from navy intelligence."

He laughs, but he's forgotten how well I know him, how I can tell it's fake. "Marks isn't a fairy, Andy. I'd know."

"That's the part I can't figure out, actually," I say. "If this was all a long plan—you knew somehow that Marks and Danny were a thing, maybe you found out on the job, investigating folks like us, putting them before tribunals. So you got close to Danny, trying to find out more, figured out the blackmail scheme, and realized if they were doing it to you, they were doing it to Marks, too. And if you had those photos, well, then your career is safe, right? The head of navy intelligence finds out about you, hauls you in front of a committee, you just tell them if you go down, so does he. You have pictures to prove it. You give those to the papers and it would be a huge scandal, ruin careers. The whole navy is just filled with queers, same as the State Department. No one wants that. You'd be untouchable. Free, in a way we never were in the navy. So did you plan all that? Or was it just an opportunity?

You saw the photos, recognized him, and swiped them while I wasn't looking?"

"Andy, I don't know what you're talking about," he says.

I stare at him in silence for a while. "He's going to kill me if I don't get the photos back," I say finally.

He's quiet, and I wonder if that's enough. If he'll just hand them over. But he blinks again.

"I wish I could help," he says, finally. So much for doing it all to protect "us," then. So much for "I love you." Just him. Always just him.

"Sure," I say. "I thought it was you, but I guess not. Sorry." I look at my feet, like I'm embarrassed. "I'm just scared right now."

"You want to come around later? We can figure it out, I'll protect you," he says. "My place?" He always liked me best when I was scared, I think.

"Yes," I say. "Give me your address. I'll come by at seven."

He smiles, and I hand him a pen and paper. He was always arrogant. Always thought he got away with it, because he usually did. He writes it down. Richmond District. When he hands me the paper, he lets his hand linger in mine for a while.

"I can't wait to see you," he says. "It'll be like old times again."

"Just like old times," I say, and I smile like a ghost.

He's got a nice little house with palm trees out front, white stucco with an archway over the door that's good for hiding in while you pick a lock. Inside, it's nice, too. Big windows looking out on more palm trees. Everything is tidy—kitchen clean, bed made with tucked corners, even the pillows on the sofa in front of the TV are fluffed, one placed in each corner, like a magazine ad. I spend a while looking around. There's no photos anywhere, no posters; the only thing hanging on the walls are mirrors.

In his underwear drawer, I find one old photo of me, naked, covering myself with just my hands and laughing. I also find photos of a few other guys, none I recognize, but I'd guess from other times in his life. A collection.

I swallow and start looking for the photos of Marks and Danny. James would keep them somewhere safe, waterproof, out of the way. I tap walls, look behind the mirrors for a safe, but don't find anything. Then I look under the furniture, under the bed. Finally, I pull down the ladder to the attic, and in there, I find a safe, tucked in the corner. I'm not an expert safe cracker, but I try his birthday, and it works. Inside are a few guns, cash, and an envelope with the photos and film. I take it, and close the safe up, then walk back down the ladder. When I get down, though, I see James, standing there, waiting.

"I thought that you were a little too forgiving," he says. "At first I thought maybe you were just looking for some fun, if you really thought he was going to kill you. A way to go out. But I remembered how angry you were the other day, after that fight. You always liked holding on to your grudges."

"And you lied," I say, holding the envelope.

"So he's the one who gave you that black eye?" I nod. "I wouldn't have let him hurt you, you know. I would have shown him the photos, told him to leave you alone. I was going to make it go away, and you wouldn't even know."

"I was a cop, James. I've gotten my hands dirty. I'm trying to make them clean now."

He rolls his eyes. "Clean, dirty. Andy, it's all the same. What's important is that with those, we could be safe. You'd be safe, I'd be safe—we could be safe together."

"You did it for us?" I ask.

"Always," he says.

"What about the other guys in your underwear drawer?" I ask.

He laughs. "Come on, we were never one of those couples, just the two of us. I liked that. I like sharing with you, too." He takes a step closer. "You liked it. You liked us together, didn't you?"

"I did," I say. "And I'm not jealous. I'm just saying, James—it was never for us. It was for you. Saving me—that would be for you. So you could keep roaming free, and maybe I'd be part of that freedom, but if you really want to protect me, if you really cared about me at all, you'll let me walk out with these. Because otherwise I'm dead. And if you try blackmailing Sam, you're dead, too. I've looked in his eyes."

He looks sad, and he doesn't move.

"I miss it," he says. "I miss being free."

"We were never really free," I say, walking by him. As our bodies pass, I feel the ghosts again, remember the way his skin felt, the callus on his finger. But it's nothing, just fog that fades the moment you try to touch it. The ghosts aren't hungry, they aren't magnets. They're just dead.

At the door I turn around and look at him. He still looks handsome, dignified. "I hope you find some way to be happy, James. I hope you find a way to be . . . less scared."

"Facing fear is what the navy's all about," he says, smiling, chin high. "I'll see you when you come back, Andy. You know you will. We'll always end up back together. You can feel it, too."

"Bye, James."

I turn around and leave him alone.

That night, I go downstairs at midnight. There's a car waiting outside the Ruby. The window slides open and I hold an envelope near it. I look into the window and see a pair of eyes, watching me. Smoke floats out.

"You want to come in?" Sam asks.

"I'll stay out here. But I have a question—how do I know it's over? How do I know you don't hurt me, anyone else, once you have these?"

"Why would I?" he asks.

"Because I know the truth about you," I say.

He chuckles, low. "What does that matter? You're just some fairy. No one would believe you. I've got a reputation. The ones who get fired, get caught, they're the ones who aren't careful enough. They're unashamed, or too swishy to hide it. But if you can play the game, you can do whatever you want."

"Until someone takes some photos," I say.

He raises an eyebrow in the dark of his car.

"You ever wish you could just live your life?" I ask.

"Like you do? That's not a life."

Part of me agrees, but it's a small part, a smaller part than it's ever been. This is a life, it's just a rough one. One where I couldn't save Danny or Donna, and I'm letting the man who killed them go free because otherwise more people will get hurt. One where a man like this, in his fancy car, can threaten me and proposition me in the same breath, and not consider what that might say about him. About me. It's a life. It's just a rough one, an unfair one, a life that wants you to give up on it. But that's not all it is, and hiding away doesn't make any of it change, not really.

I nod slowly, then hand over the envelope. I wait for him to open it, look at them, check the film. When he does, he looks back out at me.

"You would have been a good sailor, if you were just a little more ashamed of what you are."

"What we are," I say. He leans back into the shadows and I can't see him anymore.

The window closes and he drives off. I watch the car go, and

254 LEV AC ROSEN

turn around the corner. Then I look back at the Ruby. Elsie is there, leaning against the wall, smoking, and watching me.

"You know, you could have blackmailed him," she says as I get closer. "Could have figured out a way to do it without getting killed. You're clever."

"I didn't want to," I say.

"Even to an asshole like that?"

"Assholes like that are everywhere. I used to be one of them."

She tilts her head back and forth, thinking about it. "Maybe a little," she says.

"Thanks for giving me a place again," I say. "Y'know. For helping me not be a good sailor like he wanted."

"Hey, it's an investment," she says, patting me on the shoulder and steering us both inside. "And from what I saw today, it's paying off."

I smile. She's right. Word is getting out about me, and I already had three new clients come in tonight. Cheating girlfriends, missing lovers. I might be able to really earn my keep.

"If you're making real money now, though, you have to start paying for drinks," she says.

"That's not what the bartender told me," I say, and she laughs. I get into the elevator, but she doesn't get in with me, holds the door open instead.

"I'm going out to see Margo," she says. "They brought the baby home today."

I smile, my body warming at the thought of it. "What's the name?"

"Irene," Elsie says, smiling a little. "She apparently slept all day, so they're expecting her to be up all night. Already my kind of girl."

I laugh. "Well, tell everyone hello. And congratulations. I'll have to pick out a gift."

"Yeah," she says. "I will. Oh, and that bartender—I made him my manager today. Since I might be around a little less. Still behind the bar, but keeping an eye on the place. You'll help him out, right?"

"Of course," I say.

She leans in and gives me a kiss on the cheek. "Good work, Detective," she says, and then she walks away, and the elevator door closes. I take it up to my office, and go inside. Lee is waiting for me, sitting behind my desk, her feet up. On the desk next to her is a small rectangle, wrapped in paper.

"That for me?" I ask. "What for?"

"Please, you should be buying me something. That was just in here when I came in."

"Why did you come in?"

"I wanted to hear the end of the story."

"I gave him the photos. He said if I had a little more shame, I'd make a good sailor."

She laughs and takes her feet off the desk. "You already have plenty of shame. How much more can a person stand?"

I laugh and grab the package. It's only an inch thick.

"Wait," she says, leaning forward. "What if navy intelligence sent you a bomb to make it all vanish after?"

I smile and put the package to my ear. It's too thin, but I play along.

"No ticking," I say. "Plus we won't know unless we unwrap it."

She stands up and comes around next to me as I peel the paper back. Underneath is a picture frame, and in it a photo—me, James, Helen, in front of the *Bell*. A note is inside, too.

> *It wasn't all bad*
> —*H*

I smile and put the photo up on one of my shelves, the first real thing in the office.

"You sure you want that?" Lee asks. "That man was fine to have you murdered, and they both lied to you about killing someone. Not sure they're worth remembering."

I hand her the card. "Like she says," I say with a shrug. "It wasn't all bad. It's worth remembering the good. Behind glass, anyway."

"Well, I'm going to go back downstairs and make a few good memories of my own," she says. "No photos, though."

I smile and on impulse reach out and hug her. She's confused, but after a moment, hugs me back.

"Thanks," I say. "I really couldn't have done this without you."

"I know," she says, waltzing out the door, where Gene is standing.

He's dressed nicely, not for work, in a suit and tie, both a soft blue. He looks handsomer than I could have imagined.

"Case closed?" he asks, smiling. I walk close, graze a finger carefully on his wrist.

"Yeah," I say.

"Then I think it's time for our date? Where are you taking me?"

"I was supposed to pick?"

"Well, you asked me out."

"I don't remember it that way."

He smiles and takes both my hands in his.

"Let's go dancing," I say. "I want to be with you. Somewhere with friendly faces. Somewhere we can be surrounded by people like us."

ACKNOWLEDGMENTS

Books don't come about because of one person sitting alone in their room, writing and never interacting with another human being, even if that was (and still is) my dream. Books are created by a community, and while I may have written everything on these pages, so many people helped me to refine those words and then create the beautiful package that has found its way into your hands.

There are many people to thank for being part of that community, so thank you to everyone listed here, and many others.

First, my editor, Kristin, who helped me to understand the conventions of my First Ever Sequel, and explained to me things like "People might have read the first one a year ago!" and "Some people start in the middle of the series!", even if that second one still horrifies some part of me. Her guidance helped me to refine this story and make sure it didn't get pulled too strongly one way or another, that it was, first and foremost, a mystery, not a history lesson, not erotica. (It came pretty close in one draft.) Her insight, as always, was invaluable, and I absolutely could not have gotten the book to where it is without her. And somehow, she made all of it a continued pleasure. Working with her is like the best kind of party.

And my agent, Joy, my stalwart, my knight in shining armor, who is always there when I need her. When this book comes out, she'll have been my agent for twenty years!! (Yes, I got an agent for my bar-mitzvah.) And so it fits that I'll have three books coming out this year, and all of them are in honor of her and our partnership—our friendship. Aside from my husband, she's probably the person I talk to the most. She's family. And I can never thank her enough.

And while we're talking about family, my parents deserve all the thanks in the world, not just for making sure I was raised on all those old noir movies, but for the continuous support in this insane business / my insane life. I cannot thank them enough.

Troix, who joined the series when the first book was done and so only got to be an editor this time around, has been an absolute delight, not just because she's another queer voice on the team but because she's such a natural editor. Her insights and notes have helped to shape the book, and more importantly, have helped me figure out what it was I was trying to do. I can't thank her enough.

Katie and Colin deserve all the praise and thanks for creating another astounding cover. Covers for sequels, it turns out, are really hard! Which conventions do you bring over? How do you make it relate to the first cover, but still stand on its own? How do they look next to each other on the shelf? It's a lot to take in, and they did that all with such aplomb and skill, and look at the front of this book! It's amazing, they're amazing, and I'm so lucky to have them working on this series and just to have gotten to know them even better. They're just amazing people and so talented; I'm so grateful.

My publicists, Laura and SallyAnne, who have been SO, so amazing, making sure this book found its way into your hands and many other hands as well. The market is inundated with so many voices, and trying to make sure one stands out is a hard job, and one I am in no way equipped for, so I'd be completely lost without them. I cannot thank them enough, because even if this was the best book in the world, no one would know about it without them.

Likewise, the marketing team: Jennifer, the marketing queen; Anthony, the library king; Lucille; Eileen; Arianna—their jobs are so hard, making sure one drop of water in an ocean somehow stands out. They've created such a beautiful strategy with these books and have fulfilled it with so much enthusiasm and joy. Thank you so much.

Thank you, in fact, to the entire Forge team, overseen by Linda, who have just made publishing so much fun again. I've been in this business awhile, and putting out a book can be exhausting and demoralizing. But the enthusiasm and kindness you've all shown me has made me really love this part of the job again—I'm so grateful I get to work with each and every one of you, and I can't tell you how much I appreciate the zeal and kindness you bring to your jobs. Thank you.

My writing group—Laura, Dan, Jesse, and Robin—actually helped me hash out the plot to this book. I knew I was writing a sequel, and so I asked them all to read the first one, and then sort of ran ideas by them, and they helped me refine it into something I could actually make into a novel. It was so much fun, and I can't thank them enough. We've been a writing group in some form for over a decade now, and I'm just so grateful for the constant work everyone puts into it and the fun of seeing everyone, even as we're all across the country now, and talking about our work. Thank you guys so much.

And the rest of my writing community: Tom, Dahlia, Adam, Caleb, Julian, Sandy, Adib, Cale, Teri, and so many others. Having you all in my corner makes this insane career so much more manageable. Or at least, more fun.

I also want to thank John again, for bringing me into not only the bookstore, but the community. Getting to meet you in person and talk with you and really do an event made me feel like I was part of the mystery community. Likewise, thank you so much to all the other mystery writers who have welcomed me: Hank, especially, who has been my constant cheerleader, and Barbara,

Chantelle, Alex, Dan, PJ, Rachel, Wanda, Rita, Nekesa, and Walter. Thank you for making my lil gay stories feel welcome in a space I felt sure would not want them.

Finally, as with *Lavender House*, I have to thank the queer historians whose shoulders I stood on to write this novel. Again, Nan Alamilla Boyd's *Wide-Open Town* was a key text for me, one I came back to again and again. I took inspiration for the three bars in this book from three San Francisco queer bars: Shelly's was inspired by Finnochio's, Cheaters by Mona's, and the Silver Jay by Jack's on the Waterfront. Two of those bars I first read about in *Wide-Open Town*, and though I took many liberties with them, those liberties were informed by everything I read about in Boyd's book. I cannot recommend it enough.

For research about the Lavender Scare and the military both during and after WWII, I turned to *Coming Out Under Fire* by Allan Bérubé and *The Lavender Scare* by David K. Johnson. Both are excellent books that paint a fascinating portrait of contradictions that I hope I managed to portray in the book. To be queer in the military during WWII was both incredibly freeing and filled with stifling paranoia. Men openly made out on ships and were told just to move or else be court-martialed. Queer people, funneled together by the draft, found one another for the first time and created communities, even newsletters, like the queer army newsletter *The Brighton Beach Bitch* . . . and in doing so, became more visible, which made the military crack down on them more, which lead to more visibility like the Kinsey Reports, which lead to more crackdowns—in the form of the Lavender Scare, which at its height was more reported on than the Red Scare. It's a cycle we keep going through, as evidenced by the real-life Newport Scandal that Sidney was a part of. But these books made both the joy and fear of it all so human, and the stories within both chilled and warmed me. I couldn't have written this without them. Looking back on our history isn't as horrible as you might think; yes, our past is filled with hate and persecution, but it's also filled with love and hope. The men who were discovered in the military in the later years of WWII were sent to military asylums, and there they found community, threw parties, laughed. Some said it was some of the best times of their lives. Even when we're persecuted, we find family and love. That's part of the cycle, too.

So thank you to the community, not just those who made this book, but those queer historians who continue to make our community bigger and more open.

And to Chris, for being Chris.